Perfect IMPERFECTIONS

Samantha Vitale

HU
HOUSE
PUBLISHING

HEARTS UNLEASHED HOUSE PUBLISHING

Copyright © 2023 Hearts Unleashed House Publishing
The stories and events that appear in this book are fiction.
Maturity Advisory.

Text copyright © 2023 by Samantha Vitale
Cover design by Susan Harring © 2023 by Samantha Vitale
Interior book design by Samantha Vitale, layout by Susan Harring © 2023 by Samantha Vitale

For information about special discounts for bulk purchases contact:
hearts@heartsunleashed.com

Manufactured in the United States of America
Library of Congress Cataloging-in-Publication Data Vitale, Samantha.

Summary:

Nine years after the death of her best friend and having to take on the responsibility of her child, Katie is faced with even more new discoveries and shifts in her life. Between a move and a new member of the family, so much is going on for Katie, when she comes across a box. Will what's in this box undo everything Katie strived to do to heal after the loss of her best friend, or will it bring her even closer to her, even after her death? How will these changes affect the family, and how will they come together to embrace loss and grief in order to move forward? Find out in this incredible novel about family, friendship, love, healing, faith, and strength. This amazing story will have you laughing, crying, and learning more about humanity at every step.

ISBN: 979-8-9882783-2-0

[1. Young Adult Girls and Women. 2. Family and Friendship. 3. Wholesome Romance. 4. Loss and Grief.]

This book is dedicated to family, to best friends, and to each day in this 'Perfectly Imperfect' life.

A Letter From The Author

I want to express my gratitude to you, yes you! A long time ago, throughout my struggle with self-doubt and low self-esteem, I would not have fathomed that I would realize my longtime dream of being a published author.

Writing has always been my favorite form of self-expression. I love to journal, I love poetry, I love writing recipes, taking notes, and most of all, I love telling stories!

In my book *Sweet Imperfections*, I tell the story of two best friends as they learn to navigate life, how to grow up, and what it takes to face adult situations. High school! Oy! What a crazy rollercoaster that is and was for most.

Many of my readers have asked me questions like "What is Beth's story?" or "This story is a work of fiction, but you've said it is also based on some real events. Which parts are real?"

The beautiful thing about writing, for me, is that I can write whatever truths I want in my story. It is my story, both fiction and non. I am the creator, I have the power to write what I want. Tell the message I want to tell. Release things that I have held onto. I get to tell my story through a fictional lens. I take you through my journey, as well as the journey of my beautiful characters.

Writing *Sweet Imperfections*, and this amazing sequel has been very therapeutic. I hope that this book is everything you hoped for, thank you for choosing to read it.

I invite you to sit back, and enjoy.

Samantha Vitale

One

Hey sweetheart! I was going through some things in the garage and I found a box that I know you would want. Would you like for me to bring it up to you?

I rolled my eyes after reading the text, *I really didn't have room for more stuff!* She'd been on this cleaning kick for weeks, and I'd already turned down several things she had tried to send my way.

Hi Mom! What's in the box?

I didn't want to seem short with her, but she knew that we were in the process of packing. I grew concerned when she was suddenly calling me. "Hey Mom, what's going on?" I asked, trying to keep worry out of my voice.

There was a pause, followed by a long drawn-out sigh.

"Mom?" I asked again.

"I found a box of Beth's things," she said, her voice sounding off, as if she'd been crying. I realized then, how difficult it must have been for her to call me about this.

I ran a hand through my hair, took a steady breath, and sat on the edge of my sofa. I had lost my best friend Elizabeth a little over eight years ago, and was raising her daughter Gracelynn. Losing Beth had been the hardest thing I'd ever gone through.

Beth had been a sister to me, we grew up together. My family had taken her in after we found out that she was pregnant, and there was no way we were going to let her stay in the hellhole she had to call a home.

I'd been by her side through childhood, our weird pre-teen funk, and through her entire pregnancy, and in the end…I'd lost her.

"Sweetheart?" My mom's voice startled me, returning me to the present, lost in thought as I was, I'd almost forgotten I was on the phone.

"Sorry, Mom," I replied as I ran my hand through my hair again. I felt anxious. "I can come by with Gracelynn tomorrow if that would work for you? She has an appointment with the dentist."

"Oh honey, that sounds wonderful!" Mom replied.

We talked for a little while longer and when we hung up I thought about what might be in the box…I'd thought we had already gone through everything. I hadn't wanted too many of her belongings, I felt like it would be too overwhelming, so I'd decided to keep a few pictures and a mixed CD that Beth used to listen to all of the time.

I looked at my watch, I would have to pick Gracelynn up from school in about thirty minutes. When my cell phone rang I answered without looking. I knew it was my husband.

"Hello, my love," I said, a smile in my voice. It amazed me that even though we'd been high school sweethearts, and had gotten married after college, he still gave me those crazy butterflies.

"I may be a little late. I had an emergency at the clinic. I wanted to let you know so you wouldn't worry."

I smiled. Bobby was always such a kind and respectful person. I knew I was infinitely lucky to have him. We had survived several of our friends' marriages, and often heard questions like, "how do you keep your spark?" or even "I wish I had a love like yours." It warmed my heart to hear the latter, of course we had our arguments and disagreements like anyone in a relationship would, but our communication, respect, and love for one another kept us strong and committed.

I broke out of my thoughts, realizing that I hadn't said anything to Bobby. "Thank you for letting me know, honey. I will have dinner warm for you when you get home." Bobby worked at a veterinarian clinic, he'd taken veterinary medicine in college.

We chatted for a few minutes before he had to get back to work, and then it was time for me to pick up Gracelynn from school. I grabbed my purse and my keys before locking up, and headed out.

It was a beautiful early spring day, and I greeted the warm sun with a smile. I drove the few blocks to the grade school and pulled into the large line of waiting vehicles. On high alert for some crazy driver, I scanned the parking lot and kept my eyes focused ahead for the line to move.

School pick-up and drop-off was not my favorite! Everyone was in a rush, and the parking lot was always chaotic. When I saw Gracelynn pop out and join the other little ones by the fence I smiled. I could pick her out of a crowd of a thousand. She looked so much like her mother, thoughts of Beth came to mind as I sat in my car looking at Gracelynn. Her ebony curls shining in the sun, and her smile…that sweet, perfect smile! Her eyes lit up when she saw me and I grinned widely, rolling down the window and waving at her.

When I finally was able to pick her up I waited, watching as she tossed her bag beside her and climbed in to buckle up. It was so hard to believe that she was eight years old!

"Hi momma Katie." She greeted me with a brilliant smile.

"Hey baby girl! How was your day today?"

I listened intently about her day, as I drove us to the store. I needed to grab some things before we headed home, and Gracelynn loved helping me shop. She grinned as she talked about her day at school.

In the store Gracelynn picked out the fruits she wanted—apples and bananas this week. I grabbed lettuce, tomato, and cucumber. Then, I let Gracelynn pick out her cereal and juice. After grabbing a loaf of honey wheat bread on the way to the register, Gracelynn helped me pay the cashier, a kind elderly woman who commented on her being such a good help to her mom.

We got in the car, and headed home. I listened as Gracelynn told me little stories about her best friend, Lilly.

Lilly and her mom, Tracey, had moved to the neighborhood a couple of years ago, I helped bring in some groceries one day, that's how the girls had met. They were quick friends.

I studied Gracelynn in the mirror when I came to a stop at the light. She had a wistful look on her face. I didn't know what she was looking at, maybe she was just lost in thought as she sat there, looking out her window. I thought about how Beth's eyes were just as vibrantly green in the sunlight.

Gracelynn knew about Elizabeth. When she was five years old she had asked me, flat-out, who her mom had been. I'd sat her down, and we'd talked about Beth. It had been hard, I had cried, and she had cried. She'd always known that I was not her biological mom. I talked about Beth quite often, even when she'd been too young to understand.

Gracelynn has a photo of Beth on her nightstand, and in the photo she is pregnant, smiling, and holding up a pair of tiny pink shoes at her baby shower. Every night before bed Gracelynn smiles at the photo, and sometimes I catch her staring at it for long periods of time.

Since the age of six, we have been visiting Beth's grave every year on Gracelynn's birthday. It wasn't long before Gracelynn had stopped calling me Momma, and took to calling me Mom or Momma Katie. She'd been so sweet about it. She'd said frankly "you aren't my real mom, but you are still my mom. I can't call you Katie, because it sounds kind of disrespectful to me."

Gracelynn sneezed, pulling me from my thoughts. "Bless you!" I told her as I parked in our driveway. When we got out, she grabbed her backpack and I let her carry the bread. I grabbed the rest and unlocked the door. She put the bread on the kitchen table and put her things in her room.

She was raised to be tidy, as I'd been. Of course, since she was only a child, there were days when she tried to refuse to do her chores. She didn't have many, but I believed that it was good for a child to do little things around the house. A bit of responsibility never hurt, and we had a reward system in place. So, if she does a certain amount of chores she may get extra play time, T.V. time, or we may go out to eat, something along those lines.

I put away the groceries while Gracelynn played in her room, my thoughts returning to my talk with my mom that afternoon. I found that I was nervous. I didn't know what I was going to see in that box of Beth's belongings. To be honest, I wasn't sure if I even wanted to look.

I busied myself with a little bit of housework to see if I could distract myself. When I was done, and it hadn't helped, I peeked in on Gracelynn to see her sitting on her bed with the photo of Beth in her lap. I frowned and knocked on her door.

"Yeah?" she called out softly.

I sat down beside her and tucked a curl behind her ear. "You okay?" I asked as I glanced at the photo. I smiled at the memories, so vivid in my mind, even after all of this time. Beth had not wanted a baby shower, but in the end, she'd loved it.

"Yeah, I just…" she sighed, a soft, sad sound before continuing. "I just wish I could have known her."

I nodded in understanding and rubbed her back, her gentle curls brushed against my hand, and I chose to play with them as I spoke. "She loved you. You know? She was scared, but when she found out she was having a baby girl, oh she was so excited."

Gracelynn smiled, it was a sad sort of smile, and I felt it tug at my heart. I pulled her close to me. "I know you wish you could have met her. I wish you could have too. She was such a wonderful person, a fantastic friend," I said as I looked at the photo.

Gracelynn set the photo down beside her and leaped into my arms. I held her close, and held back tears. She needed me to be strong for her, and I always tried my best to give her exactly what she needed.

"I love you Momma Katie," she said softly after some time, and she got up off my lap.

"I love you too honey, now and always." When she sat back down beside me, she leaned against my shoulder. It felt good to be here for her comfort. After a while, Gracelynn was in much better spirits and I offered to watch a movie together.

I let her pick one out, and when I put it in, making sure she was okay, I went to the kitchen to work on dinner. I prepped the salad and tossed some seasoning on the chicken I'd gotten out the night before, and put it in the preheated oven.

Once the salad was chilling, and the chicken cooking, I sat with Gracelynn on the couch. I smiled at her, watching her facial expressions—how she'd raise her eyebrows, or frown in concentration on a certain scene. She smiled at me, and I knew she'd caught me looking at her. She snuggled up to me, laying her head on my shoulder. Her hair smelled like strawberries. Once I'd told her that her mother had loved strawberry shampoo, she'd insisted that I get her the exact kind Beth had used.

Gracelynn didn't have many connections to Beth's family, and it made me feel sad, and almost guilty. I had been leery of allowing Sheela any time with Gracelynn as a baby. I'd given her a photo of Gracelynn to keep, and she did get the chance to at least see Gracelynn a couple of times.

Beth's mother Sheela had passed away from liver disease when

Gracelynn was almost a year old. I hadn't attended the funeral, Beth's mother had not been there for her, though I had never wished any harm to come to the woman, I couldn't quite bring myself to go to the service.

Gracelynn had asked about Sheela, and I had told her that Beth had struggled a lot growing up, that she didn't have a very good relationship with her mom.

I, of course, spared Gracey the details of her mother's past. Going into detail about what Beth had gone through, that would be too much for a child to take in. Too much for her to understand, and it was hard to talk about.

Beth's Aunt Beck reaches out once in a while though, she'd been down to see Gracelynn a couple of times during the summer breaks, and she sent letters from time to time. I am happy that she has that connection to Beth. Gracelynn enjoys her visits, and for that I am very thankful.

I stared at the screen. I just wanted to turn my mind off for a few minutes. The day had been busy, and I suddenly felt drained. I leaned my head back and allowed my eyes to close. I focused on the sweet smell of Gracelynn's hair and the sounds of the T.V. I took the time to allow myself to relax. I wasn't too good at relaxing; seemingly always in hustle mode. Bobby constantly reminded me to relax, even Gracelynn has used the phrase "chill out" several times.

When dinner was ready, Gracelynn and I sat at the table together. She gave the salad a look that clearly stated she didn't want it, but she took a small helping and ate it anyway. After we finished, I cleaned up, and kept the chicken warm for Bobby. Gracelynn did her chores that consisted of cleaning up her room, and wiping down the table. Sometimes I'd let her help with dishes, and she'd take out the trash when needed.

I didn't ask her to do anything aside from cleaning up her room and the table though, I needed to keep my mind occupied, and sometimes doing housework would do just the trick. After she finished with chores I saw to it that she took her shower.

That evening Bobby got home later than he'd planned, Gracelynn had already gone to bed. I sat with him at the dining room table while he ate his dinner, and raised a brow when he insisted on doing the dishes that he'd dirtied.

I stood and watched him as he cleaned his few dishes, taking in his wavy blond hair, and muscular body. His cute boyish features had long gone, but his eyes were still lit up with mischief. He was the same in spirit as he'd always been—the kind, warm-hearted, wonderful soul that I fell in love with so many years ago.

"How was your day, love?" he asked, after sitting on the couch beside me and propping his feet up with a soft grunt. I took that moment to snuggle up beside him. I curled my legs up and leaned my head against his chest. I closed my eyes, inhaling his scent. He always smelled so good, like sunshine on a warm day.

"It was okay, thank you," I mumbled into his chest. "Gracelynn was sad this evening, she was looking at her photo of Beth." My mind went back to that morning's conversation with my mom, and I knew I needed to get it off of my chest.

Bobby held me closer when I mentioned Beth, he'd been by my side through my losing her. He has helped me through a lot of my grief, he's always been so very supportive.

"Mom called this morning. She said that she found a box of her things." I felt him shift and knew that he was looking at me, so I sat up to face him.

"I thought you'd gone through all of her stuff?" he asked softly, his blue-gray eyes full of compassion.

I nodded and pulled my knees up to my chest. "I thought so too, but she called and said she'd found a box, and wanted to know if she could drop it off. I told her I would just come over since Gracelynn has her dentist appointment tomorrow morning anyway." I shrugged.

I felt Bobby's fingers slide against my arm to rest on my hand. "Do you want me to come?" he asked tenderly.

"If you could take Gracelynn to her appointment, I could go through the box without her there? I feel like I should find out what is in there before she sees anything." I bit the inside of my cheek in thought.

Bobby nodded and pulled me to him. "I will take a personal day," he stated, having made up his mind.

That night in bed, Bobby snored quietly beside me, and I listened to the ticking of the clock while I stared up at the ceiling. Moonlight filtered through the window curtain. I focused on taking a few deep breaths. My mind felt so full, I could hardly ignore it. I closed my eyes, begging sleep to find me, and after a few hours, it did.

Two

The next morning, while Gracelynn watched cartoons with Bobby, I enjoyed a steaming cup of coffee and made french toast for breakfast. Bobby took Gracelynn to the dentist, and was to meet me at my parents house after her appointment. I drove slowly on the way, pondering the box of Beth's things. I frowned in thought as I turned onto that familiar road toward my parents' house.

We only lived about an hour away, and we were getting ready to move into Bobby's aunt's and uncle's farm. They had asked Bobby if he was still interested in taking it over, because they were both getting too old to do it anymore, and Bobby of course said yes. He had always wanted to take over the farm.

I had a position offered to me at Sweeties, the old cafe I used to work at when I was a teenager. I'd miss working for the church, but decided it would be nice to be back home. Plus, if I decided to go back to work at Sweeties it would be something to do. I had loved working there, so long ago. I enjoyed the smell of fresh coffee, the old-fashioned root beer floats, I loved the customers, I loved how at home I had felt because I had a good relationship with the owners. They had been so excited to learn that I was coming back, and I felt honored that they had asked me. I didn't want to make a rushed decision, though. I wanted to get settled in at the farm first.

Of course, Bobby had stressed multiple times that I didn't need to work if I didn't want to. Besides, I'd have plenty to keep me occupied. He knew that I enjoyed working and have always liked having a little something to do, and I'd told him I would think about it for a while before I made any decisions. The more that I thought about it, the more the idea of staying home and doing what I wanted to do sounded rather nice.

I pulled into the driveway, shut off the engine, and stared at the house for a few moments. So many memories, *every time I come I'm so overwhelmed with memories. Some wonderful, some sad.* I unbuckled and got out of the car. My mom opened the door and stood on the porch, waving at me with a huge smile on her face.

When I got on the porch, she embraced me in a big hug. I closed my eyes and inhaled her familiar scent, and when she let go she led me inside. She'd rearranged a little here and there, but everything was basically the same as it had always been.

"Hi, Mom!" I said as I set my stuff down, and after saying a quick "hi" she hugged me again as if it had been a year since we'd last seen one another, even though it had only been just under a month. I didn't mind, I really missed her.

I took my jacket off and put it on the coat rack beside the door. After we talked for a bit, Mom opened the guest room, which had been repainted a pretty country blue color and turned into an office. "Wow, this looks nice, Mom," I said as I took in the transformation.

"Thank you, honey. Your dad and I decided it was time for a makeover."

My eyes zeroed in on the box sitting beside a small, gray loveseat against the far wall. I walked over to it and looked down. It had Beth's name on it and I cocked my head in thought. "I wonder where it came from?" I said out loud.

"I'm not sure, honestly I don't remember ever seeing it," Mom replied, with a hand on her hip as she studied the box, a slight frown on her brow.

I sighed audibly and sat on the loveseat, placing the box right in front of me. My heart began beating so fast, I felt like it was in my throat. I didn't want to look inside just then, so I looked at my mom instead. "What's in it?" I asked, chewing my lip nervously.

"I didn't have the heart to really look, sweetheart," she confided with sad eyes, and gently patted my knee. "I am going to check on lunch okay? You go on ahead whenever you're ready," she said softly, and she left me to it.

I took in a breath, and rotated my neck. *Why was I putting this off?* After a quick shake of my head, I opened the box. I peeked in slowly, taking in each item.

Her red and green flannel pajama pants.

Her tattered and old navy blue hoodie, that had been at least two sizes too big on her. I smiled as I folded it.

Three CD's that had the words "Mixed Tunes" written on them in bold blue permanent marker. The sight of her handwriting made my heart squeeze. I took a minute to breathe, and put them on the couch beside me, before continuing through the box.

An empty wallet.

A little collection of keychains with no keys.

The last thing in the box was a soft fleece blanket. I picked it up and held it in my lap. It didn't look familiar. I frowned at it, smoothing my fingers over the soft violet fabric. I stood and unfolded the blanket, my eyes widened in surprise as something hit the floor between my feet with a loud thud.

I looked down, and raised my eyebrows at what had fallen out. It was a book with a worn cover, that was a soft, velvet blue.

I took a deep breath and opened it.

"Dear Diary" it read, and I quickly slammed it shut. I placed a hand

to my mouth and held the book to my chest, my throat closing with emotion. I hadn't known what to expect, but I hadn't expected this. I didn't even know that she'd kept a diary! *Why should I know?* I asked myself. A diary was a personal thing, not something someone really prattles on about.

I held onto it a tad bit longer before softly placing everything back in the box and closing it. I left the box there, and walked out of the room.

Following my nose into the kitchen, I found my mom fixing a salad, so I stirred her homemade chicken noodle soup that was simmering on the stove. I closed my eyes and allowed the sounds and smells of the moment to pull me from my inner turmoil.

"You okay?" Mom asked softly as she diced up a plump, red tomato on the cutting board.

I exhaled softly, slowly continuing the stirring of the soup even though it wasn't necessary. I just needed to keep myself busy. "I'm okay," I muttered, the sudden tremble in my voice betraying me.

"I'm sure that was hard for you, sweetheart." I looked over as she scraped the tomatoes in with the rest of the salad.

I stopped stirring the noodles and covered the pot with the lid, moving to the counter where she worked on grating colby jack cheese over the salad. I sat down and watched her busy herself with the rest of the salad preparations, suddenly feeling rather light-headed. I assumed it was from the shock of finding that diary. I massaged my temples, and felt my mom's hand on my back.

*Damn…*I was going to cry. As my shoulders slumped, Mom sat down and wrapped her arms around me.

What came was not a soft gentle sob. No, I was full on ugly crying!

I don't know how long we sat like that as I cried, but when I was finally reduced to tiny hiccups, my stomach was upset and my nose was running. My mom handed me a tissue and I wiped at my face. *Where did she get the tissue so quickly?*

"Thank you," I sniffed.

When I felt like I was done I glanced at my mom. Her eyes glittered with tears, and bless her heart she was giving me time before she said anything. My mom has always been a fixer. When someone was upset, or something went wrong, she wanted to fix it. Even if it wasn't fixable. Like this.

"Sorry. I didn't mean to lose it…I just…" I shrugged, not knowing how to explain myself.

"You don't have to apologize for being sad, sweetheart. Crying soothes the soul. If you didn't show some emotions after going through her things, I would have been concerned." I snorted a small laugh. "I've been thinking about that box since you called me yesterday. Wondering how we missed it, wondering what was in it, if I truly even wanted to know what was in it."

I squeezed the tissue in a tight fist before continuing. "I didn't expect to find what I found." I closed my eyes and took a steady breath as my voice broke. I really did not want to start crying again!

"Do you want to talk about it?" Mom asked as she stood to stir the soup before turning off the heat and placing the lid back on.

I swallowed hard, taking a moment before responding. "Most of it was just odds and ends, a couple CDs, an unused wallet, her favorite hoodie…I found a blanket, and when I unfolded it her diary flopped out onto the floor." My voice cracked, and a couple of new tears escaped as I explained to my mom and I wiped them away with a trembling hand.

My mom gripped my shoulders and softly kissed my forehead. "Did you read it?" she asked. I shook my head and cleared my throat. I needed to calm down before Bobby came with Gracelynn, I glanced at the time.

"I'm going to go clean up." I said, my voice barely more than a whisper.

Mom gave me one more shoulder squeeze and began setting the

table up for us to join her for lunch. I headed to the bathroom and gently closed the door behind me, turned on the faucet, and filled my hands with cool water to splash on my face.

I looked at myself in the mirror as I cleaned up, and I opened the medicine cabinet to grab the eyedrops. My eyes were badly bloodshot, and I knew it would worry both Bobby and Gracelynn. After I looked and felt more presentable I joined my mom back in the kitchen.

"Thank you, Mom," I told her, giving her a hug before helping her set out drinking glasses.

Just as we set the last glass on the table, Gracelynn came running through the door first to hug Mom. "Hi Nanna!" she squealed. Then she walked over to me, to give me a hug too. I kissed her cheek and helped her put her jacket on the coat rack.

Bobby came through the door next, a sweet smile on his face. He kissed my cheek and then gave my mom a hug. "Good to see you, Mom," he said, before shrugging his own jacket off and putting it beside mine.

"It smells amazing in here!" Bobby complimented as he took the lid off of the pot and inhaled deeply. "Mmmm," he said as he placed the lid back on. He looked at the table with a smile. "You don't have to cook for us every time we come over!" He looked pointedly at Mom.

Mom placed a hand on her hip and jutted out her chin. "I absolutely do!" she stated sternly.

Bobby laughed and gave her another hug. "You know we love it."

Mom softened and smiled widely. "I'm glad, because your dad is out golfing, Paul is out with his girlfriend, and I could use the company."

"Girlfriend?" I asked, curious about how my little brother was spending his time these days.

Mom rolled her eyes and started serving the soup. "Yeah, this is his third girlfriend in two months!" she groaned.

I giggled. "And you and dad were worried about me!?" I joked, batting my eyelashes innocently. Mom playfully threw a pot holder at me. We all laughed, Bobby gave me a wink, and of course my stomach fluttered. *Lord how I love him!*

"Honestly, I can't keep up with all these girls!" Mom said as she finally sat down with her own bowl of steaming soup.

"I'm sure he is just being an average boy," I suggested quietly and Bobby nodded with a passive shrug. We passed the salad around as we talked. Gracelynn ate quickly, and then with permission, went upstairs to my old bedroom, which was now her room whenever she stayed the night or we visited.

Once we were finished with lunch, we enjoyed some light conversation, before we began helping Mom clean up, although she stated several times she didn't expect us to clean since we were guests. "You raised me to be clean, and besides, we wouldn't ever leave you with a mess," I said matter-of-factly as I started the dishwasher.

Giving up, she kissed my cheek and thanked us both as she put away the leftovers. We stayed for a while longer before it was time for us to get back home.

"Can't I stay the night with Nanna and Grandpa?" Gracelynn asked as I handed her her jacket. Mom looked at me with raised eyebrows.

I looked at Bobby. It had been a long time since we'd had any real time alone together, and it was Friday so Gracelynn didn't have school in the morning. I pursed my lips in thought. "If it's okay with Nanna," I replied.

My mom hardly had to think about it. She instantly nodded, and Gracelynn tossed her jacket in the air with a "whoop whoop." We all laughed. I took the box from the office, and grabbed my jacket. Holding that box in my hands, I felt a tug at my heart.

Bobby took the box carefully with a curious frown and put it in the car while I said "bye" to Mom and Gracelynn. They waved "goodbye" on the porch until they couldn't see the car anymore, and I settled back in my seat looking at the road ahead.

"A night to ourselves! What to do, what to do?" Bobby said playfully, wiggling his eyebrows.

I laughed, I couldn't help it. "What would you like to do?" I asked, after my smile began to fade. He turned toward me with the sun in his gorgeous gray-blue eyes, and smiled his sweet smile.

"I want to make love to my wife," he said, his husky voice washing over me. My eyebrows raised in surprise as my cheeks heated.

"We might be able to make that happen," I replied with a smile and a wink. He growled playfully. It felt good to have this time with him. We loved being with Gracelynn of course, but it was healthy to have time alone too.

We drove in comfortable silence the rest of the way home, and when we got home it wasn't long before I was in my husband's arms. He was strong, but soft in the right places. His heart pounded as I ran my fingers through his hair. He did the same to me, and placed a small kiss on my neck. His breath on my skin made me tingle, my toes curled of their own accord.

We were tripping over ourselves as we kissed one another through the house, chuckling as we found the bedroom door. Bobby opened it and surprised me by swooping me up and into his arms to toss me on the bed. I squealed as I landed with a soft bounce, and then grinned as he bounced beside me, and kissed me passionately without a word.

Much later, we curled up on the couch with a movie and pizza for dinner. The box that had been forgotten had been brought in and placed in the small hall closet.

We ate our pizza, and watched the movie in silence. After the movie was over we simply enjoyed one another's company. We talked about our day, about Gracelynn, and discussed the pending move.

It was getting late and Bobby had to work, so I assured him it was okay for him to go on to bed without me. I was in need of a shower, and time to wind down; to process, and reflect on the day's events. I have never been the kind of woman to be able to go to sleep without a fuss. *Do women do that?*

After Bobby went to bed I climbed into the shower and let the water beat down over me. After I was done, I dressed in my favorite thin cotton pajamas, and brushed and braided my hair. I took a look in the mirror. I honestly hadn't changed much since high school, my brown eyes stared back at me in the mirror. A few new laugh lines around my eyes, longer dirty blonde hair, fewer freckles. My body was still in good shape as well.

I quietly made my way into the living room. Bobby wasn't normally a light sleeper, but I didn't want to wake him by stomping about. I sat on the couch with my journal and wrote for a while with my legs curled under me.

Even after pouring my thoughts out onto paper I couldn't seem to get tired, couldn't seem to get Beth's diary out of my mind. So, I journaled about that also. *Was it wrong of me to almost want to read it? Would it be so bad if I buried it beside her, among all the letters I wrote to her in the past? How would Gracelynn feel about it? Should I give it to Gracelynn?* I swallowed past a hard lump in my throat. It had taken me a long time to heal after losing Beth…all the work I had to do to heal from the anger, the sadness, the absence of her, the *why!*

The sadness never really went away if I was being honest with myself. I felt sad for my loss of her, for Gracelynn's loss of her. But, I had reached a good place. I could remember her in the best moments; celebrate her as who she was as a person, and all of those sweet memories that we had shared together.

I closed my eyes, and a little voice inside me whispered. *"Just read it. You have to at least try."*

I stood, and walked across my living room floor, softly opening the door to the closet. I lifted the lid of the box with a conflicted sigh. I shuffled around until I found the blanket. I unwrapped it slowly until the book came out into my hand, and held it to my chest as I made my way back to the couch.

I sat criss-crossed, and I looked at it, turning it over in my hands. I felt its weight, and felt its warmth. I ran my fingers along the worn surface and squeezed my eyes shut as I opened the hard cover, taking a deep breath before I opened my eyes to read.

Three

Dear Diary,

Or whatever the hell I'm supposed to say...

This feels so dumb! Probably because the school counselor suggested it...she says I should start writing from as far back as I can remember. That it might help me heal from my past? She gave me this diary with the hope that I would use it. I kinda like the feel of it, it's almost velvet, and it's blue.

Anyway, since I don't have anything better to do, here goes nothing.

There was a time when my mother didn't always drink, and once upon a time, my dad was with us. We were a normal family.

Until around the age of 8, I had a happy, and mostly blissful existence.

I remember the day well, I had come home from school, and my dad patted his lap. I sat on it happily, smiling at him as I always had.

He had the weirdest look on his face. "I have to go, Elizabeth," he told me. I remember feeling confused. "Where are you going? Can I come with you?" I asked.

He shook his head. "You have to stay here, with Mom." I remember him beginning to cry, and I wrapped my arms around his neck, begging him to stay. He gave me a hug, put me on my feet, and he left anyway.

I remember my mom screaming at him, screaming "Take her with you! I can't do this on my own!" I'd never heard her scream before.

He never looked back.

He never came back.

From there, things only got worse at home.

Home was no longer somewhere I wanted to be. Home wasn't safe, home wasn't comfortable. Home wasn't home anymore.

I closed the book and exhaled a breath that I hadn't realized I'd been holding. I wiped away tears from my cheeks, and I carefully tucked Beth's diary back inside the blanket. I placed it tenderly in the box in the closet, and I went to bed.

I didn't go to sleep right away, of course. I just lay there, staring up at the ceiling, listening to Bobby's light snoring. Relishing in the comfort of his warmth, as I thought of Beth. I kept thinking about what I'd just read. Elisabeth hadn't ever really talked about her dad. All I knew was that he left not long after we met in the third grade. I remembered comforting her, well, comforting her as well as eight-year-old me could.

I woke to an empty bed and a note on Bobby's pillow beside me.

Honey,
You looked so peaceful, I didn't have the heart to wake you. Your mom called and said she'd bring Gracelynn home after lunch.
Enjoy your day, beautiful!
Yours, Bobby

I set the note back down with a smile, and stretched my sleepy body. I took a moment to glance at the time. It was almost 8am! My eyes widened in disbelief. I couldn't remember the last time I'd slept in. Though, after the night I had had, I supposed I shouldn't have been too surprised. It had taken a long time to shut my brain off before I could get any kind of real sleep.

I got up and shuffled into the kitchen, needing a strong cup of espresso. Bobby had gotten me this fancy coffee machine for Christmas last year, and I just loved it! Well, I loved it after I was finally done being intimidated by it. *Why did they make things these days with so many buttons and gadgets?* I pushed the buttons I needed and didn't have to wait long before I had the perfect cup.

I blew at the steam and took a sip with my eyes closed. *Smooth as silk,* I sighed in contentment before I set the cup down to cool while I made a quick breakfast. Moving around the kitchen, still half asleep, I washed an avocado, mashed it along with some garlic seasoning, pepper, and a pinch of salt, and slathered it on my wheat toast.

Once my breakfast was ready, I sat on the sofa with it and my coffee and I enjoyed the quiet of the morning. It wasn't often that I had the opportunity to enjoy a quiet morning. My mornings were filled with getting Gracelynn ready for school, or fixing her breakfast before she watched morning cartoons on the weekends.

Still feeling tired, I placed my empty plate in the sink and made myself another cup of coffee. This time, adding a bit more foam, and a tad of chocolate syrup for a sweet treat. Coffee in hand, I sat on the sofa once again with my legs curled under me for some journaling time.

I often wrote in the mornings, it was amazing what could be brewing in your mind first thing. This morning however, I wrote about the only thing I could really think about, Beth's diary.

I had felt myself wanting to read more last night, but it had been late and I knew that I wouldn't have gotten any kind of sleep had I kept reading. I wasn't sure how to feel about reading more….a girl's diary is her secret companion, a personal place for feelings, for reflections, to vent. Even though Beth was gone, and it was a material thing, to read it almost felt wrong. It felt as if I were invading her privacy.

On the other hand, when I had read it…it had almost felt as though she were talking to me. Oh, how I missed our talks. Good, bad, sad…I missed it all, every bit of it. Beth with her warm smile, and soulful, brilliant eyes, her bold personality.

When I finished journaling I went to the bathroom and washed my face. These past couple of days were wearing my emotions thin. I studied myself in the mirror. I was buzzing from two cups of espresso, and somehow I looked exhausted.

I decided to get dressed, choosing a cozy red sweater and a pair of black leggings. I tossed my hair up into a messy bun and put on a little makeup in hopes that it would put a pep in my step. I needed to wake up, I had some packing to do, and I wanted to clean up the house before Mom came with Gracelynn.

I turned the music on, choosing to dance about as I began packing some things that we didn't need out right away. I ended up filling three good-sized boxes from the living room. *How do we have so much stuff!?* I thought to myself.

When we had broken the news to Gracelynn that we were moving to the farm, she had been sad because she'd miss Lilly and her teacher at school, but she'd told me she was happy at the same time. She loved the farm very much, and she already knew which bedroom she wanted.

I had sat with her and dried her tears, assuring her that she could keep in touch with Lilly, that just because we were moving didn't mean that they couldn't be friends anymore. I told her that we could still arrange playdates and maybe they could even still have sleepovers once in a while. Certainly not as often as they were used to, but Gracelynn had been happier after our talk.

I packed one more small box of knick-knacks, turned the music off, and took a break. I grabbed a glass of water and sat down on the recliner. I knew if I sat on the sofa, I wouldn't want to get back up, *that thing is way too comfortable!*

I glanced at the clock. Mom would probably call me when they were on the way so I kept the music off while I cleaned up the house, starting in the living room and working my way around to the bathroom. Cleaning almost always helped to keep my mind busy, and when I was satisfied with how the house looked, I sat down on the sofa.

Glancing at the time, I realized it was still quite early. Mom wouldn't fix lunch for another hour at least. I decided to put my shoes on and take a walk. I checked the weather first, and seeing that it was already going on 70° out, I chose to change clothes before I left. There was no way I was going to need a sweater.

I locked the door behind me and headed for the park. The park here was small, and rather quaint with lush green grass, and the wild daffodils were surely on their way to blooming. The walking path was surrounded by thick, tall trees with big fat leaves, providing good shade from the full sun. It was one of my favorite places in town, and my go-to place when it was nice enough to walk.

It wasn't long before I made it to the park, and I smiled to see the daffodils were definitely in bloom. I admired the combinations of yellows, whites, and pinks. *So pretty,* I always thought they kind of looked like tiny trumpets.

I walked slowly when I made it to the path, taking time to appreciate the trees, the warm sunshine, the singing of the cardinals, and the robins as they explored the treetops. I took in a fresh gulp of air. Spring was one of my favorite times of year, and always made me feel happy. It was easy after all to feel happy with all of the fresh new life growing after a long, cold winter.

I felt my mind begin to clear with each step I took, focusing on the sound of my sneakers on the pavement, my steady breathing, and the quiet whisper of the wind through the trees. I felt myself relax, and sighed with relief. I truly loved nature.

After some time, I found a bench overlooking the small river that ran through the park, and sat in the sun. I watched how the sunlight glittered on the surface of the water. I closed my eyes and felt nature around me. I never felt more connected spiritually than I did in nature. I found myself drifting back to the words I'd read in Beth's diary.

"What do I do?" I asked out loud, my eyes still closed. "Do I keep reading? Do I bury it with the letters I'd written to her? Do I give it to Gracelynn?" I asked these questions out loud to myself, to Beth, to God. I squeezed my eyes closed, and swallowed past the hard lump in my throat.

When I opened my eyes, I knew my answer. I felt deep down what I needed to do. There was a whisper in my soul that craved to know more about the life Beth had written about in those pages. If everything happens for a reason, then maybe I was supposed to find this diary, maybe I was supposed to read it, maybe to reconnect with Beth.

When I got home I made myself a quick sandwich and a glass of orange juice. I set them on the coffee table in front of the sofa, and gently opened the closet door. I grabbed the blanket, unwrapped the diary, and took it with me.

I tucked my legs behind me, and I opened the diary to the next page. With a deep breath, and a new purpose, I began to read.

Dear Diary,

Ugh! I really don't want to think about my past. It is so much easier to sweep it under the rug and try to pretend nothing happened. To pretend I don't remember the things that happened to me, and around me.

But, I said I'd keep trying, so...here we go again.

To say things got worse is an understatement! After Dad left, my mother basically lay in bed for days. I cleaned the shitty trailer house we were forced to move into after we lost the house. There was no way we could afford to stay there. I missed the house, missed my bedroom, with its cotton candy blue walls, I missed the space, and the security. More than anything the security! I didn't want to hurt my mother's feelings, so I never talked about it.

I made her coffee, and sat it beside her. Her eyes were open, but I don't think she saw me. I made her a bowl of ramen. I wasn't good at cooking at the age of eight, but remember feeling proud of myself for making it. She didn't touch the soup. I had felt sad, because nothing that I tried ever seemed to make her feel good.

For days, I'd go to school and come home, and she'd still be right there in that damn bed. I remember that I'd felt scared, I felt like she was angry at me. I felt like it was my fault that Dad left.

"Mom," I said one day. Sitting at the edge of her bed, and as usual, she didn't acknowledge me. I honestly had felt like yelling at her, because I was scared.

"Mom, I'm sorry that Dad left," I whispered.

I watched as a tear crawled down her cheek. Watched her

wipe it off. She closed her eyes, and she didn't say a word. I stomped off into my bedroom and shut my door behind me.

I felt angry, at Dad for leaving, at Mom for just laying there... for making me worry.

I felt so alone.

Then, one day I came home from school, and Mom was sitting on the couch. I was so surprised, I remember standing frozen in the doorway as I looked at her. Her hair was a mess, and the trailer stank...but she was out of bed! It was a step in the right direction.

Or so I thought.

"Where have you been?" she asked, her voice sounded weird. I figured it was because she hadn't talked in a while.

"I was at school," I told her hesitantly as I took my bag off of my shoulders.

"Go take a shower, and get ready for bed" she practically yelled.

I frowned, "but, it's the middle of the day," I said, I remember feeling so confused.

"Do what I ask!" Her voice was so loud, echoing in the trailer.

"What about dinner?" I questioned softly.

"You ate at school," she said with a cruel shrug.

I remember crying in the shower. I remember going to my room and curling up in my bed, I lay there for a while with my eyes squeezed shut feeling like dad leaving was somehow my fault. Feeling like my mother didn't want me. I heard music, and sudden laughter coming from outside.

I went to the window and looked out, surprised by what I saw.

My mother was dancing, she was laughing, and she was with a bunch of guys. People I didn't recognize. I sat on the edge of my bed. It was the first time I'd ever gone to bed hungry. This was the first time in all of my life that I didn't want to be with her. I remember feeling so angry, and confused. Not understanding what was going on. I was scared, and very much alone.

As I lay in bed I covered my head with my pillow to drown out all the noise. My mother had changed into someone that I didn't even recognize. I came to the realization that night that I was afraid of her.

Four

Dear Diary,

After that first time I'd seen my mother hanging out with a crowd of men, it became part of the norm.

I was sent to my room often right after school. Forced to listen to loud rambunctious music, sounds of laughter at jokes that I didn't understand.

I felt invisible. Mom always smelled of alcohol, and the trailer was almost always full of people coming and going. It was full of smoke, and terrible language. Full of people who didn't know me, and didn't care to know me.

My mother said things like "Nevermind her" as I'd come out for the bathroom, or to get myself whatever was available to eat.

Most of the time it wasn't much.

After about a month, I got used to it, and my room became my sanctuary from the swinging door of men. I locked myself in most nights. More often than not I went to bed alone, scared, and hungry.

On the off nights it was just her and I, she'd make dinner. (usually mac n cheese, or a peanut butter sandwich.) and once in a while she'd even ask about school.

Often, I would talk about Katie. About her family, and how much fun Katie and I had at school. My mother hardly listened when I went on and on about my day. Most of the time when she looked at me, I felt like she looked through me. As if I weren't really even there.

I've always thought Katie's family was perfect.

I never said it, but I was so jealous of her life. Was, Ha! Still am. They are the nicest people I have ever met. Katie's family has been a Godsend, if there is a God...and I have to believe there is because there has to be more to this life than this...Katie has so much faith, I just wish I had that too.

The fact is, Katie and her family came into my life at exactly the right time, and I can't imagine my life without them.

I turned the page, my vision blurring with unshed tears.

Dear Diary,

Sometimes I feel so unbelievably alone. I know I have Katie, and there is school, but when I'm here, in this "house" I feel invisible, I feel unimportant to her, like I don't matter. Most days, I feel as if I am living in a nightmare. Sometimes I find myself praying that this is all a bad dream, and when I wake up, everything will be fine.

Then reality hits, and I know beyond a shadow of a doubt that this is my life, this isn't just a nightmare. As much as I would love for this all to be one crazy bad dream, it isn't.

Again I am struck with how fortunate I am that I do have Katie. She is the one constant, the one form of stability that I have in my life. Without her, I fear that I would be truly lost.

She is the very thing for which I have to be grateful for, each and every day. She may never know how much I love, appreciate, and need her.

Dear Diary,

Today is not a good day. I can't think about my past right now, not while my present is so screwed up!

My mother is high.

She's high, and my stupid step-dad is drunk as well as high...I had to come out of my room because I was starving! I hadn't eaten all day, trying to hang in my room, but I just got so hungry, I had to get something.

I made a sandwich. Peanut butter since we have little else, as usual.

He touched me.

I grabbed a change of clothes and locked myself in the bathroom, forgetting my hunger. I scrubbed and scrubbed. Still, I can feel him.

His hand was on my ass!

My mother was too stoned to even notice!

I HATE IT HERE!!!

I swallowed hard and took a sip of water, wiping the tears off of my cheeks. It was so hard to keep reading. Already I was learning things that I hadn't known. Beth had told me a lot, and I had seen a few things firsthand, but I hadn't known this. I hated that she'd been so alone.

I closed my eyes for a moment to steady my nerves. *Oh Beth! I am so sorry you had to go through this! I wish you would have told me!* My mind was screaming, my chest ached for my friend, my sister.

I opened my eyes, took a deep breath, and turned the page.

Dear Diary,

It's been a couple of days since I've written. Im' okay...Thankfully he hasn't touched me again. I don't think he even remembers doing it, and that really scares me. What if he does it again? What if he does something worse?

I didn't tell Katie. I didn't want her to worry about me... pretty sure she is always worried about me though. My Aunt Beck tried to get me to move in with her not long ago. She knows my mother has a drinking problem...maybe I should have just said yes...

I wouldn't know what to do without Katie though. She is the only friend that I have...She is like a sister to me, and her family is the family I will never have.

Maybe I screwed up by not going with my aunt.

Maybe I can change my mind.

Maybe I should change my mind.

What would Katie think?

I don't know if I could do that to her, to any of them! I'm not sure I could ever leave and forgive myself for doing so.

Also, there is still this stupid, ridiculous notion in the back of my mind...This tiny little shred of hope.

"What if everything changes?"

"What if it gets better?"

I feel dumb for wanting to believe it, after going through so much, for so long, to still have hope that things will be okay...am I crazy?

Maybe I am.

Dear Diary,

I used to pretend that I was Katie's real sister. I have a nice room, the air is always clean. There is almost always laughter to be heard. Stories are told, dreams are shared, there would hardly ever be a bad day, and when I did have a bad day, someone would always be around to comfort me. To talk about it, and to help me through it.

I wish I could be close to my mother as Katie is close to hers, I wish that like Katie, I didn't live in a stupid filthy trailer house, in a shitty part of town, that I didn't get picked on about my clothes, and about my mother.

That I wasn't often referred to as "trailer park Beth."

People suck sometimes...they don't take the time to understand a situation before they judge you. They make you feel like it's your fault that you are in the predicament that you're in. We don't get to choose what we are born into...

You don't get to choose your parents.

That is all out of your control...but when I am old enough to be on my own...I will have control. I will have control over my future! I will never, ever live in this condition again. No sorry excuse of a home, no shitty neighborhood if I can avoid it...

I will never (if I have a family of my own, that is) subject a child to the life that I have had to live.

I promise myself that much. Just because you grow up a certain way, or that you are raised a certain way, I have to believe that we get to make our own choices...my parents screwed up, they chose wrong. I won't make their same mistakes.

Dear Diary,

I remember going outside to play one summer day, Katie was on vacation with her family and I had been so bored. It was a hot day, but I didn't want to be inside.

I didn't want to be around any of the noise, the smoke, the booze...so I went outside.

I sat in the sun, on an old tree stump, away from the trailer. The sun felt good beating down against my skin. I remember closing my eyes to listen to the birds in the trees, and hearing the funny chattering of squirrels. It had been a simple pleasure.

I remembered walking about, playing with sticks, pretending I was in an enchanted forest. Pretending that life was beautiful, and grand.

I started getting hot, getting thirsty, so I went back to the trailer.

It was locked.

I beat on the door, for what felt like forever. I started crying, I started to panic.

No one opened it.

I found what little shade I could, there wasn't much escape from the sun though... and my skin is so delicate I burn quickly.

When she finally let me in after what felt like an eternity, I grabbed a glass of water, my hands were shaking so bad I could hardly hold the cup.

My mother in a cruel tone said "You look like shit, why didn't you come back in?" I looked at her, not knowing what to say, I was so angry, so confused...she'd known she locked the door. Why would she ask me that? Was she so drunk that she couldn't remember locking her child outside? I had been out there for hours!

Tears streamed down my cheeks, I remember the burning trail they left on my sunburnt face. I remember I had glared at her and threw the cup in the sink.

"You locked me out! You didn't open the door!" I showed her my arms. "Look at me!" I screamed at her.

She hit me across the face.

I bet if I closed my eyes I could remember exactly the way that it had felt.

My skin was so burnt I could hardly move without crying. I could feel blisters begin to form all over my arms, my face, my legs. I grabbed the aloe lotion out of the bathroom, I remembered using it when Aunt Beck had taken me swimming once.

I winced as I rubbed it all over myself in my bedroom.

It was the worst pain I'd ever felt. I have never told a single person about this.

I feel that some things just aren't meant to be talked about, and I'm scared that if I did talk about it, I'd relive that pain.

Oh God, Beth!

I closed my eyes and held the diary to my chest as new tears continued to stream down my face. I wiped at them, and when my phone rang I jumped, my heart racing. I took a steady breath before I answered.

"Hi Mom. Yeah, no I'm fine. Yep, I will see you soon." I knew she was worried about me, there was no way I could hide the fact that I'd been crying. When we hung up I went to the bedroom and put Beth's diary in my nightstand drawer. Then, I rushed to the bathroom to get myself cleaned up.

I needed to calm down, I definitely didn't want Gracelynn worrying over me, nor my mom. *I'm not ready to talk about it!* I thought. I grabbed a random book off of the bookshelf that hadn't been packed away yet, and began to read. I needed to try to clear my mind before Gracelynn came home.

Sometimes, I really hated crying because I felt like I couldn't stop. I was still very much feeling all of the emotions from the pages in Beth's diary, and I could feel the threat of more tears. I closed my eyes for a moment, deliberately slowing my breathing pattern.

Inhale.

Exhale.

Five

Dear Diary,

There was this one time when I actually tried to run away! I hadn't made it very far, only a couple of blocks before I had chickened out and snuck back inside. I wasn't even noticed, my mother was asleep in her room with boyfriend number 4? Number 7? It was impossible to keep track those days.

In all honesty, my respect for her left along with my dad. Sometimes I find that I am still angry at him for leaving. I don't understand what made him leave. I probably never will.

Did my mother have a drinking problem before he'd left? Had she always been like this? Maybe I hadn't noticed, maybe I hadn't paid enough attention, there had to be something I missed.

Sometimes I wonder how life would be if he had stayed. Sometimes it's easier just to blame him though. After he left, everything went wrong. We used to be happy, used to be normal. I do still think about getting out...maybe moving in with my Aunt Beck in Oregon, but it breaks my heart at the thought of moving so far away. It has to get better, it just has to. It can't be all bad! Can it?

away. It has to get better, it just has to. It can't be all bad! Can it?

Dear Diary,

Kids suck and boys are so immature!

I didn't have a lot of clothing to choose from. What I have is stuff from thrift stores my mother went to. I wish she would have taken me along, because most of what she picks up is either too large or too small, and is almost always in bad condition and embarrassing!

I have one favorite hoodie. It's navy blue, and it's huge on me, but I like it because it kind of feels like a hug.

I have a total of three pairs of pants that fit well, and a dress that I will never wear. I am not what anyone would call a "girly-girl."

I got sidetracked...anyway, back to where I'd started. Kids suck, and boys are immature.

I got picked on a lot as a kid, because I never "fit in," my clothes were grungy, hand-me-downs. They were worn and torn, and so they called me things like "smelly Beth, or "stinky Martin," even "Trailer Trash." The last one hurt the most. I never smelled bad. My clothes were, what was the term...dated?

When I started puberty I got picked on by boys a lot more often. I wasn't as pretty as other girls. "But you could be pretty if you wore more make-up," "you could be really pretty if you changed your hair." "You could be more pretty if you wore better clothes."

This constant "could be pretty" tore at my self-esteem, I wasn't pretty enough for boys. I wasn't pretty enough to have a lot of friends. I wasn't pretty enough to have a good life.

Where the hell does that come from? Who said you have to be pretty to have a good life, to make something of yourself? I guess, the more of something negative you hear, the more you really begin to believe it…The more you really begin to doubt yourself.

But here is the thing. I have been thinking about it, and I think I am pretty. Who gets to decide what pretty is? Regardless of my tattered clothes, and less than popular status, I'm not bad looking.

My hair is long, dark and curly. My eyes are like my dad's, bright green, they are actually my favorite feature. I'm not fat, and I'm not too thin, I'm somewhere in the middle. I'm not tall, but I'm not short either. I don't wear a lot of makeup, because I don't like the way it feels. Heavy, hot, cakey…

I've never given a ton of thought to my looks, but I can't honestly consider myself unpretty.

The name calling got to me more than I'd let on. I'd never show them that it bothered me. Sometimes it made me cry. Or that sometimes it had made me hate myself, and made me doubt that I'd ever be "pretty enough."

They'd call me names, and I'd pretend I hadn't heard them, or just keep walking away.

The thing is, I really don't like confrontation. Maybe that comes from spending so much time isolated in my room. Away from everyone, except for when I'm at school, or when I am with Katie. Which is a lot these days.

I feel wanted when I'm with Katie's family, like I belong there, like I'm part of the family. I have never felt judged, or "less than" when I am with Katie and her family. They treat me like a normal person. Anne is super sweet, she's like the mom everyone wants. Well, she's like the mom I want…

I read every chance that I could, between Gracelynn, Bobby, packing, and daily chores. Any spare time I had, I devoted to reading Beth's diary.

I talked to Bobby about it, finally. After crying over what I'd read one night, he'd held me, and with tears in my eyes I talked about how much of Beth's life I really hadn't known about…

I admitted to feeling guilty about the fact that Beth stayed because of me! What if she had moved in with her aunt? How different things would have been…but when I thought about that I cried harder, because I couldn't imagine a life without Gracelynn.

Bobby had comforted me, he held me close and let me cry. He whispered sweet words in my ear and rubbed my back. He told me that it was okay, that Beth did what she thought was best for her, that I didn't have any control over that.

I knew he was right, I hadn't had control over what Beth had decided to do. I knew that all I really could have done was be the best friend I could. To be there for her whenever she needed me, and I felt like I had always done that to the best of my ability.

It had taken me a long time after losing her. To get through the denial, the anger, the pain, and the constant overwhelming absence of her. Gracelynn, my angel…without her, I don't know if I'd have really ever come out of such depression.

There were days, especially in college, that I had wanted to give up, that I had thought about letting my parents take Gracey. Times when I had thought that I couldn't raise her, that I wouldn't be enough for her.

I let my eyes drift as Bobby held me. Concentrated on the sound of his heartbeat, the strength of his arms around me. The smell of his skin, and the sound of his steady breathing. I eventually succumbed to sleep.

Dear Diary,

I remember the very first time that Katie asked if she could come to my house to play. I had felt so scared, so very afraid to say a word. I actually sort of froze, and I remember stuttering as I came up with something along the lines of "I don't think my mom would like that so much."

Katie had taken it in stride. She had just nodded, her cute honey-blonde pigtails flopping behind her as we resumed our playing at recess. I had felt so relieved that she hadn't asked any questions.

It wasn't until a while later that I finally broke down (quite literally) about my mother. The way I lived. When I broke down in front of her, instead of making me feel embarrassed, Katie made me feel loved.

She'd hugged me, and she told me she would always be there for me, no matter what. So far, she's lived up to her word. Her whole family has been there for me, without fail.

Hell, if I could move in with them I would in a heartbeat. I'm sure that I'd probably only have to ask! But here is the thing...I don't like asking for help, and I don't want anyone to take pity on me (that ship has sailed I know). I don't want to be seen as a charity case, life is hard enough as it is.

I guess I might try again to get some sleep. I have school tomorrow, it's going on like one a.m. and I have an awful headache. I hope there isn't a test or something that I've forgotten about. I don't particularly like school, but I don't want to fail either.

Dear Diary,

My mother's "friends" are retarded! Right now I have the pleasure of listening to this terrible rage type music. Like, scream singing! My ears are pulsing, they hurt so bad. This is NOT music! The bass is up too high, the whole trailer is vibrating with it. All I want to do is shut it off, but I am not leaving this room!

There are too many people here. When I went to the bathroom, my mother had been sitting on my step-dad's lap. There were 4 other guys sitting on the couch beside them, and at least 10 other people standing around.

The trailer looks like shit...The air is thick with smoke, the counter cluttered with old food and unwashed dishes. It smells rancid.

I hate it here!

Maybe I should text Katie, and see if I can stay the night with her. I'm sure her parents wouldn't mind. Lord knows my mother doesn't give a shit, she probably wouldn't even notice I was gone.

Honestly, I don't really think I even need to ask her permission for anything anymore. Who is she to tell me what to do anyway?

She obviously doesn't care. If she does...She has a piss poor way of showing it! Hell with this, I know it's like 7 pm, but I know Katie and I know her parents. I have always been welcome.

Okay, I sent the text. Katie is quick to respond so I'm sure that I will hear back soon. I can't be here tonight. My head is screaming in pain. I just want to take a shower, and sleep in peace.

Katie just texted, I am going to get ready to go. Katie is going to drive over to get me. Her parents let her drive their Buick, which is awesome. Katie is like the most responsible person my age that I know. I honestly don't remember a time that she's gotten in trouble.

Sweet

Perfect

down-to-earth Katie.

I don't know what I'd do without her, or her amazing family!

I closed the diary and squeezed my eyes shut for a moment. Reading her words, "Sweet, perfect Katie"…it brought me back to an argument we had had so long ago. For some reason, it was still fresh in my mind, as if it had just happened.

Beth had been pregnant with Gracelynn, she had told me I was perfect, and that I had the perfect life, and perfect family…and I had taken offense.

Yes, I do have a good family, and I had been raised in a much better situation than Beth had, but I wasn't, and never have been perfect. I smiled at the memory of us apologizing to one another, and I remember thinking…my family really was as close to perfect as it could probably get, and compared to what Beth had…My family was probably the most perfect she'd ever come close to seeing.

I remember a long time ago, I'd been jealous of Beth too. I'd been jealous of her boldness, and her tenacity. Elizabeth had a strength in her that I'd always seen, but for some reason she really had never acknowledged it. She had thought of herself as weak for needing help.

As I read the pages of her diary, I saw strength and determination, I saw hope, and though she was never religious, I know that she had faith, because no matter what she went through, no matter what she'd endured, she stayed, and she stood strong. As strong as she could, for as long as she could.

I set the diary in my nightstand and shut the drawer. I had taken a pause in packing, because we decided that we should let Gracelynn finish out the school year before moving. It would be a busy situation, because we would have to make the drive to the farm often, to tend to it and make sure it was running well.

There were hands on the farm that Bobby had known for most of his life, so he trusted each of them. There were only a couple more months to the school year, and it would be better for Gracelynn to finish her year out where she was instead of moving her into her new school, so close to summer break. So, I had begun going through some things and decided that it was time to declutter.

There were things that we didn't really need, nor use anymore. I could donate them to the church and local thrift stores. Things that I didn't feel like packing up and moving with us. Moving is a good time to get rid of things, and I had been needing to do that for a while.

Since Gracelynn was over at Lilly's for the afternoon for her playdate, and Bobby had gone to the farm, I had time on my hands to do something productive. I went to our bedroom and changed into some older jeans, and a t-shirt. I tossed my hair into a high ponytail deciding to start with the attic. It had been a long time since I was up there last, there was no telling what I might find.

Frankly, I didn't like being in the attic, or in any dusty, confined areas. I decided to take my phone with me. I could find a podcast to listen to, or some music to keep me motivated with my task. I put my phone in my back pocket, and grabbed my water bottle. It was my favorite, despite being pink, because it had a measuring table on the side to keep track of my water intake. One of the gals at Bible Study had gotten it for me as a birthday gift, it was rather neat.

I climbed the steps carefully, they squeaked and groaned with each step I took. I clicked on the light and coughed at the dust accumulation in the air. I looked around, not as crowded as I had worried. Only a few boxes and bags. I grabbed my phone, and loaded up some 80's music to work with. I placed my bottle and phone down on an empty crate, and took a seat on the dirty old floor. I tried to ignore the claustrophobic feelings that the attic gave, and put my mind on the task at hand. I came across some things that made me wonder *why the heck did I keep this?* Like, hair rollers…*where did I even get these?* I laughed as I put them in a corner. Next I found bottles of old, half-empty nail polish, broken crayons? *Honestly!* I decided right then to make three piles.

1.   Donate

2. Keepsake

3. Throw away

By the time I was done, I was covered in dust and unfortunately, cobwebs! I felt like my skin was crawling, I felt sticky, and quite desperate for a shower. Aside from that, I also felt really motivated, pleased with my productivity, and made a mental note to continue to do this going forward.

I descended the stairs quickly, cringing as they creaked under my weight, and when I reached the dining room I set my phone and empty water bottle on the table. I immediately went to the bathroom. I checked everywhere for spiders, I couldn't stand those nasty little alien critters! My body did an involuntary shiver as I searched. Thankfully, as I'd not found a single creepy-crawly, I turned the water on and climbed in.

Once I was done with my shower, I wrapped a towel around my head and headed to the kitchen to find something for lunch. I hadn't realized it had gotten so late! I opened the fridge with a hand at my hip contemplating what I wanted. I opened the crisper drawer and got out some lettuce, cucumber, and tomato, and made myself a salad with the vegetables that I needed to use up.

After I got my salad together, I crunched some crackers over the top and lightly dressed it with my favorite Greek vinaigrette. I refilled my water, and sat at the table. Usually I don't sit at the table when I'm alone, but I did it for a change of pace.

I ate in silence, chewing each bite slowly, taking in all of the flavors of each vegetable with every bite.

Once I was finished with my lunch, I rinsed out my bowl, and decided to sit down on the couch with the diary once more before it was time to get Gracelynn from Lilly's. I tucked my legs underneath me as I cozied up against the decorative pillow. It felt so good to kick my feet up after hard work. With a soft sigh, I opened up the diary and flipped to the bookmarked page.

Six

Dear Diary,

They say everything happens for a reason, well I'd like to know what the hell the reason is for me having to live like this! Why am I in this situation? What good can possibly come of living here?

My mother is in the other room, with some dude...They are getting high, of course. I've never seen this one before, but he scares me. His eyes, huge, weirdly shaped and so dark they are almost black. He creeps me out, I can feel the evil pouring off of him.

I feel it in the way he looks at me, in the way that he holds himself. The moment he laid his dark eyes on me, just that one little moment that I came out of my room to get this bag of stale chips. He'd looked at me as if I were something to be consumed.

My God, I'm terrified!

What if one of these days, she will meet the wrong person and she will end up getting hurt, or killed...What if one of them hurts me?

What if it's this asshole?

I've been locked in my room since I grabbed the chips. I'd felt his eyes on me the entire time, and though it had been a moment, it had felt like an eternity.

If everything happens for a reason....Then why does it have to be so bad? Why does it have to hurt so much? What is the reason in that?!

Why is it always me? I swear the only thing good in this shit-show of a life I have, is Katie. Without her I honestly don't know what or who I would be.

I do know one thing.

<u>I will NEVER be anything like my mother.</u>

Dear Diary,

This guy...he has been here for days. I look forward to school because it means I can get away from him for eight hours. Yesterday was sadly not a school day, and I couldn't stay at Katie's because she was out with her family. I mean...I'm sure I could have asked to tag along...but I hadn't. I know they have always been there for me, but sometimes I feel like a burden. I don't want to be the tag along...

Today I got home from school to this guy sitting on the couch. It was unfortunate that he was sitting in his underwear. Eww! Oh my god! He is so disgusting!

He had looked at me as if he were trying to take my clothes off with his eyes alone. It made my arm hair stand, my skin prick, my stomach roll.

How could anyone feel comfortable in his presence?

He scares the shit out of me...I feel like something is going to happen. Though I don't exactly know what. Maybe he will just end up robbing us blind. I wouldn't put it past him, and I would be thankful if that was all he did.

My gut tells me differently.

My gut is telling me to watch my back. Every time he looks at me, I have a desperate urge to run. I'm going to listen to my gut.

Dear Diary,

The guy had stepped out for a while and so I used that time to come out of my room. I'd heard him talking with someone outside, and was thankful for a moment to come out. My legs were sore from being curled up for so long. I'd literally spent hours in the same position.

Even his voice seems to set me on edge, sort of like bringing me into a panic attack. I've never experienced that before from a single person. How can my mom not notice how creepy he is? Does she even care?

I broke down, I begged my mother to make him leave. She laughed at me. She told me that I don't get to tell her who comes in and out of her house.

I called her a bitch. Not the first time I've thought it, but it was the first time I called her that.

The sad thing is, she hadn't even reacted. She hadn't said a word. All she had done was look through me and glued her eyes on the tv. I feel like screaming at her. I feel like shaking her, I need her to wake up, to grow up...but I know that won't ever happen. I feel like running away. I feel like moving in with my aunt, just to get away from her, away from them.

Again I listen to this stupid little voice, this little thing inside me that says "you can't run."

Maybe I can't run. Maybe for some stupid unknown reason, I am supposed to go through all of this hell.

I don't get it, I probably never will. I mean...who the hell has any answers anyway?

I've thought about going to the cops...to report my mother, though I am not sure what good that would do.

I am afraid I'd be forced into foster care, or forced into moving in with my aunt.

Neither one of those sound like a good plan to me.

Maybe I should beg Katie's family to take me! I'm just not sure how much longer I can be here...

"Oh Beth!" I sighed out loud. "You were never crazy, God how I wish you knew that," I said to the empty house, my voice seeming loud in my own ears. Gracelynn was at school, Bobby was at work. I had been going through some things and had decided to take a break, and keep reading the diary.

Once again, I felt like I was trespassing.

Once again, I felt like maybe I should stop reading.

Once again, I talked myself back into it.

I tapped my fingers against the velvety surface of the diary on my lap. I was torn between getting back to work, and reading more. Scared to read more because I was terrified that something really awful had happened to Beth. Another secret she'd kept from me… these pages were full of things that I never knew.

My throat felt tight, making it hard to swallow. I looked at the diary nestled in my lap, I hated that she had had this life. I made a fist and hit the diary. I felt a familiar surge of anger, and not being able to help it…I cried.

I cried in anger, and in sadness. Beth had not deserved the pain she had endured. Her mother had not deserved her. I rocked back and forth, taking big, deliberate breaths to calm myself down.

Beth had deserved all the good the world had to offer. I hugged the diary close, as close as I would if I were hugging her instead. I had loved her so much. For all that she was, for all that she would grow to be…my chest ached for her.

It ached for the pain she went through, it ached for the child that she didn't get to raise, my chest ached with the absence of her once again.

I hadn't cried so much in a year as much as I had cried these past few days reading Beth's diary. It brought on so many emotions.

Emotions, both new and old. *Would the pain stop? Would the absence of her ever really go away?* I wondered to myself as I massaged my temples slowly, making small circles with light pressure. I'd gone and cried myself a headache. NO, I don't think the absence will really ever go away, but I know for a fact it does get easier with time. I always hated that old saying "time heals all wounds." I feel like time doesn't necessarily heal all wounds, we heal through the process of grief. It's not the same thing. In any case, it was getting these wounds ripped back open that I had a difficult time with.

I looked down at the diary, still laying in my lap. I picked it up, and I flipped through it. So many unread pages left. *Do I have the courage to keep reading?* My long, drawn-out sigh filled the empty room. I knew in my heart that I couldn't stop…not now.

RING RING! My chest leaped and I almost tossed the diary up in the air. I let go of a breath I hadn't realized I'd been holding and set the diary down, picking up the phone. I cleared my throat before answering.

"Hello?"

"Hello, Mrs. Farris?"

"This is she."

"Hi, this is Julia Reynold, Gracelynn's English teacher. I'd like a moment with you if you wouldn't mind."

"Is Gracelynn okay?" I asked, my heart accelerating as my mind instantly thought of a billion bad things that could have happened.

"Oh, she's fine, we had an assignment and I wanted to know if you'd be available to chat a moment today when you pick her up?"

I sighed with relief, feeling the tension in my shoulders begin to release. "Yes absolutely. I'll see you soon."

We hung up and I decided to put the diary away. There was no way I was going to be able to read more, especially if I were about to have a meeting with one of Gracelynn's teachers. I needed to clear my mind.

I glanced at the clock. I had about an hour left before it would be time to head out, so I decided to run a bath. A soak in the tub felt like just what I needed to calm down, and release all this tension.

I poured lavender epsom salt into the running water and padded off to the bedroom to collect a fresh change of clothes. I decided on a pair of nice jeans with a pretty top, there was no need to be overdressed.

I tested the water, toes first, before gliding in slowly. The water was just on the edge of being too hot. It was perfect because when the muscles relax, you feel better mentally as well as physically. It was something I'd learned from my counselor in college, years ago while I continued to battle depression after losing Beth.

I took a leisurely drive to the school. I wondered what the meeting may be about. I made it to the parking lot and found a good place to park, away from the crowded pick-up line.

I locked the car, and walked in. The mixture of cafeteria food, glue, and musty old textbooks assaulted my nose. My shoes clicked against the linoleum as I walked down the left hall toward Gracelynn's English classroom. I looked up to locate the names on the signs in the doorways.

I entered Mrs. Reynold's class slowly with a tap on the open door. She smiled softly in a friendly greeting and welcomed me into the room. She motioned for me to have a seat, and I felt a little silly as I sat in one of the tiny chairs and looked up at her. I suppressed a giggle at the fact that I felt like a child sitting in that little chair. The only big chair in the room was her desk chair.

"We did a poetry assignment, and I thought you would want to read Gracelynn's poem." Then, she slowly slid a piece of notebook paper onto the desk in front of me.

I smiled upon seeing Gracelynn's neat handwriting. Pretty good for an eight-year-old, in my opinion. My breath caught in my throat, and tears pricked at my eyes as I took in the words she'd written.

Seven

<u>My Mommy is an Angel</u>
By Gracelynn Martin-Farris

My mommy is an angel

looking down on me.

She left me before I knew her

I was told she left peacefully.

My mommy is in heaven

I just want to say hello.

To tell her some things

She never got to know.

My favorite color is blue

And I love music too

My hair smells just as hers did.

I never got to say I love you

I never held her hand

You see

My mommy is an angel

she left me with her very best friend

Katie is kind

She is the only mom I know

But I wish I could meet my real mom

The more I begin to grow

I suppose she's with me in ways

I have her smile

I have her eyes

Katie misses her too

Sometimes she even cries.

I cry too, but Katie says that's ok.

Katie says tears don't make a person weak

Sometimes they help us through the day.

I hope she knows that I think of her all of the time.

If my mommy is an angel in heaven

Then she's with me everywhere.

Katie says I carry her in my heart

a place she will always be.

If my mommy is an angel

Then I know she must be watching over me.

"I'd love it if Gracelynn would read this at the assembly next month. It's completely up to her, and you of course." Mrs.Reynold said after I'd set Gracelynn's poem down on the smooth surface of the desk.

I blinked tears from my eyes, my throat thick. I cleared it. "Sorry, that was…" I took a deep calming breath before I finished my sentence… "unexpected."

Mrs. Reynold nodded before saying "Gracelynn is such a sweet soul, she's always been at the top of the class as you well know. I think it would be good to share with everyone, I'd love it if you both gave it some thought."

I nodded, and thanked Mrs. Reynold for sharing. The final bell rang as I walked out of her class and I pinched the bridge of my nose with my eyes squeezed shut for a second.

I heard "Momma Katie!" and my eyes flew open to see Gracelynn walking quickly toward me. I smiled involuntarily and scooped her up in a hug. "What are you doing inside?" she asked as we walked together to her locker.

"Well, Mrs. Reynold needed to see me," I told her matter-of-factly, and stood to the side as she grabbed her backpack and shut her locker. She looked up at me with such expressive eyes and I smiled. "Everything's fine," I assured her.

We made our way to the car and we both got in and buckled up. "How about an ice cream?" I asked, and felt the corners of my mouth tug at her excited smile, and the very enthusiastic nod of her head.

When we got to the little ice cream shop I ordered an ice cream cone for Gracelynn and ordered myself a small cone as well. We sat at a secluded booth by the large windows that overlooked the water park.

"So, Mrs. Reynold let me read your poem today," I told Gracelynn as she took a lick off of her ice cream.

Her already large eyes grew wide, and she licked her lips before saying. "Did you like it?" her hopeful voice tugged on my heartstrings.

"Oh honey, it was so beautiful! You did such a good job, I am very proud of you." I felt my throat tighten and I swallowed hard.

"I felt very sad, and that was just what came out," she said with a shrug and another slurp of her ice cream.

I nodded in thought, and we finished our ice cream in silence. On the way home Gracelynn stared out her window.

"I'm sad that I never got to know her," she said suddenly.

My chin quivered as I looked in the rearview mirror. Her eyes, so large, and so sad. "I wish you could have too, sweetheart," I said, trying to keep my voice from wavering.

That night as I laid next to Bobby, I felt restless. My mind was full with thoughts of our pending move, thoughts of Gracelynn's poem, and thoughts of Beth. I stared at the shadows of the trees playing on the walls of our bedroom. I listened to Bobby's light snoring, enjoying his warmth and the comforting presence of him beside me.

Eventually I must have fallen asleep, because my alarm's beeping jolted me upright. I turned it off and squinted in the light now streaming in through the bedroom window. When I heard something thud, I jumped out of bed, pulled on my silky soft purple bathrobe, and padded quietly toward the sounds coming from the kitchen.

Smells of coffee and breakfast wafted through the air and I sighed, a small smile playing on my lips. I peeked around the corner and took in the sight of my husband standing in the kitchen, took in his grey sweats, bare feet, and the fact that he didn't have a shirt on was definitely not lost on me. His muscles flexed as he whisked eggs in a large mixing bowl. Unable to help myself, I walked up to him and pressed myself against his back, wrapping my arms around his waist.

"Mmm, morning baby!" he said, in that sexy, sleepy voice—a voice that sent shivers down my spine and made my toes curl.

I inhaled the fragrant air before replying "Good morning love! I'm surprised that you're home."

Bobby chuckled, and moved to pour the egg mixture into the skillet on the stove. I reluctantly let him go, but with a smile I fixed myself a hot cup of coffee. I leaned against the counter and watched him work on breakfast for a while, not bothering to help. He was doing just fine.

"I took the day off, we haven't had much time together for a while. I'm sorry I forgot to turn the alarm off. I was going to wake you with breakfast in bed," he said as he dished some eggs onto a plate, and popped some bread in the toaster. While the bread was toasting, he grabbed the butter, and plopped some hot crispy bacon onto the plate. When the toast was finished, he added it to the plate and passed it to me.

"Thank you, honey," I said as I took the plate from him. "Not just for this wonderful breakfast, but for taking the day off. I miss you," I told him softly.

Bobby leaned in to give me a peck on the lips. "You're welcome, now go sit and I'll join you in a minute."

"Is Gracelynn still asleep?" I asked, glancing at the clock. It was just after 7:00 am. But she was normally at least beginning to stir by now.

Bobby smiled as he joined me at the table. "Yeah, I checked on her a while ago. Snug as a bug."

I raised my eyebrows, it was strange but wonderful sharing breakfast alone together. Certainly a rarity these days.

We ate our breakfast in comfortable silence, and I took note that Bobby touched me any chance he got. A brush of fingers against my thigh, a small touch on my arm, our feet occasionally meeting underneath the table.

It's amazing that even after all of this time, he could still make me feel just as he had the day we'd shared our first kiss.

I smiled, I could feel him looking at me. I allowed my leisurely gaze to travel over the sun-kissed skin of his chest before meeting his eyes. He was smiling seductively.

"What would you like to do today?" he asked as he took our empty plates to the sink.

I leaned my back against the chair, and rotated my neck before looking back at him. He was looking at me so intently as he leaned against the counter with his arms crossed against his chest, that I was reduced to nothing but a hard swallow.

That seemed to suit him, because he sauntered over to me, a lion stalking its prey. I felt my heart quicken and my breath catch as he was suddenly looming over me. His eyes, dark with passion, seemed to caress me.

Something delicious tickled in the pit of my stomach as he held his hand out to me. I took it gladly and let out a small yip of surprise as he scooped me into his capable arms and carried me off to our bedroom.

Sometime later as we lay breathless, cuddled in each other's arms in bed, we both smiled as we heard the telltale signs of Gracelynn. She was coming down the stairs. Bobby got up after he kissed my forehead and told me he would take care of breakfast for Gracelynn.

I didn't complain, I was quite comfortable indeed. Though after some time, I stretched lazily before getting up.

Bobby's day off went quickly, as it always did, but we enjoyed it to the fullest. We spent our day loving one another's company as we watched Gracelynn play with her friend Lilly in the park. We went to the diner to eat lunch after dropping Lilly off back home, then went to the small zoo, and even went out for ice cream before coming home to watch a movie.

Bobby and I made dinner together with the music on, and we giggled as Gracelynn came into the kitchen and joined us for some dancing. She helped with setting the table, and I allowed her a soda with our meal.

We stayed up late after we had tucked Gracelynn into bed. Though we were both tired after the full day that we'd had, it was a good kind of exhaustion and neither one of us were ready for the day to end.

We held hands as we talked. We talked about a variety of things, and in quieter moments, we took in the compatible silence of the room.

I told him about Gracelynn's poem, and for what seemed like the millionth time of the day, I thanked him for taking the day off so that we could be together. It had been quite a while since we had had a day like that. We talked for some time as we enjoyed a rare glass of wine.

When we finally headed to our room for bed, Bobby rolled me onto my stomach and gave me a back massage. I closed my eyes and allowed myself to relax as he worked on sore muscles. I focused on the feeling of his smooth fingers making circles on my skin. I took in the smell of the sweet citrus lotion that he applied as he worked on my shoulders, and then worked his way down to my hips.

After he was done, I told him to lay down so that I could return the favor. He complied with a smile, and I giggled at his grunts of satisfaction. I sat on his bottom as I kneaded the tension in the muscles of his back. Enjoying the feel of his taut skin beneath my fingers. I allowed my hands to wonder of their own accord, and giggled when I found a ticklish spot.

He rolled over, making me fall to my side with a surprised laugh, then he leaned over me. I sighed as I looked into his eyes in the dim light of the room. They were bright bluish gray, and full of humor, but as he pressed himself against me they grew darker with renewed passion.

Later, in the aftermath of our lovemaking, truly exhausted, we held one another close as we fell to sleep.

Eight

Dear Diary,

I am not my past...

I am not my parents

I am not their mistakes

I am not what I go through

I feel like if I keep telling myself these things, I will start believing them. I am so tired of feeling scared...so tired of feeling invisible...I am so tired of living this stupid life in this stupid place, with these stupid people!

I just want to be normal.

Normal Beth, normal family, normal home!

I don't like asking for help, but I don't know how much longer I can stand being here. My mother barely looks at me, and when she does...it feels like she is looking through me. Does she hate me? Does she blame me for Dad leaving?

What did I do to make her hate me? Why does it feel like...it's my fault somehow. I don't understand.

Dear Diary,

Katie and I sat at lunch today and talked quietly at the table. I ate my food fast, without really tasting it. My stomach made dreadful noises when I swallowed. I know Katie had to have heard, but she hadn't said anything. Katie knows I don't get to eat much at home. I've confided in her more than I have confided in anyone.

Katie invited me to stay the weekend with her, and I told her I would. I am beyond asking for permission anymore. Hell, I don't think my mother even knows I'm here most of the time.

The guy that was over finally left. I haven't seen him in a couple of days, and I've slept better for it. I hope he doesn't come back...I feel like something is going to happen, I feel on edge, I feel so afraid when he's here.

I am fixing to get ready to go to Katie's, it's Friday and she is going to pick me up soon. I already threw some clean clothes in my bag for the weekend. I did my laundry yesterday after school at the laundromat. I'd used some money that I had found under the sofa cushions. It had been just enough to get my load of laundry done, and buy a soda from the vending machine there.

At least I am able to bring some clean clothes for the weekend over at Katie's. I would be so embarrassed wearing dirty clothes around her family, in their nice home.

Unfortunately I have had to wear dirty clothes before. To school!!

It was embarrassing, but unavoidable. I'm not the skipping school type. Mostly because I don't want to end up in some foster home. I don't ever want to be part of the system. My life is bad enough without belonging to the state.

Dear Diary,

The weekend went by way too fast. I wasn't ready to come back to this stupid place after school today. I had stayed at Katie's house from Friday evening to this morning. Katie did my makeup and I did hers before we went to school together. It had been such a good weekend. Full of fun and laughter...I soaked up every moment.

Her parents took us to the mall and Katie bought me a pretty, soft, blue shirt that I had had my eyes on in one of the little shops. The fabric is soft cotton and it looks good on me. The color seems to bring out my eyes.

I don't have very many good pieces of clothing, and it means more to me than she will ever know. I felt a little silly, standing in front of my mirror. I was looking at the way the shirt fit me. Taking in curves that I didn't really notice until I put the shirt on. For the first time in a long time, I feel pretty.

Dear Diary,

Self affirmations.

The school counselor told me to try to do some self affirmations. She says "the more positive things you say about yourself, the more you might just start to believe it." It's funny cause I've already tried this. Maybe I need to do it more often? I don't know.

I tried to give myself a self affirmation this morning. I told myself "I am strong, I am brave, and I am beautiful." I felt absolutely ridiculous talking to myself in front of my mirror. So, I closed my eyes, and I repeated the affirmation.

When I opened my eyes, I was surprised to find that I was crying. I wiped at the tear and studied it on my finger before I glanced back up at myself. I did feel strong, and brave because of everything that I've gone through.

I don't know anyone who has gone through what I've gone through. I know there are more unfortunate people. Some people are more unfortunate than myself, but I am not going to compare trauma...that's not something anyone should do.

Before I went to school I looked back at my reflection, and I said the words again.

"You are strong, you are brave, you are beautiful."

Maybe the counselor is right, this affirmation stuff might help. Something has to!

Dear Diary,

He's back, and I'm scared as ever. I have locked myself up in my room, honestly if I had a bucket I would use the bathroom in here so as not to go out of my room and see him. I feel like he's watching me all of the time, and even though when I come out of my room I'm only out a short time, it feels like his eyes are on me for an eternity. It makes my skin crawl, my heartbeat erratic...I am going with my gut about this dude. The fact is, he is not safe, and I am not safe with him here!

I popped out for a quick sandwich earlier. He was sitting on the couch beside my step-dad...His eyes were on me the whole time, I could feel it without looking. I zoned in on my sandwich. I spread my peanut butter on, then the jelly as quickly as I could without being noisy, and without a big mess. I'm curled up right now, my door is locked but I'm so terrified I'm shaking.

I'm scared to close my eyes, scared to sleep with him not too far from my door. I didn't feel hungry after his eyes were all over me, but I forced the sandwich down and followed it up with a large drink of water. The water has been sitting here since last night, but I don't even care. I'm not going back out there tonight.

I can't.

Dear Diary,

Something happened.

I was getting ready for school, and I left the safety of my room for the bathroom. There was no way I could hold it until I got to school.

He followed me into the bathroom....

He shut the door and leaned against it. I moved away from him as far as I could in the small space. I had wrapped my arms around myself, I swear it felt like my heart was going to beat right out of my chest. I stood there, panicked and stock-still.

He took his pants down, and told me to look at him, and he told me that if I didn't look he would hurt me.

I looked without actually really looking. On the inside I felt sick, I felt scared, and violated. It was as if I was outside of myself...because I had just stood there, looking without really seeing, as if it hadn't happened to me. Maybe I was in shock?

Apparently he felt satisfied because he yanked up his pants and he laughed at me before shutting the door behind him. His cruel laugh rang in my ears as I slid down the wall of the bathroom, clutching my stomach...I was late for school but I made it. He isn't here right now thank God, but still, all I want to do is run.

I closed the diary, and squeezed my eyes shut. Tears streamed down my face, and I did nothing to hide them. My heart was pounding so fast. I had felt as if I myself were on the outside looking in. Seeing her standing there, petrified in her bathroom as that pitiful excuse of a man tormented and scared her.

I felt like I couldn't breathe. I set the diary down and sighed, a loud sound that echoed in the silence of the room. I placed my face in my hands, trying to get this terrifying image out of my head. I felt disgusted and my soul ached.

Oh Beth, how I wish I would have known! We could have done something to help you! Why didn't you say anything? I cried, rocking back and forth. I felt my fists clench, and forced myself to take some deep breaths.

I didn't want to read anymore, so I got up and made myself a hot cup of tea and decided to open up a coloring book. I needed to do something, anything to get my mind off of everything. I wished that I could turn back time, to make everything right for her. Beth had deserved all of the beauty the world had to offer, and she'd gotten so very little.

She'd been taken just before it got better, brighter, and so very beautiful. It wasn't fair, and even after all this time, I still feel angry for the life that she'd had to live. I know that we don't get to choose the family we are born into, but why had she been made to go through such a hard life?

Nine

Dear Diary,

I bought a fake ID from someone at school...I don't know what I'm going to do with it yet, but I have one. I had shamelessly stolen money that was sitting in the living room. I don't know what gave me the idea. I didn't really think, I just did it.

I heard a rumor that one of the football players made these fake IDs, and they were definitely being used for getting into bars, and maybe even used at liquor stores. Anyway, I was surprised how quickly I had it in my hand. Of course, I tucked it away as soon as it was given to me. Now that I'm looking at it, haha! It doesn't look anything like me. On the card I am Penny Bigsby from Newkirk, Oklahoma. Age 22, 120 pounds.

I wish that I could change my identity for real. Not just on some fake card, but as in 'this is not my life,' but then if this wasn't my life, maybe I wouldn't have Katie. I can't imagine that. I definitely won't be telling Katie about this! I can just imagine the look on her face, or what she might think of me. I don't want to see or hear it. Does that make me a bad friend?

Maybe it does...I just can't bear the thought of her being disappointed in me. I guess I bought the ID because I wanted some kind of control over my life...like...as a way of telling myself that I can do what I want.

I don't know if that makes any sense...but it's too late to go back on it now. I know, I could just get rid of it. I probably should get rid of it, but it's still tucked carefully in the back pocket of my jeans. It's almost kind of thrilling in a way. I've never done something like this before.

Dear Diary,

He tried to get into my room last night. I know it was him. I had been laying there, looking at the moon from my window, when suddenly I heard the floorboards creak.

Slowly, the door handle turned and my breath caught in my throat. I had brought my blanket up to my chin, gripping it in a tight fist as I watched and heard the door handle rattle.

Thankfully he hadn't tried for long, and as I heard him walk away, I breathed a long sigh of relief. I think if he had tried any harder, he would have gotten in.

Needless to say, I didn't sleep for shit last night, and it was extremely difficult to stay awake in school today. In fact, Katie had had to wake me up a couple of times in class, and even at lunch!

As I lay here, I think I have caught my second wind...go figure. Maybe I will try to read. I should sleep better since HE isn't here tonight.

Dear Diary,

I can't...I just can't be here, I have to find a way out tonight! They are all drunk. HE is back, and tried to get into the bathroom while I'd been in the shower. I heard him as I washed my hair. "Let me in, beautiful. I won't hurt you. I just want to watch."

Sick bastard!

I ran to my room after my shower. Leaning against my locked door.

He's been tapping on my door off and on. I hate the sound of my name on his lips.

I'm scared shitless.

I feel like he is going to eventually do something bad to me... and there isn't a damn person in this house who will notice, or probably even care.

My stupid phone is out of minutes... I can't call Katie.

I have to get out of this place, now!

Dear Diary,

I screwed up...I screwed up big time!

I snuck out of my window last night. I couldn't take it any-more. He kept tapping on my door. Kept saying my name, asking me to let him in. I had thrown on my nicer looking jacket after braiding my hair, and putting my old makeup on. Taking extra care to make myself look older. I even painted my lips strawberry red. I sometimes listened to the preppy girls, I picked up on some tips. I'd been quick, and as quiet as I could getting ready.

I'd put my fake ID in the back pocket of my best fitting jeans...I squeezed myself out of my window. It hadn't been a very hard escape, minus the window seal pressing against my stomach as I had slid out.

I ended up in a bar...the fake ID worked! I hadn't expected it to be that easy. There was a guy there, he was cute with sandy blond hair and kind brown eyes, he was flirting with me. He bought me some drinks, we talked and danced to the jukebox music in the smoky bar for a couple hours.

I was nervous but he was nice, made conversation. Mostly about his dog and his truck. I didn't really care. My head was spinning, I felt dizzy and disconnected...That part was nice, I was Penny Bigsby last night...I wasn't Elizabeth Martin with her shitty life. I was Penny, 22 years old and free, a woman, not a girl.

I let him take me to his house. A small place, but it was clean and didn't smell like smoke. It was quiet too, and his dog was cute, a small fuzzy breed. We sat on his worn couch talking for the longest time, when we suddenly started making out. How I ended up on his lap with my lips dancing with his, I don't remember.

I didn't even know his name, how old he was, what he enjoyed doing. He was a stranger.

I lost my virginity to a stranger.

I am so disappointed in myself...but there was a reason I did it. A girl's first time should be her choice...I didn't want my first time to be with HIM, and if I am to be raped, at least I won't be a virgin. He doesn't get to take that from me!

The guy had been gentle at least, he didn't hurt me, though I am sore....God, I'm such a screw-up! None of this is okay.

Once again I had to put the diary down to collect myself. I rested my face in my hands and contemplated the diary. I hate that she had to go through this! I hate that she had had this stupid miserable life before we finally took her in!

My fists clenched in renewed anger. *Why had we waited?* I obviously knew some things, the things that she'd been willing to tell me. I know my parents had on a few occasions, wanted to call the cops, or report it to Child Services.

I had begged and pleaded for them not to. Beth was scared to end up in a foster home, and I didn't want that for her either.

But why hadn't we done something sooner? Why hadn't I encouraged her to move in with her aunt in Oregon?

I'd been a selfish child! I hadn't wanted her to be so far away. Again as I cried, I reminded myself had she left, we wouldn't have Gracelynn. *I can't imagine a life without her in it.*

I glanced at the time, surprised that it was only a little after eleven o'clock. I still had quite some time before I had to pick up Gracey from school, and Bobby was at the farm probably until around dinnertime. I glanced at the diary, before getting up and opening the front door. It was getting warm out. I decided to pack myself a sack lunch, I grabbed an old blanket from the linen closet, and made myself a tall to-go cup of sweet iced tea.

After my hair was up off my neck, and everything was ready, I drove to the park to have a picnic. I'd never had a picnic by myself before, but it sounded nice. The diary lay on the seat beside me along with everything else.

I found a nice place to park and walked to my favorite spot in the sun. I laid out my blanket and stretched out on my stomach. It felt good, and for a moment I lay there enjoying the sun's warmth against my skin. I took a few breaths with my eyes closed, and then I settled in and opened the diary.

Dear Diary,

I haven't really had any energy.

To be honest, after losing my virginity I feel depressed, and angry with myself. I wanted my first time to be with someone that I loved. I definitely hadn't wanted to do it with a complete stranger!

I had acted out of fear...and it wasn't until now that I started really panicking... he hadn't used any protection!

HIV-AIDS

STDs

Pregnancy

These thoughts are churning my stomach, I feel like such a failure! How could I have been so stupid!?

Dear Diary,

I screwed up so bad, and there isn't a damn thing I can do to take it back...what's done is done.

I feel sick to my stomach. I keep telling myself it's stress, and depression that has me so wound up. I mean, my life is definitely not rainbows and butterflies!

I want to talk to Katie so badly about this, it's literally eating me up inside. I think maybe that's why I haven't felt good these past few days.

It's been over a week since I lost my virginity. Nothing significantly crazy has happened around here.

Same shit different day.

My mother yelled at me this morning because I guess I was in the shower too long, and she needed to use the bathroom. She'd all but shoved me out of the way to get in once I'd opened the door.

HE hasn't been around, and I've been so unbelievably grateful for that. I don't think I could take another night of him trying to get into my room, or saying things to me behind closed doors, or following me into the bathroom.

I might just literally vomit at the sight of him.

I blame him, I blame my mother, and I blame my father. I blame them all for everything that is going wrong in my life!

I'm so pissed! I can hardly stand the sight of myself. When I glance in the mirror I see my mistakes, I see someone that I don't even really recognize anymore. My hair is an unruly mess, my eyes are heavy and red-rimmed from lack of sleep and crying. I have dark circles under them, the once bright green is now faded, dull. My face is pale.

To put it bluntly, I look like shit!

Katie is probably worried about me. I miss her, but I just don't want to see her. I know that if I do I will blather on about everything and I want to forget about it.

If only that were so easy.

I could barely stomach the chicken salad sandwich that I had packed for myself to eat, but I took a break from reading to eat it. I listened to the birds, and the slight wind in the trees, I watched as the sun glinted on the surface of the water.

It was nice to know that she had wanted to talk to me, because she had taken quite some time before she'd finally broken down. I closed my eyes, I remembered the day as if it had just passed.

We were sitting on my bed and she was crying. She told me how she'd lost her virginity to a man she'd met in a bar. It was the day that she had told me that she was pregnant.

I opened my eyes and took a deep breath. I remember feeling angry at her, at the same time that I felt desperately sad. I cleared my throat, willing myself to get back out of the past. Sometimes it's so hard not to look back, especially now that I am reading Beth's diary. I can't seem to help myself.

In a way, I am glad that I decided to read it, to finally know the truth about what she had gone through. It was incredibly hard to read most of the time. I felt scared, guilty, hurt, and angry…and yet, I also felt connected to her in a way that I never had been before, I felt loved as I read about how much my family and I had impacted her life.

Honestly, I think it is this feeling of connection that keeps me reading, despite how terrible most of it is.

I leaned my back against the tree I was laying under, after finishing my sandwich. I decided I'd been laying down long enough. I brought my knees up to my chest as I opened the diary once again.

Ten

Dear Diary,

I went to the free clinic today, since I have been feeling so sick. I can hardly eat, and in fact, I have even stopped going to school. I called the secretary and told her that I was really sick. She told me to get well and that had been it. Every day for the past couple of weeks I've been calling and saying I'm sick.

I'm surprised they haven't called child services...Didn't this count as truancy? I'm glad of course that they haven't, but at the same time I wonder...Do they even really care? Sometimes I think maybe it would be better if they did...my mother would be arrested for sure.

Anyway, I went to the clinic and told them I'd been feeling very sick for the past couple of weeks and I thought I should see someone. The nurse asked me personal questions, and I had to pee in a cup.

About twenty minutes later, the doctor came into the room.

I asked what was wrong with me. She said "Elizabeth, you're

pregnant." She handed me a handful of pamphlets on being a new mother, talked to me about my options, and sent me on my way. I feel like the world is closing in on me.

Oh my God... I'm pregnant!

I can't even take care of myself, how in the hell am I going to take care of a child? I am a child!

I'm such a screw up! What am I going to do? I don't know the first thing about having a kid, let alone raising one.

I can't breathe...

What have I done...

Dear Diary,

It's been a while since I've written, but I have better news. Even though I am pregnant.

I moved in with Katie and her family! They had basically kidnapped me. Katie had boldly stormed in and told me to come with her. Katie's mother, Anne, had taken Katie and I to help me move out after I had finally confided in them about being pregnant. I won't lie, it had been so damn hard telling them. Probably the hardest thing I've ever told Katie.

Katie had looked so sad, and shocked, and actually kind of angry when I had told her the news. I'd been surprised when she'd been so supportive, I guess I shouldn't have been that surprised really. Katie's always been so unbelievably kind and caring!

Anyway, long story short, I am finally out of that stupid place, with those stupid people, living that stupid life!!

They got me out! They rescued me!

Dear Diary,

Ugh!!! I feel so gross and I am so tired...Like all of the time. I told Katie I wanted to quit school, and I thought she was going to have a conniption. I, of course, am staying in school. I can't help but feeling the way I do though, I feel sorry for myself.

I wear loose-fitting clothes most of the time, even though I'm not really showing yet. I'm terrified that someone might notice weight gain. I'm not extremely tiny or anything, but I've always had a small frame. I just...I know that when I start getting "The bump" people are going to notice.

I know that soon, I won't be able to hide this pregnancy.

I've been made fun of most of my life. And I am still worried about what people are going to think, or say. Why is that? You'd think after so many years of being made fun of, and called names, it wouldn't affect me so much... But it does.

Just the thought of it is making me nauseous. Well, more nau-seated than I already am.

I wouldn't think that's possible...

Dear Diary,

School sucks, I'm tired all of the time, I want to cry for no real reason, I'm always hungry but I can't keep anything down. I hate being pregnant! What if it's like this the whole time?

Anne says that it will get better, the morning sickness shouldn't last very long...but Damn! I've been feeling this way long enough! When does it end?

On the plus side though, Katie's family is so amazing to live with! I wish I'd done this years ago...

Seriously though, why hadn't I just asked them to adopt me? It's not like my mother would have bat an eye about it.

She probably would have signed the papers and thrown a party when I was gone! Honestly, I wouldn't put it past her...I bet she hasn't even tried looking for me!

Hell, she probably hasn't even noticed I'm gone.

Dear Diary,

Anne gave me some dissolvable tablets that made the nausea disappear in a matter of minutes. OOOH MY GOD! I feel so much better. I mean, I could complain that I don't like the orange chalky flavor it leaves behind, but honestly it's a small price to pay to feel this amazing!

I've been eating a lot of eggs, which is so weird because I don't even like them. I mean, who the hell looks at something a chicken pooped out and thinks "yum?"

Well, I guess I like them now, or at least the baby does.

I feel like a different person...It's all so surreal.

In other news, Katie has a boyfriend!!!!! She is going out with Bobby Farris, this is so cool! She's been crushing on this guy for like EVER! They look cute together, I always thought they would, and I'd always told Katie that he liked her. I'd see the way he would look at her when she wasn't looking. I am happy for her, but at the same time, I feel kind of jealous...I hate that about myself.

Katie deserves this! She is the most amazing person that I know. She deserves every bit of happiness. If he ever hurts her though, I will kick his ass! I think he knows that. If he doesn't, he will soon because I will straight up tell him!

I let out a loud laugh, hugging the diary to my chest. I closed my eyes *"I love you so much!"* I said to the wide, endlessly blue sky. I stood up and stretched my body, feeling sore from leaning against the tree for so long.

I collected the picnic items, and walked them to my car. Then, I decided before I headed back home that I would take a walk around the park. It would also give me time to reflect on Beth's diary, and time to clear my mind before I picked up Gracelynn from school. I had over an hour to spare.

I took my time walking, taking in the sights and smells around me. Nature has always given me a sort of peace that nothing else seems to measure up to; feelings on a spiritual level that I've never even felt at a church, or anywhere. I decided long ago that nature is my real church. It's the closest connection that I can find to God, the universe, everything.

I contemplated thoughts and feelings as I walked. I felt my body loosen up, as if a great weight was lifting off me and I could breathe easy. Maybe it was the sun, maybe the fresh air. Maybe it was from reading these past few pages of Beth's diary. Whatever it was, it felt good.

Once I finished walking the path, I headed back to the car and leaned against the seat to catch my breath before driving.

I drove slowly, enjoying the languid feeling of the moment. It had been such a wonderful and slow going day. It felt so good being in nature, and feeling so close to Beth again. I closed my eyes briefly as I waited in the ever-crowded pick-up spot at the school.

I wish Beth could have gotten to know the beautiful person that she'd brought into this world. I wish Gracelynn could have gotten to know how amazing her mother was. I let out an audible sigh, opened my eyes, and smiled as I saw Gracelynn pop out with her friend Lilly.

Bobby came home in a good mood, although I could see from his eyes that he was exhausted after his day at the farm. Gracelynn was also tired, her eyes drooping as she tried to stay awake for the movie we were watching.

We'd decided on Twilight, because of course I had told her once that it had been one of her mother's favorite movie series. There were a few scenes in the movie that I personally didn't feel she was ready for, and I giggled to myself when she covered her eyes during the kissing scene, mumbling "eww gross!" even as she peeked through her fingers. Bobby had fallen asleep not even midway through the movie, so Gracelynn and I cuddled together.

I was surprised that she stayed awake through the entire movie. Once it had gotten past the worst of the "mushy stuff" Gracelynn seemed really into it. After it was over, I got up and stretched before turning off the DVD player and the T.V. Then, I walked Gracelynn upstairs to her room. She didn't want to be tucked in, so I kissed her forehead before wishing her goodnight.

When I turned out her light, it occurred to me just how much she'd grown up. I smiled, a sad sort of smile at this realization. She wouldn't need me as much soon, and would prefer time with her friends. I'd have to get ready for that. I peeked in at her, seeing that she was already nestled in and sleeping. I carefully shut her door and headed downstairs.

Bobby had woken, and was running his hands through his hair when I came down. He smiled at me, kissed my cheek, and told me he was going to bed.

"I'll be there after a bit, honey," I told him quietly.

I sat on the couch for a little while with my journal. My pen moved gracefully over the pages as I poured out my thoughts and feelings. Once I was finished, I turned off the lights and headed to bed.

❖ ❖ ❖

Dear Diary,

I haven't written in a while, I guess nothing really comes to mind other than my recent poor life choices.

Katie, Anne, and I went to the hospital and I got a doctor. Her name is Dr. Ray. She is really nice, and I like her a lot. Her eyes are kind, and she didn't make me feel any certain way about being pregnant. I had feared that she would look down on me or something, but she hadn't. She'd been kind, and gentle. I don't think I could have handled a male doctor. The thought of that kinda freaks me out. I don't want a man in my personal space!

I got to see the baby. I hadn't liked the fact that in order to see, I had to drink lots of water, and that I could not go to the bathroom so that they could get a good image. Honestly, I felt like I was going to pee my pants...I hope it wasn't obvious that I was squeezing my legs together the whole time.

I got to hear the heartbeat, it was beautiful and we all cried. My appetite is growing rapidly, and I am clearly getting the "baby pooch." Anne thinks it's adorable. Katie is so weirded out, I can tell. She's still unbelievably supportive though.

Katie and Bobby go out a lot more now that they've been dating for a while. It feels good to see her so happy, but again I find myself from time to time, jealous.

I feel like a third wheel around them. Though I definitely shouldn't. It's just that it has always been me and Katie. Not me, Katie, and Katie's boyfriend.

It's most likely just the hormones...I'm lonely, it would be kinda nice to have a boyfriend...PSH! No one is going to want to date a seventeen-year-old pregnant girl! That's just too much, I think...hell it's too much for me and I am the one going through it!

Seeing the relationship that Katie and Bobby have formed, has really inspired me though. They are rather perfect for one another, it's as if they were meant to be. It makes me excited for my future, because I hope to have a love like that one day.

Katie's parents have also taught me something. I'm learning what healthy relationships are supposed to look like. Growing up in my household, I never really got to see what a good relationship looked like.

I don't remember seeing my parents fighting, I do know they yelled sometimes. My mom didn't like to "make waves" as I recall. I feel like my dad actually didn't spend much time inside, now that I think about it. He chose the garage over the house more often than not, when he wasn't working.

Anyway, if he loved me, why did he leave me and never come back? If she had been going on that downward spiral while they were together, why hadn't he taken me with him? Why leave me with her?

I have all these questions, and no desire to seek him out to get any answers. I truly feel like if he cared, he would have come back. If he cared at all, he wouldn't have left me in the first place... Would he have? Does he have a wife and kids somewhere else? Does he even think about me?

UGh! Now I'm crying, and I need to go do something...I'm not sure how this writing feelings down is helping anymore. I just feel sad.

Dear Diary,

Katie and I got into an argument. I was immediately angry with myself, it wasn't even really an argument I guess, and now that I'm thinking about it, I don't even remember how it started! I just need to apologize and get over myself!

I think I miss our friendship...The way it used to be.

Before the pregnancy

Before Bobby

Everything is changing so much, so fast...And I don't feel like I can keep up. I've never treated Katie this way before...she's probably crying, I feel terrible.

I feel stupidly jealous, and very selfish right now, and I think I am going to cry...Ha! Nothing new there! I feel like lately all I can do is cry.

Stupid hormones!

Eleven

Gracelynn recited her poem at the assembly, and she received an award! Even though I'd read the poem…I had cried like a baby! Bobby had cried too, sitting there holding my hand as we looked at our beautiful daughter on stage. She seemed so confident up there in front of all those people. She was so courageous, and I was so very proud!

After the assembly, we took Gracelynn out to eat, her choice. I hadn't expected her to pick McDonalds of all places! Afterward, we went out for some ice cream and then we went back home and I allowed her to stay up late to watch a movie.

While Gracelynn watched her movie, Bobby and I held hands at the kitchen table and talked. It was a little over a month before school would be out for the summer, which meant that it was almost time for the big move.

My mom had talked us into letting Gracelynn spend some time with her while we got moved and settled in. She thought it might make it easier on us, as well as Gracelynn. The move wasn't something that Gracelynn was truly happy about yet.

She was spending a lot of time with Lilly now that summer was almost here. She was still very worried about losing their friendship.

I felt upset about it, but really…what could I do? We were moving, everything was in place, and definitely in motion. Bobby had been taking loads of things that I already had packed up and ready to the farm house.

I could tell he was excited, and I was also ready for the new chapter in our lives. I worried that Gracelynn might take some time to really adapt. I thought once she realized she could still see Lilly from time to time, maybe she would relax and accept the change. She does love the house, which I hope helped tremendously!

Dear Diary,

The secret is out! People know that I am pregnant and the rumors are spreading like wildfire.

I hate school!

Katie is a huge help, she and her family have been amazing... They always have been, but now more than ever.

I need them now more than ever too! I have a baby inside of me, a living thing growing inside of me!

Sometimes it feels so surreal! And while most of the time, I feel crummy, irritated, sad...and lonely, I also feel just the slightest bit...excited.

I don't know how that is possible, but there it is. The excitement is there, and building. Even though I'm too young for this, I feel like this is my chance to do something good. I know that Katie's family will help with the baby, I am not going to be all by myself! But...eventually, I will be raising my baby, and he/she will never ever go through the hell that I went through!

I am not my mother, I am not the mistakes of my past, and my child will have a beautiful life.

Dear Diary,

My goal to keep writing every day is failing miserably, but honestly I am just...tired, and I don't care. I feel like I am no longer concerned about talking about my past. I don't want to keep reliving it! It happened, and it was horrible. But it's over! I've acknowledged what happened, I've felt all the feelings, all the emotions...why must I wallow in it? Why constantly harp on that old pain? I just...I don't understand how it is supposed to help me heal.

Obviously I still think about it, but it doesn't have the impact it used to. I don't feel like writing about it anymore. I want to write about being pregnant, and living with Katie and her family. I want to write about happier things, focusing on all of this negativity is really bumming me out.

So, on to a better and happier topic! I love my room...MY ROOM! They even painted it for me. It's amazing! Everything in this room is bold and colorful and yet somehow, Anne made it all go together. The room is all vibrant reds and oranges, there is cream and gray in the pillows and curtains. It all just...works. Anne is awesome at this stuff. No offense at her current job title, but I think she should decorate houses for a living!

I feel at home, and that in itself is the best feeling I've had in a very long time.

I still get talked about at school, but even that is dying down! For that, I am beyond happy, I don't like being looked at and talked about, and finally I don't feel like I am in the direct spotlight anymore.

It feels kinda good, looking at the new and better things that are going on in life. Focusing on all of the negative things has just gotten me feeling more tired.

I know that in life we have to take the bad with the good, but I kinda need a break from the bad...that's almost all that I've ever known.

Now I'm feeling kinda melancholy again...damn these hormones.

I smell food, so I'm gonna go investigate!

After I finished a couple of pages in Beth's diary, I put it away. Bobby was already headed to the farm, but Gracelynn would be up soon. I wanted to make her some breakfast, and take her to the park for some good quality time together.

I padded off to the kitchen, whipped up some eggs, and got some ham slices in the frying pan. Gracelynn walked in, her hair a wild mess. She rubbed her eyes, and looked at me sleepily as she sat down at the counter on her stool.

"Good morning," I told her with a smile, setting a plate of scrambled eggs, with cheese, ham, and toast in front of her.

"Good morning Mom! This looks yummy," she said, and dug in.

My eyes rose as I watched her gobble her food and I felt myself smile. "You must be hungry this morning!" I said as I sat beside her, with my own plate.

After our breakfast, I put Gracelynn's hair up for her, something that she only sometimes allowed me to do. Then, after I cleaned up the kitchen, we headed out to greet the day together.

The weather was already warm, the sun shone brightly in a cloudless blue sky. Gracelynn excitedly chattered in the back seat about what she wanted to do for the day, and asked if after we were done at the park if she could go to Lilly's. I had hoped for the day alone together, but as I looked into her hopeful, green eyes I couldn't bring myself to say no.

"I will call and ask," I told her.

I watched as Gracelynn began to swing for a while and suddenly she stopped to look at me with a hand at her hip…"Aren't you gonna swing with me?" I joined her on the swingset, my stomach disagreeing with the movements after a short time. *What is it about becoming an adult? As a child, I could do this for so long! Now, it just makes me nauseous and dizzy,* I thought to myself.

I slowed the swing down so that it was barely moving and watched Gracey. How her curls bounced as she swung back. The way the sun caught the amber flecks in her beautiful green eyes. The smile on her face, that could light up even the grayest of days.

I closed my eyes for a moment, and then looked up at the wide open sky. Such an excellent day to be out in nature, and any day was a perfect day to spend time with Gracey.

"Momma Katie?" Gracelynn's voice broke through my thoughts.

"Hmm?" I asked, turning my attention toward her.

"Are you okay?" Her eyebrows rose in concern and though it was sweet, I wondered why she was asking.

"I'm doing wonderfully," I said as I smiled at her.

"You looked kinda sad," she said, before getting up off of her swing.

"I'm sorry honey, I didn't mean to worry you. I was just thinking about how pretty it is out here, and how happy I am that we are here together," I told her truthfully.

This seemed to soothe her worries, because she smiled and took my hand. Together, we ended up going to the slides. *Oooh Lord!* Trying to squeeze myself in enough to go down a slide with her was difficult.

Gracelynn laughed heartily when I made it down. "You looked like a hot dog!" she said, her face pink and her eyes watering.

"Oh my! How do I look like a hot dog?" I asked with a snort of laughter.

Gracelynn laughed again. "You were all squished up and your body was flat, like this." She laid down and squished her arms tightly to her sides in the attempt to imitate me. The expression on her face did me in. I doubled over laughing.

"Ooh my goodness!" I managed to say. Gracelynn held her hand to her mouth as she laughed with me.

We took a walk after we were done playing on the equipment, and we studied the water together. On the way back to the car, we watched as some ducks waddled up to the water. Gracelynn laughed and imitated a duck walk.

"Hahaha! You are so wonderful, you know that don't you?" I asked her as she took my hand.

"I suspected as much," she said matter-of-factly.

I snorted, she definitely had her mother's wit! "I love you so much! Don't ever forget how special you are, okay?"

Gracelynn settled in the car, and buckled up as I got my own seatbelt on and started the engine. She looked tired, her cheeks a pretty pink from the sun.

"You want some ice cream?" I offered. Her eyes lit up and I smiled. I took that as a yes, and headed in the direction of the ice cream shop downtown.

"I need to go to the store before we get back home though, okay?" I told Gracelynn as I parked the car.

"Okay! Can I get some avocados?" She asked.

"Absolutely!" I said as we made our way into the ice cream shop. It was quiet, and I was surprised on as warm a day as it was, I figured it would be busy. I glanced at the time, It was earlier than I had thought. I was thankful that we had come before the crowd.

After our double scoop of ice cream, we headed straight to the store. Gracelynn got out happily, and I smiled at her excitement. Most children her age seemed to despise going grocery shopping. She had always been eager to go, even when she'd been younger. I also loved how when most children begged for a candy bar she would ask for something like avocados! Beth had liked guacamole, but hated avocados by themselves, I remember her claiming that they tasted like a very sad banana. I smiled recalling the memory.

I put a couple pounds of hamburger in the cart, some turkey lunch meat on Bobby's request, a loaf of bread, and some fruit. Gracelynn picked through the avocados until she found a couple that felt good. I had taught her the proper way to check if an avocado was ready to be eaten.

Once I grabbed the eggs and milk, we were ready to check out and head home. Gracelynn helped me load up the groceries in the trunk, and then we unloaded them together when we made it back home as well. I took the majority, and handed Gracelynn the keys so that she could unlock the door. I called Tracey to see if Lilly was able to play, but she'd informed me that they were out of town, so I let Gracey know. She'd been a little disappointed, but thanked me for calling to ask.

After all of the groceries were put away, Gracelynn made herself a snack. I cut the avocado for her after rinsing it off, and Gracelynn squished the avocado into a bowl, and mixed in some salsa and ranch. Then, she grabbed the corn chips off of the counter and made herself comfortable at the table.

"Would you like to eat your snack with a movie?" I offered.

"Yay! Thank you, Mom!" she grabbed her chips and dip, and I poured her a cup of juice before following her into the living room.

I let Gracelynn choose what she wanted to watch, and I chuckled when she pointed to the next Twilight movie. I'd seen these movies so many times, but I didn't mind. It made her happy that I put it in and settled down on the couch beside her.

That night after I said goodnight to Gracelynn my phone beeped and I picked it up to see a message from Bobby. It was getting late, it was a relief to finally hear from him.

I love you baby, be home in a couple hours. Sorry it's so late, don't wait up.

I hated him driving alone at night. Bobby is an excellent driver, but I worry because I know the deer are getting thick.

I love you too honey, thank you for letting me know. Please be careful, okay?

I will be careful, I promise. I am gonna get a bite to eat. I hope you and Gracey had a great day together.

I'm glad you are eating! We did have a wonderful day, we miss you.

Miss you both too, love, I will be home before you know it.

I sighed and put my phone down, I had known that this would be a challenge—Bobby going to work, and then spending time at the farm. So, why was I being so emotional about it? I guessed, I missed being with him. With so much going on, our days together were few and far between.

I decided on a bath to relax my nerves. For some reason I felt a bit edgy. I attributed that to Bobby driving at night, and it being a long and eventful day. I started the water, and added some extra bubbles for supreme comfort.

I got in and sank down into the tub. Closing my eyes and allowing myself to breathe, I soaked up the silence, and felt my muscles relaxing bit by bit. One thing I was ready for however, was the huge attached bathroom to the master bedroom at the farm. It had a tub big enough for the two of us—round and marble, and perfect!

I spent a while in the tub, feeling each part of my body relax. I thought about the farm and spent time focusing on my breathing, and being in tune with myself. I got out and lotioned my body, paying attention to my knees and elbows, as they tended to crack when they got too dry.

I'd started learning about the importance of self-care in college from my counselor. She helped me a lot, through my grief and learning to find myself again…after I lost Beth, I really felt as if a whole piece of me went with her. My counselor taught me that I needed to practice self-love. She said, do one thing each day that is just for you.

There are still days that I tend to forget about myself, with the hustle and bustle of life. I make excuses for myself, but I do try desperately to do at least one thing a day for me. Self-love and self-care are so very important.

I closed the bottle of lotion and slipped on my favorite pair of pajama bottoms and a soft cotton t-shirt, leaving my hair wrapped in my towel. Then, I made my way into the kitchen to fix myself a hot cup of tea. My body and mind felt relaxed, but I didn't feel quite ready for bed.

After I made myself comfortable with my steaming tea, I brought out the diary. I set it on my lap and took a couple of sips of tea, taking time to taste the peppermint, and feel the way it soothed my throat on the way down. The simple pleasures truly made me happy, even something as simple as enjoying a hot beverage.

With a new sense of calm and purpose, I opened Beth's diary, and began to read.

Twelve

Dear Diary,

Wow. I got terrible at keeping a diary...oh well. Nothing much has changed, except for the size of my jeans!

I am getting undeniably rounder, and soon I will be five months pregnant. Anne says I will be feeling the baby move very soon, and I have an appointment to have an ultrasound. I am both nervous, and weirdly excited.

School really sucks! I am still learning just how immature kids my age can be! Katie tells me that the talking will stop. I know she's right, but I really do hate it...I got called a slut the other day...I didn't tell Katie.

This diary seems to be full of things that I haven't told her...I kinda hate that.

I just don't want to complain all of the time. She is juggling a lot right now too, with it being senior year, work, and her boy-friend...I just want to be respectful. I feel like all I do any more is complain. I hope she isn't getting tired of me! Course, she would never say as much. Sometimes I honestly feel like I really don't deserve her, but I am always so thankful. I truly hope she knows that.

Great...Now I am crying!

Dear Diary,

I felt the baby move! Katie actually cried when she felt it. It made me happy that she was excited. The baby moving around feels so weird, it's like this fluttering sensation. Now that I am trying to put it into words, it's hard to describe.

I am looking forward to my appointment next week! Maybe I will be able to see if I am having a boy or a girl. Anne says there shouldn't be a problem being able to tell the sex, but that sometimes the baby can make it difficult to see?

I don't know...all I know is that this is so surreal! I seem to be at a loss for words, which sucks...I just feel weird, and excited, and emotional.

Gah! The emotions! I am so tired of crying. I cry when I laugh, cry when I'm hungry, cry when I'm tired...I cry because I'm crying! Anne says that is normal too. I am thankful for Anne, she's been a mother to me. Katie's whole family is absolutely amazing. I am honestly blessed to have them all here for me.

Happiness is a much better topic to be writing about than the crap I used to fill these pages with.

I closed the book with a soft sigh on my lips. It's not often that I get through a couple of pages without crying. I took my empty cup to the sink and rinsed it out before heading to the bedroom.

Glancing at the time, I frowned, I hoped Bobby would make it home soon. After I put up Beth's diary, I crawled into bed and cozied into the sheets. The bed felt really empty without Bobby, so I scooted closer to the middle and tucked the blanket in behind me a bit.

I curled up and breathed in deeply. I could smell his cologne on the pillows beside me, and it wasn't long before I felt myself drifting.

I rolled over when I felt Bobby lay down next to me, and my eyes opened slowly. I smiled at him and yawned. It was late.

"Hi honey. I am so sorry it's so late! Go back to sleep," he said as he kissed my forehead.

I yawned and snuggled up to him, smiling as he wrapped his arm around me, drawing me closer.

"I love you," I whispered.

Dear Diary,

I'm having a girl! It's official! Well, I mean...It feels more real now. Knowing that I am going to have a baby girl. These months are going by fast, I'm really scared but excited at the same time.

I just hope that I am a good mom to my little girl. I know that I will try as hard as I can to be. She deserves everything! She will have everything! She will grow up knowing that she is loved, she will be provided for. She will never have the life that I had for so many years.

My little girl will have an amazing life, surrounded by so much love and happiness. That's all I want for her.

Anne is taking me shopping, of course Katie is coming too, though I suspect she feels awkward. She seems weird around me sometimes. I may just be paranoid. Our friendship is so very different now that I am pregnant. It's like...everything is centered around the baby, and nothing is what it used to be.

I hope she learns to be okay with that, and knows that she is and always will be my very best friend.

Dear Diary,

I haven't written in a little while. I feel overwhelmed, scared, and excited, and nervous. I have so many thoughts and emotions...And they all end up draining me of energy.

The baby moves around a lot now, sometimes it actually kind of hurts. The kicks have only gotten stronger and more frequent. At night, it is the worst. I'm trying to get comfortable. It's as if she is doing complete somersaults in my stomach. Maybe she's trying to get comfortable? Maybe she's squished because she doesn't have enough room...?

I really don't know how to explain the feeling. I wish I could be more detailed, even if just to look back on this someday and remember exactly what I was feeling, and experiencing.

Baby girl is definitely growing, and I feel like a freaking cow. All I want to do is eat, and sleep. I make sure to exercise though, and I still go to school. The rumors have basically stopped, I am thankful for that. I think everyone got bored, I have long since stopped showing that what they say bothers me.

They still look at me, but I think they are probably just curious.

I have noticed a lot of people want to touch my belly and it feels admittedly, a little creepy. I wouldn't tell anyone that though, I just smile and let it happen.

Maybe I need to learn how to create some boundaries? Anne says that it is normal not to really like all of the attention, I think that it's because I'm not used to it. I don't really like the attention, not as much as I may seem to act like I do. I don't want to hurt anyone's feelings.

I honestly don't think I could handle hurting anyone's feelings.

These crazy moods are the worst, and I think that if I knew I had hurt someone's feelings, I would cry...when I cry, I feel like I won't stop.

Katie's home, I think I'll talk to her for a while about her day. I need a distraction, I think I'm bored, and I really don't think I have much more to write about at this moment.

Dear Diary,

<u>Gracelynn Michelle Martin</u>,

I feel so much better putting a name to her, at first it felt silly when I started talking to my stomach, but Anne told me it's good. That she will remember my voice! That is so freaking cool! To think that she will know my voice when I hold her for the first time. She will automatically know that I am her mom.

I haven't even met her yet, and I am so in love with her!

Katie had made a list of names with me...she'd taken her time. I think I may have made her feel kind of pressured into it. I really hope I didn't make her feel that way.

The list of names was actually pretty fun, and I love the name Gracelynn...

She is my amazing Grace.

Dear Diary,

Oh my gawd! My mother showed up out of nowhere. I am so mad! After all of this time, it was basically as if she hadn't even realized I was gone. Or, she didn't really care.

It was embarrassing to come back from church, and lunch with Katie's family to see her sitting on their porch. I feel like she invaded their space.

I felt as if I couldn't breathe, and then...for some stupid reason I had wanted to talk to her!

I guess it wasn't that I wanted to talk to her, so much as I think that I just wanted to hear what she had to say for herself. I mean, I have been gone for months! Plus, she didn't know I was pregnant and what was even weirder is she hadn't even looked surprised to see me that way.

Of course, she was drunk. I could smell the booze on her straight away. It made me want to gag. I practically had to hold my breath to keep from getting sick. Also, I was embarrassed because she yelled at Katie, and she got ugly with her parents.

I hope she never comes back! She acted as if she was upset because I'd left. She'd said something along the lines of how I was her only child, and she didn't understand why I had left.

Is she for real? She hasn't acted like my mother since my dad left, almost ten years ago! I had to suffer being treated like that for almost ten years of my life! She had no right talking to me, or Katie and her family like that. Drunk or not, there is no excuse.

She called my baby a bastard!

I am so mad that I'm shaking! What nerve she had to come over here and say those things to me! And to treat Katie and her family like that!

I just want to go to bed...I am overwhelmed, pissed off, and really tired all of a sudden. I hate getting emotional! I just can't believe that actually happened. I feel embarrassed. I know I shouldn't but I do!

I pray nothing like this ever happens again. She will have nothing to do with me, or my baby. I won't have her around my daughter.

Dear Diary,

This weather sucks, it's snowing from like all directions! I don't understand how it can seem like snow is coming from the ground up...I'm happy to be in such a wonderful home because I'd be freezing in that stupid trailer! It's so warm and cozy here.

Anyway, school was canceled because of this terrible winter storm and today, Katie and I both are sick! I feel bad because she tried so hard to stay away from me so that I wouldn't catch her cold, and I still ended up getting sick anyway. I hope no one else gets it, this is awful!

Anne is taking good care of us, she keeps going from me to Katie to see if we need anything. She made homemade chicken noodle soup, and even though I wasn't hungry, I couldn't say no. It tasted really good and I ate most of it.

Hopefully we feel better soon, I haven't been sick like this for a while, and Katie is hardly ever sick at all. I think I can count on one hand the times she's been sick since I've known her.

I'm going to lay down and try to get some sleep, I'm not really tired but there is nothing else to do while I'm stuck in my room. I'm not going to expose the whole house.

Thirteen

Dear Diary,

Anne really out did herself, and though I didn't really want a baby shower...it really was very beautiful. I am huge, and I had to sit through most of it. Honestly, I was scared to move with so many people there, I would have probably knocked someone over! I am surprised by how many people came.

Everything was pretty, and oh my goodness, everything was so pink! I got really amazing gifts for the baby, and some of the women from church got things for me too. I even got money, though I don't really plan on spending it just yet.

I can't imagine the baby will really need anything for a while, we have a whole room with stuff from the baby shower. It had been a huge mess to clean, and of course with me being as big as I am, Anne didn't want me doing a lot. She let me help a little with the clean-up and now here I am laying down because everyone insisted I should rest.

They probably aren't wrong, my feet hurt. I feel like I have a mountain of a belly, I can hardly see to tie my own shoes! So embarrassing! Still, as I watch Gracelynn move around inside me, I can't help but feel anything but pride. How is it possible to love someone so much?

a mountain of a belly, I can hardly see to tie my own shoes! So embarrassing! Still, as I watch Gracelynn move around inside me, I can't help but feel anything but pride. How is it possible to love someone so much?

Dear Diary,

Well, I am on bedrest, and I had to move into the guest room downstairs because it's getting too hard to climb the stairs. I feel like a helpless blimp.

I did have some bleeding. It scared me so bad! I thought I was going to have her a bit too early, and then I thought something was really wrong with her, or me. Dr. Ray says it happens sometimes though, and to try to rest and drink a lot of water.

Also, I am having Braxton hicks. Oh they hurt so bad! If being in labor feels like THAT, and worse, I am scared shitless!

Every time I have one of these stupid little contraction things I want to scream! Thankfully, they are slowing down...Katie has been so scared, and though it hurts I try to act like it isn't so bad.

This bed rest sucks, but at least Katie has been bringing me homework...crazy how I am excited for that, I gotta do something! It's monotonous, laying around all the time. I just want to get up and walk around. I go to the bathroom and get to walk a little obviously, but can't do much until Dr. Ray says that it's okay.

Dear Diary,

Lane Fields is pregnant! She's pregnant and she's texting with me...and she's asking for advice.

Lane has always been one of the more popular girls. She's not quite what I would call preppy really, she is actually kind of a badass. She hangs out with the popular kids, her attitude is terrible. I never expected to become friends with a popular girl, let alone someone like Lane Fields.

Everything is different. I am a mom, and I am trying to help Lane see the good things about being a mom. She actually confessed to me that she was thinking about abortion. Her family, I guess, isn't really there for her. Maybe that's why she's always acted bitchy to everyone. I don't know...I guess, I was wrong to judge. Being a little judgmental of others comes quite naturally, but I try hard not to be.

I guess I kind of feel bad for her. Plus, her boyfriend is pretty much an airhead. Okay, so, Admittedly he is cute, but a total idiot! Most boys our age really are immature. Drake (Lane's boyfriend) doesn't know she's pregnant yet, but she did tell me that she is going to talk to him about the baby. Especially since she is thinking hard about keeping the baby now since we've been talking.

Katie was quite surprised when I had started talking to Lane, and she doesn't know what's going on. I promised Lane I wouldn't tell anyone, and I don't plan on breaking that promise. As I told Lane, it is up to her to start telling people, not me.

I do feel a little guilty, I have a lot more secrets from Katie than I have ever wanted to have...but there are some things I just don't feel like talking about. Even to Katie, who has always been there for me. Still, she knows me better than anyone. If she ever finds any of this out, I hope that she understands my reasons for not talking about these things. Maybe one day I will let her read this diary.

Okay, I'm going to go do something else. I'm getting sad, and sore. Maybe I should walk around the house for a little while, I've been laying around for too long as it is.

Now that I think about it, I might get myself something to eat, I'm kinda hungry again.

I closed Beth's diary with a sigh, and placed it on the coffee table. Lane and I had gone our separate ways after graduation, and had lost touch not long into college. After Beth passed, we had formed a close friendship. In fact, I had been right there in the delivery room with her when she had her own baby. I remember it like it was yesterday. Funny how so much time can go by, but memories have the ability to make it seem as if no time has passed.

I shut my eyes because they felt tired. I'd been reading for quite some time, curled up on the couch. Gracelynn was with Bobby at the farm, and I had wanted to go, but I'd chosen to stay home since I wasn't feeling well. Truth be told, I hadn't been feeling well for over a week. My body felt tired, and I had been sick as well. Bobby insisted that it was the flu bug that was going around.

Whatever it was, I was growing tired of it. Gracelynn had made me a sweet get well card, and for the first two worst days, Bobby had stayed home with me. I felt awful, and upset that I wasn't well enough to do any packing, or anything fun with Gracelynn. I'd not spent much time with her because I didn't want to risk getting her sick. So, Bobby took care of everything as I mostly rested.

Honestly, I didn't get sick very often at all, so when I did, I was not great company. I found it odd though, that I'd been feeling terrible and neither Bobby nor Gracelynn showed any oncoming symptoms.

A sliver of a thought crossed my mind. My eyes widened as my mind started racing. *That couldn't be right! Could it?* I opened my purse and pulled out my personal calendar.

I felt my heart accelerate, the room seemed to be spinning. I sat down and drew in a few deliberate breaths. *Had I forgotten to take my pill?* I opened my circular disk and peeked, nope I was right on track.

My mind swirled as I put on my shoes, grabbed my purse, and drove to the pharmacy. I walked through the aisles, until I found what I was looking for. I grabbed one, paid for it, and brought it into the bathroom. I paced the linoleum floor while I waited. It felt like hours instead of mere minutes.

My eyes widened when I looked down. *Oh my gosh!* My heart thumped harder in my chest as I stared. I threw it in the trash, paid the nice lady for a few more and drove home. Once home, I drank two full glasses of water, doing my very best to ignore the bubbling nausea as I downed the water. I walked around the house, slowly and deliberately.

When the urge finally came, I rushed to the bathroom with the little brown sack. For some reason it felt as if the bag weighed a lot more than it did, but I knew it was probably from sudden adrenaline. *Calm down,* I told myself.

I forced myself to wait, thinking that maybe if I waited longer I'd get a good reading. *Maybe that one was wrong?* Half an hour later I went back into the bathroom and glanced down. My eyes widening once more in renewed shock as I glanced at each one.

Six total…each one positive. I looked in the mirror, taking in my tired eyes, and my pale face.

You're pregnant! My reflection mocked. I squeezed my eyes shut. Now wasn't the right time! We had too much going on right now to even think about having a baby.

How did this happen? "This can't be right, I'm on the pill!" I said out loud, to the empty house.

I placed a hand on my abdomen softly, gasping for air. I threw the tests in the garbage and walked it to the can outside, and picked up my phone. It was time to make a doctor's appointment. These store-bought tests could be faulty. Something in the back of my mind laughed at me and I tried as hard as I could to ignore it. Still this voice in my head sneered *six tests and you still think it's not real?* "Argh!" I yelled, as I threw my hands up in frustration.

Fortunately, I was able to make an appointment for the follow-ing morning after insisting that it couldn't wait. Gracelynn would be at school and Bobby would be at work. Unfortunately, I wasn't in a very patient mood. I needed this doctor's appointment, I didn't want to wait a whole day!

Of course, I wanted a baby… But not now! I wanted one when we were completely settled, when Gracelynn was a little bit older, when we had plenty of money, and plenty of room.

Now was the most imperfect time!

I flopped down on the couch. My lower lip began to tremble and I took another deep breath. *Calm down, Katie!* I told myself. I squeezed my eyes shut again, in silent meditation for a few moments.

After a while, I decided that I had better try to eat. I hadn't eaten anything but toast for the day, and it was going on one o'clock in the afternoon. I slowly made my way to the kitchen and opened up the cabinets. Nothing looked good, so I opened the pantry. *There! Chicken noodle soup is good for a sour stomach,* I thought with a twitch of my lips.

I opened the can and poured the soup into a small pot, setting it on the stove to boil. While it was warming, I grabbed some soup crackers and then grabbed one of the bottles of ginger ale that Bobby had gotten me. I poured a glass, watching as it bubbled toward the rim and I sipped at the fizz, taking time to appreciate the pleasant taste.

I curled up on the couch with my hot soup and soda, and I turned the T.V on. I needed to distract myself while I ate. First of all, I didn't feel the least bit hungry…second of all, I needed to slow my mind down. I was starting to develop the worst sort of headache!

I sipped my soup slowly, trying to breathe through the rolling of my stomach, and after the first few bites I began feeling a little better. I took a drink of my soda and stared at the screen. I wasn't sure what was on, but it was at least distracting. Some sort of thriller or other I gathered, as the young woman was running down the road in the dark, in a thin nightgown. Beth would have snorted, or laughed. I just watched as I waited for someone to pop out at the woman. The music was getting louder, and that was a typical indication that something was about to happen.

After I finished my soup and my stomach was mostly settled, I shut the television off with heavily lidded eyes and curled up on the couch for a nap.

When Bobby got home with Gracelynn I was just getting awake. I had slept for over an hour. When I stood, my stomach squeezed, my throat constricted, and I sped to the bathroom, not missing Gracelynn's wide concerned eyes.

Bobby rushed in despite my protests and rubbed my back as I got sick. *So much for lunch!* I thought blandly as I flushed the toilet, and washed my face and hands. After assuring Bobby that I was okay, I brushed my teeth, and rinsed my mouth out.

"I'm sorry, honey. I thought I was beginning to feel a little better after eating," I told Bobby as I plopped down on the couch and curled my legs to my chest. He sat beside me, I scooted over and laid my head on his shoulder.

"Maybe you should make a doctor's appointment," he said after a moment of silence. I nodded and glanced up at him.

"I made one, they will see me in the morning."

"Would you like me to go with you?" he asked. I knew he was worried. I gave him a small smile, but as I thought about this afternoon I felt a moment of panic.

"Nah that's alright, honey. If it's something important I'll give you a call. If it's just the stomach bug there is no sense in you missing another day of work."

There was no point in jumping the gun and telling him that I may be pregnant. I wanted to be sure before I said anything, to anyone.

"If you're sure," he said as he smoothed my hair back from my face. "I've been worried about you. You're hardly ever sick, babe."

I closed my eyes and sighed. My body was drained and honestly I felt like I could sleep all day. "I'm sure," I mumbled, before I drifted off yet again.

Fourteen

"Well, Katie, what seems to be the problem? I understand you haven't been feeling well?" Dr. Farenthrope sat in his black chair and looked at me with kind, brown eyes. I was in the exam room; my knuckles white as I clenched the edge of the bed.

"I haven't been feeling well for over a week now. Bouts of nausea and vomiting, dizzy spells, fatigue. I feel hungry, but when I eat I get sick." I paused and cleared my throat, looking just past the doctor's shoulder. "I need a pregnancy test. I took a few at home but those are faulty sometimes, aren't they?" I asked. My voice sounded hopelessly small.

Dr. Farenthrope nodded. "Certainly, they can be faulty." He paused before continuing. "When you say a few?" he asked.

"Six tests," I admitted.

"Well, Katie…" he started with a soft laugh. "I know that the store bought tests aren't always accurate, but six positive tests? I think it is safe to say that you are pregnant," he stated matter-of-factly.

I frowned in frustration. "Can we do a test anyway? I am on the pill! This can't be right!" I spoke a little too loudly in desperation. Dr. Farenthrope smiled his kind smile and nodded.

"Yes, Susan here will get you set up. I'll be back in a few minutes."

He and the nurse left, and I was left alone in the small room. It was a pale yellow, with country blue trim, I noted. Meant to be cozy I'm sure, but it did nothing to calm my nerves.

The nurse tapped on the door and came in with a small plastic cup with a lid. She instructed me to use the bathroom and to bring it to her when I was finished. I nodded, taking the sample cup from her with a shaky hand.

I made my way to the small bathroom after being told where it was located, and used one of the wipes to wipe the toilet before doing my business. I never liked public bathrooms, even one that looked as clean as this. This bathroom was painted a pretty shade of rose pink, offsetted by gray trim. I liked the color palette and thought it would be nice in the guest bathroom at the farm.

I held the cup awkwardly, deciding I may as well get it over with. After I was finished I washed my hands. I looked in the mirror. I wanted to know for certain, but now that I was here…I didn't feel ready to know.

Chicken! A little voice nagged at me in the back of my mind. I sighed before I nodded at my reflection as if to prove that I wasn't a chicken. Squaring my shoulders with my chin up high, I left the bathroom with the cup, gave it to the nice lady who wrote my name on it, and then made my way back into the exam room.

It felt as if I were there forever when Dr. Farenthrope finally came back in with his nurse in tow. I gave him what I'm sure was an awkward smile, my heart kicked in tempo as he rested in his chair. I felt rather impatient at that moment as I waited for him to say something. *No no, just take your time!* I thought irritably.

"Well, Katie. You are definitely pregnant. Judging by your last menstruation cycle, that would put you at about three weeks."

I opened my mouth to say something, but closed it again and swallowed. My mouth suddenly felt like cotton. My hand came up to touch my flat stomach in disbelief, even though I knew now without a doubt that it was real.

I left the doctor's with a handful of pamphlets, a prescription for prenatal vitamins, and another prescription that Dr. Farenthrope said should help with the nausea. I drove to the pharmacy and walked the aisles as my prescriptions got filled.

I felt weird, as if it were all a dream. I was seeing and hearing the happenings around me, but I wasn't taking anything in.

When my last name was called, I made my way to the receptionist's desk, handed over the insurance card, and paid what I owed for the prescriptions. I listened, but it sounded as if I was listening to her under water as she read the instructions on the medication. I gave the woman a smile and thanked her before heading back to my car.

When I got in I placed the bag in the passenger seat along with the pamphlets I was given on becoming a new mother. I put my head against the steering wheel and took a few breaths. I felt dizzy, confused, and so scared in that moment, all I really wanted to do was cry. As if on cue, I was crying.

After I calmed myself down, I drove home taking several side roads so that I could take my time. When I got inside I placed the items in my nightstand drawer behind Beth's diary and closed it. Then, I made my way to the kitchen for a glass of water. I drank it quickly, and poured another to take with me to the living room. I perched on the edge of the couch, taking in the silence, taking in the morning I'd experienced. My lower lip trembled and new tears stung my eyes.

I am the type of woman who likes to have a plan. We had too much going on at the moment, it was not the time. I wasn't ready. *Get ready, because it's happening*. I heard in my mind. I threw my head back against the back of the couch and closed my eyes with a heavy sigh.

Oh my God! What will Bobby think? How will Gracelynn feel? The questions popped into my mind in that order, and my eyes flew open to the wide white ceiling. I groaned loudly, I felt like cursing, I felt like stomping my foot like a petulant child. I did none of those things. I instead chose to sit there and sulk.

It wouldn't do me any good to throw a fit. I'd probably cry again though, but it was okay. I started thinking of the time back in college when I had been sitting with my therapist. She had told me to "Sit with my feelings. To acknowledge them, and that it was okay to have them."

"My feelings are valid!" I told myself out loud, feeling a little silly as my voice cut through the silence. I sipped at my water, and made my way to the kitchen to grab a roll of crackers. I remembered my mom when she was pregnant with Paul, and also Beth, eating crackers to calm their stomachs during pregnancy.

My eyes widened when I heard Bobby's truck pull into the driveway. *He's home early!* Then I remembered, I hadn't called or texted him. My heart did a weird flutter in my chest and I bit my lip. I wasn't ready to tell him…but I had to! I couldn't keep something like this to myself. Not from my husband, he had to know. My heart thumped harder when he opened the door. I stood and smiled at him when he came in. He returned the smile, coming up to put a hand on my back.

"Are you okay? I've been worried!" He kissed my clammy forehead.

I nodded, taking in his gray-blue eyes and slightly wind-tossed hair. I grabbed his hand in mine and led him to the couch. He seriously needed to sit for what I was about to tell him. Hell, I needed to sit!

"I'm sorry I didn't call or text, love. I'm okay though," I assured him, and saw the relief in his face immediately.

Then he frowned. "So what's wrong?" he asked.

"Well…" I started with a shaky breath. "They did find a little something," I told him with a nervous laugh. I felt his hand grip my thigh as he waited for me to tell him the news. I saw the concern in his eyes, and the tenseness of his jaw.

"I'm pregnant!" I blurted out quickly, and surprisingly loud in the short space between us. I needed to just say it and get it over with, that was the only way.

Bobby swallowed, hard, his eyes widening in shock as he looked me in the eyes. I waited, my eyes equally wide as I contemplated his reaction. Time seemed to stretch between us.

Suddenly I was wrapped in his arms, and when he pulled away he was smiling.

Smiling?

Oh my gosh! He's happy? I thought as I saw the tears in his eyes, the smile in the corner of his mouth.

"We are going to have a baby?" he asked, in wonder. "Did you forget your pill?" he asked, a slight frown on his brow.

I shook my head and shrugged. "Dr. Farenthrope said it happens sometimes."

"How are you feeling?" Bobby asked as his hand came to rub at my back. The warmth of him felt good, but felt like I was going to cry again.

My chin quivered as I looked up at him. "I don't know how to feel…really. I'm scared, and I'm confused, and I didn't know how you would feel, and I don't know how Gracelynn will feel, what she will think." I said this all in one rushed breath.

Bobby cradled my face in his warm hands, and then took me into his embrace once more, smoothing my hair. "Shhh" he soothed. "We'll figure it out okay? Everything is going to be alright."

When we pulled away from one another after some time, he was smiling. A full-on smile—he was definitely happy about this news.

I hadn't expected that.

Didn't he realize that right now was such a terrible time? I frowned. "Right now really isn't a good time to be expecting a baby, Bobby! We are getting ready to move, taking on a lot of new responsibility at the farm, getting Gracelynn settled into a new home, and eventually into a new school…and all of the unpacking," I said in a panicked rush.

He just nodded with a silly lop-sided grin on his face. I threw my hands up in exasperation.

"Would you say something?" I practically yelled at him.

Bobby jerked his head up in surprise. "I love you," he said, taking my hand in his. "I am so in love with you Katie, and I am happy. Look, I know that right now may not be the right time…but is it ever really the right time? All I know is that I love you, and I want this baby!"

His arms were around me again, and I was crying, but some of the tears were happy. I had to admit, it was a little bit exciting.

"We're going to have a baby," I said as I cried, and when I looked into Bobby's tear-filled eyes, I felt myself fall in love with him all over again. I felt a little bit better, it felt good to know that he was happy about this news. I only hoped that Gracey would be happy as well.

Dear Diary,

Lane and I have become really good friends, Katie now knows that she is pregnant. I am happy that Lane had asked me to tell Katie because honestly it had been driving me nuts not telling her! It's crazy though, that someone else my age is actually going through the same thing that I am. It's kind of nice that someone can relate. Well, a lot of women obviously can relate, but it's nice that someone my age can understand how I feel.

I feel like a cow! Honesty, I am hungry all of the time. I can't bend over anymore. I've been wearing house slippers so I don't have to worry about laces, and more often than not I just go barefoot.

I feel swollen everywhere. Katie denies that I am, and constantly reminds me that I'm not fat. I know that I'm not, it's all baby weight, but it is A LOT of weight. I'm kind of scared she is going to be a big baby.

What if she is really big? What if I have to have a C-section? I don't want one! I don't want any kind of drugs either. The more I think about it, I honestly want to do this all naturally. It seems crazy, but I think it's what I need to do.

Dear Diary,

I had my doctor's appointment and Dr. Ray says that everything is on track. I am finally off of bedrest, but I still don't overdo myself. I get plenty of exercise walking around the house, and sometimes I go outside when it's nice enough.

Most of the time I spend my days reading, sleeping, eating, and rubbing my beach ball of a belly. I do what school work Katie brings home, and the rest is done online. Katie's family got me my own computer. I had cried like a baby when Anne brought the new computer box to me in my room. Anyway, the school work helps keep me occupied.

Gracelynn isn't kicking much anymore, not like she used to. Dr. Ray says that I'm in my "nesting phase." Like I'm a hen about to hatch her eggs? Anyway, she said it's because it is getting closer to time.

I feel like I've been pregnant forever, I only have a couple more weeks to go. Anne has been working on a nursery. I know it is supposed to be a surprise, but noise travels. I hear her all the time upstairs banging away...and though the door stays closed, sometimes I catch a whiff of fresh paint.

I'm excited to see it when it's finished, I like to fantasize about what it will look like, and how it will be when my baby girl is in it. I can't help but dream up ideas about the different colors, and the baby furniture.

I know it will be beautiful. Anne is really good at painting and decorating, she's got a real talent for it. I kinda hope that not everything is pink...oh well, even if it is pink, it will be perfect.

Dear Diary,

I haven't written in a few days. I've been so tired, and really sore. I feel like this baby might literally fall out of me at any moment. Occasionally I feel sharp pains in my back, and I feel like I want to pee all of the time. It's just this constant pressure, especially when I'm walking around.

Speaking of being up and walking around, I need to go to the damn bathroom again. Ugh! I am so ready to have this little girl.

It's almost time.

I keep having to remind myself that it is almost time. She will be here soon, I just feel like every day is getting longer and longer. The closer the time, the further away it is feeling. I feel like the universe is toying with me.

I really gotta pee, I can't hold it anymore!

Dear Diary,

I am full of energy today, I'm not sure what I am going to do about it, but I do know I need to do something.

It's more like, I have to do something, I can't really explain it, I just want to be busy. Maybe I will bake some cookies, or help Anne with something around the house. Sometimes she lets me sweep, and run the vacuum cleaner. Now that I'm closer to my date she is so anxious about what I'm doing and why.

Most of the time, she tells me that I need to do some walking around because the exercise is good for me, but then if I do too much she is on me about it.

There seems to be no happy medium, I know though, that she is just being cautious, and that she is worried. Katie is as well, though she is good about not constantly hovering. She checks on me a lot, but she knows when I need company and when I need to rest.

I think I will go ahead and make my way out of this dang bed, and at least go to the living room. There has to be something that I can do. I'm starting to feel like these four walls are closing in on me.

My throat tightened when I turned to the next page. It was blank…

Blank

Blank

Blank

I continued to flip through but there was nothing, I knew the story from there. I remembered it as if it were yesterday and not almost nine years ago. She had been so full of energy that day. We were cleaning together listening to music when suddenly she just collapsed. She'd been taken to the hospital right away. She'd been dehydrated. Everything else was okay, we were told…and then I got the phone call that she was in labor.

My world was turned upside down that day. I closed my eyes and set the diary on my lap. Tears rolled down my cheeks in renewed grief. She never got to hold Gracelynn, to see her lovely, bright green eyes. To watch her grow into the beautiful child she is now, she won't get to see her grow into the beautiful woman she will undoubtedly become.

I placed a hand on my stomach. The morning sickness had gotten a bit better thankfully, my chest was sore though, and I was still really tired most of the time. I sighed and flipped through the diary again, this time flipping all the way to the back.

I gasped, my eyes widening in surprise.

Two folded pieces of paper were tucked in the back of the diary. How had they not fallen out? As many times as I've opened this diary, they had stayed tucked and hidden.

My hand shook as I grabbed one of the pieces of paper. The front of it read *Katie.* I carefully opened it up and with a hard swallow, I began to read.

Fifteen

Dear Katie,

I am writing to you because these days I find it easier to write what I am feeling rather than to talk about it. That may seem a little silly, especially since we've always been able to tell each other so much.

I really didn't want to share this diary...I was scared. Scared about anyone seeing it, scared about anyone knowing all of the crazy crap that happened...but, then I realized it isn't all crazy. There are some good things too!

There are things that I have never told you. Secrets that I have kept. I didn't ever plan to keep so many secrets, I just found it so hard to talk about. So, I wanted to give you this letter, along with my diary. I want you to read it, I want you to know the things that I could never say out loud. I wanted to tell someone what happened, in case anything ever happened to me.

The only person I've ever been able to talk to is you.

I trust that you would never judge me, about the way I felt

when I was going through so much. My past was so full of darkness, and I hate that I kept it from you.

I want you to know that you took me out of that darkness Katie, you saved my life. You saved me in so many more ways than you probably realize. I love you so much! Thank you for being my sister, my best friend. I hope that you understand why I kept some of this to myself. I hope and pray that you will forgive me.

I am healing from my past because of you, and also because of this diary. I know it may seem weird, but getting this stuff out has helped me so much. When you read this, you will know everything about me! I feel good knowing that now we have no secrets between us!

I know that you will understand, because you always do. After you read this diary, please give it back to me? I don't know yet if I will burn it, keep it, or what I want to do with it.

I love you Katie, never forget that okay?

Always,

Beth.

K&B forever!

I cried hard as I folded Beth's letter back up, and put my face in my hands. She had wanted me to read this diary. As I read, I felt her presence. I could almost see her sitting there, pregnant as she was, writing this letter to me with a secret smile.

I wiped at my eyes and cleared my throat before I looked back down. I grabbed the other folded letter and opened it with a shaky breath.

My sweet Gracelynn, it said. A gasp escaped my lips, and I tucked the letter back inside the diary in surprise. *Why would there be a letter to Gracelynn? Had Beth thought she was going to die?* I wondered suddenly. *No! Of course she hadn't!* I chastised myself. My throat constricted again, and I quickly put the diary down on the coffee table. I was going to make myself sick if I didn't calm down.

After some time, when I felt more at ease, I opened the diary and held the letter to Gracelynn. I wouldn't read it of course. It wasn't my place, and I absolutely wouldn't read it without her permission.

I put the diary up, I needed to get out of the house. There were still a couple of hours left before school was out. I looked at the time and twitched my lips. I grabbed my purse and car keys making a decision. I was going to go to Mom's. I hadn't told her about the baby yet, and Bobby promised he'd leave it to me before we started telling people.

I drove to Mom's without the radio on, just me and the long road, thinking about how to break the news to her. I had wanted to tell her as soon as I found out, but at the same time I had wanted to wait. I guess a part of me had still been in denial. I knew I needed to tell her. Soon, I wouldn't be able to hide it. I was already showing some small signs of motherhood.

My stomach slightly rounder, my breasts slightly bigger, I could no longer stand the smell of bacon, or anything with tomato! That sucked because I really did love salsa, I hoped that it would pass and I'd be able to have chips and dip again!

When I pulled up in the driveway, my mom opened the door and waved. It was almost as if she were expecting me and I hadn't even texted her to let her know I was coming! I took a deep breath as I turned off the engine and got out. The warm air hit me in the face, summer was fast approaching.

I got up to the porch and Mom embraced me in a hug. "Oooh my girl! I'm so happy to see you, what a nice surprise!" She paused and looked at my face, frowning slightly. "Come inside, it's unseasonably warm today."

I nodded and followed her into the house, it was nice and cool and I smiled as the air hit my hot skin. Mom disappeared as I put my purse by the sofa, and she returned with a cold glass of water.

"Thank you, Mom." She sat down and patted the seat on the couch next to her. I took it, setting the glass on the coaster.

"Sorry I didn't call or anything, I just wanted to get out of the house, I hadn't realized it was getting so warm out. Crazy to be this warm, it's not even summer yet," I admitted to her.

"Sweetheart, you don't have to schedule an appointment or anything! You are welcome home any time." She gave me another hug, and I held on just a little tighter.

When we pulled away her eyes studied my face. "You do look rather pale and tired sweetheart. Are you okay?" she asked.

I took another drink of water and nodded. "I'm okay I promise, but I do have to talk to you about something."

Just as I was about to open my mouth, Paul came in with a blonde-haired, half-dressed girl on his arm.

"Well I'll be damned, hey sis!" he said as he came in. I hardly recognized my little brother, I had to do a double take. I instantly felt bad that we hadn't stayed in touch. *When had he gotten so dang tall?* I thought as I shot off the couch and gave him a hug, kind of shoving his presumed girlfriend in the process. I apologized to her quickly, she rolled her eyes and I instantly didn't like her attitude.

"Mom, Katie, this is Sadie. My new girlfriend." I could FEEL my mom rolling her eyes! We both smiled and greeted her politely. She flipped her bleached blonde hair off of her shoulder and gave us an obviously forced smile. "Nice to meet y'all. Pauly is so sweet to show me off to his family." She dramatically batted her eyelashes up at him.

I found myself wondering where in the world Paul had found this one. I knew I was probably being too judgmental, but she did not give a good first impression. Paul tugged her hand and led her upstairs to his bedroom.

"Leave that door open!" Mom shouted, and I heard Paul grunt.

"Aahh Mom!" I covered my mouth before laughing out loud.

Mom and I made our way back to the couch, and she plopped down with a loud sigh.

"Honey, I don't know what to do about that boy!" she stated matter-of-factly. I shrugged and shook my head.

"I'm sure he's just being a teenage boy…I got lucky with Bobby," I said with a soft smile.

Mom's features softened and she nodded enthusiastically. "Yes you did. I am so thankful that you found the love of your life. He's always made you so happy, and has stuck by your side all of these years. Reminds me of your dad and I," Mom said, she looked wistful as if recalling her past.

"How is Dad?" I asked.

Mom smiled. "He's been alright, he works too much, and I'm trying to get him to go ahead and retire."

"Yeah, he's always been a hard worker," I agreed.

Mom patted my leg, and shifted more comfortably on the couch. "So, what were you needing to talk to me about honey?" she asked.

My mom never liked to beat around the bush, if there was something to talk about, she wanted to hear it and she always gave her full attention. I loved that about her, but at that moment, I felt myself prickle with sweat. I was nervous. I took another drink of my water, and put it down before I faced her. "Well, Mom. I came over to tell you that…" I paused, and a small smile touched the corner of my mouth. "I'm pregnant."

My mom's eyes shot up in surprise, and filled with tears as she scooted closer to pull me into a hug. "Oh honey! Oh my gosh! When did you find out? How far along are you?" she asked in a rush.

I felt guilty then, and looked away.

"I've known for a little while…I just wasn't ready to tell anyone. I guess I was kind of in denial. With so many things going on right now, honestly I wasn't ready to admit to myself that it was real."

Mom stayed quiet and nodded as I talked. I admitted to being about two months along and her eyes widened in both disbelief and awe. She gave me another hug after I finished answering her questions.

"Well, I can't say I am happy that you kept that to yourself, but I am so proud of you, and I am so happy for you, and for Bobby. Does Gracelynn know?" Mom barely took a breath as she spoke.

I shook my head. "You're the only one, besides Bobby, of course," I admitted. This seemed to make her happier. She patted my leg again.

"You're going to do just fine, sweetheart. I know you are about to move, but your dad and I will help any way we can. We are going to have Gracelynn here for a little while, while you guys get things settled at the farm. I can come over and help you unpack. Oh honey, this is so exciting! Gracelynn will be thrilled!"

I looked at my mom, and tears filled my eyes. "I'm scared to tell her, and I'm scared she might feel a certain way about all of this. Her whole world is changing as it is with the move. She is worried about her friendship with Lilly and starting a new school…now there will be a new baby. I…I don't want her to feel left out."

My mom nodded. "Honey, I know it may be hard for her at first, but I think Gracelynn will find happiness in it. She will be a big sister, and that is a great feeling! Just make sure to tell her soon okay? She won't want to be out of the loop."

I knew my mom was right of course. Gracelynn liked to be in the know.

"I plan on telling her today actually," I told Mom as I took another sip of my water.

I stayed and visited for about an hour, and decided I had better be on my way back home so that I had time to get Gracelynn. Mom gave me a bottle of cold water for the ride back, and I had hollered up to Paul that it was good to see him. I smiled when he came downstairs for a hug before I left. I could still see some child-like features in his face, but also the man he was becoming.

On the way back home I breathed a sigh of relief. It had actually felt good to tell Mom that I was expecting a baby, once I got over the fear of telling her. I always told my mom everything, so I don't know why I had been so scared about this. I guess, it made it more real to say it out loud.

"The tricky part is telling Gracelynn," I said out loud as I waited in the parking lot of the school. I was really early, but it didn't matter. I didn't want to go home just to turn around and get back out again. Besides, getting in and out of the heat made me feel sick to my stomach and so far it had been a good day without all of that.

I leaned my head back against the seat and sighed. It was getting too warm in the car, so I got out and stood beside it. I leaned against it, and lifted my head up toward the sky as a slight breeze caressed my skin.

"Hi Katie!" a familiar voice had my face turning to the left. Lilly's mom Tracey was getting out of her car. She walked up to me and I offered a smile.

"Hi there, how are you?" I asked.

"Not too bad, busy as always," she replied as she ran a hand through her auburn hair.

I looked at her with a smile and nodded in complete understanding. "It's hard to believe school is almost over."

"It is, Lilly is so worried that she won't be able to see Gracelynn after she moves. I do hope you all will stay in touch."

I felt sad and a little guilty. "Of course, actually I wondered if we could arrange a playdate or something soon. Maybe a sleepover?" I suggested.

"You know, that sounds fantastic, and actually I don't have anything going on the last day of school. If you would like, Gracelynn is more than welcome to spend the night with Lilly. I know Lilly would just love it."

I smiled at her, it had been a while since they had had a sleepover. "Thank you so much, I know Gracey would love it as well."

The final bell sounded and we both looked at the building. "I guess I'd better get in line," she said quickly, and headed toward the doors.

I met Gracelynn with a hug and helped her with her bag. It was heavy, she explained, since she cleaned her locker.

After Gracelynn got buckled in I asked her if she would like to go to the park before we headed home.

She shrugged, "Sure, I guess."

I drove us to the park and picked my favorite spot. I smiled as I saw more flowers growing, and surrounding the area were dandelions. Tons of dandelions. It made me remember a time when Gracelynn had been around four years old and I had taken her to this very spot. We'd sat down together and made wishes on dandelions as we watched them fly away after we'd blown on them softly.

"Mom?" Gracelynn brought me out of my thoughts. I unbuckled my seatbelt after apologizing, and I walked with her up to the dandelions. "Remember a long time ago we used to make wishes on these?" I asked her.

Gracelynn nodded and picked one up. She squeezed her eyes

shut, brought it up to her lips, and blew. We laughed as the fuzz swirled around us before catching a soft breeze and flying away.

"Well, aren't you going to wish on one?" she asked with a small hand on her hip. Her green eyes caught sunbeams as she looked up at me expectantly. I got the impression that she learned this hand on the hip, from her grandmother. I smiled softly.

"Oh honey, I already have everything I ever dreamed of." I leaned down to pluck one. I blew it softly with my eyes closed. Praying for strength to tell her the news, and praying that she'd be happy about it.

"I do have something to talk to you about," I told her as we made our way to the bench overlooking the water. We watched the dandelion puffs float about before they faded away in the distance.

Gracelynn turned toward me, giving me her full attention. It was silly, but I felt nervous under her scrutiny. Her expression was so like Beth's that I wanted to look away, but couldn't.

"Well, it seems as though you are going to be a big sister," I blurted out. It was the easiest way I could think of to say it. Gracelynn turned away for a moment, blinking in the sunlight and seeming to be lost in thought. After what felt like ages watching different emotions cross her face, a soft smile tugged at the corner of her small mouth.

"I'm gonna be a sister?" she asked, her voice almost a whisper.

"Do you like that?" I asked, hope in my voice. She leaped onto my lap and hugged me tight.

"Wow! I get to be a sister!" she suddenly slid off of my lap and looked at me with concern. "Did I hurt you?"

"No honey, you didn't hurt me. Come back here!" I opened my arms to her and she entered them gladly with a giggle. "Is the baby why you were so sick?" Gracelynn asked, she turned to me, her eyes wide and so bright.

"Yeah, that is why I wasn't feeling good," I admitted to her.

"Well, it's better than a stomach bug I think!" she said, giving me another hug.

We sat like that for some time before Gracelynn told me she was ready to go home. I was a bit surprised she hadn't wanted to play in the park. Though, I guessed she was probably tired from her day at school and processing the news.

When we got home I got us both a glass of water, Gracelynn drank hers quickly and got herself another glass and drank it all before heading upstairs to her bedroom. She had reluctantly started packing up her room the other day, and as I heard her moving around upstairs, I assumed she was back to packing.

After I finished my glass of water, I decided that I should get some packing done as well. I was still sorting through stuff, and getting rid of the things that I didn't want to hold on to. I was ready for a fresh start. I looked forward to us moving to the farm and now that I was pregnant I looked forward to being closer to our families too.

I grabbed a box so that I could begin packing up the hall closet, and I wrote "Closet" on the box in permanent marker. I'd been marking all of them, so that it would be easier to unpack later.

In just a short while, school would be out, and though I did not like moving, the more that I thought about it the more excited I became.

I stuffed most of the closet items in the one box, keeping only our light jackets hanging in there, just in case. After I stood and stretched, I grabbed another box and began working on some of the dining room as well. With the move coming so quickly, I wanted to get all of the things we don't need right away, packed up.

I began thinking of this move as a new chapter in life, a new beginning. Change isn't always easy, but it is important. I hummed in thought as I took down the books from the cabinet in the dining room and placed them carefully in the box. I looked forward to unpacking at the farm, I looked forward to making it ours. I stretched and took a peak at the calendar on the wall, my eyes widening. I'd been so busy and hadn't realized that Gracelynn's birthday was this coming weekend! I had to get prepared!

Later that night, I smiled as I placed a hand on my belly, snuggled in bed next to my sleeping husband. Feeling decidedly happy about this unexpected pregnancy. Scared of course, nervous even, but happy—happy that Gracelynn would have a little brother or sister of her own to grow up with.

I remembered how Beth had always referred to me as her sister, I know that she'd wished she had brothers and or sisters growing up. In heart and spirit, Beth was my sister. I wiped a stray tear off my cheek and closed my eyes welcoming rest after a long and busy day.

Sixteen

We drove to the cemetery to see Beth. I stood close, but not too close to Gracelynn as she sat beside Beth's headstone to read her the letter that she'd written. She wrote one for every visit. I gave Gracey a hug as she wiped her tears, and I gave her time before we headed out. She didn't know what we had planned and I smiled as Gracelynn looked around curiously until we pulled up to the Pizza Palace.

We orchestrated a big pizza party. My mom and dad as well as Paul came, Bobby's mom and dad were able to come, and Lilly as well, and she was going to spend the night. Gracelynn opened presents after we ate. I was so pleased that she had such a great time. I couldn't believe that she was already nine! *Where has the time gone?*

❖ ❖ ❖

On the last day of school, I picked Gracelynn up and we went back home. The house was mostly move-in ready, the boxes had been driving me crazy but I was excited to get this move done. Bobby had been taking small loads with him to the farm over the last couple of weeks. It was outstanding, the amount of stuff you could collect over the years.

I listened to Gracelynn talk about her last day, and saw the sadness on her face as she realized that that was it. She would be in a whole new school, and I could see in her eyes that she was worried.

"We will have a great summer, I think you will enjoy your new school, and honey, you will be able to see Lilly," she nodded, her face rather gloomy, and turned her attention to the living room window.

"Speaking of Lilly," I stated, and immediately had her attention. "Tracey says that she would love to have you sleep over with Lilly tonight if you want!"

Her excitement was palpable as she ran to me for a hug. In the middle of her hug, she pulled back. "Am I hurting you?" she asked, her face now full of concern. I tucked a soft curl behind her ear and smiled. She was so sweet and considerate.

"You aren't hurting me one bit," I squeezed her a little tighter, and then tickled her back. She giggled and wiggled away from me.

"When can I go to Lilly's?" she asked excitedly.

"As soon as you're ready!" I laughed as she ran for the stairs before I could finish my sentence.

It had only taken Gracelynn about five minutes to get a bag packed before we headed out the door. I decided to walk with her instead of drive, it was a nice day out, not too hot at seventy degrees.

She practically skipped the whole way there, it was only a few blocks but I imagined if I had done that, my legs would be killing me. Gracelynn rang the doorbell and Lilly opened the door so out of breath I assumed she ran. The girls giggled and I got a half goodbye as they took off, presumably to Lilly's room.

Tracey and I laughed as we watched and heard their exuberant screeching. I thanked her again for suggesting this for the girls, and she offered me a ride home but I declined with a soft shake of my head.

"It's such a beautiful day, I'll just walk back. You all have fun, and call if you need anything at all."

I walked slowly back home, soaking up the warmth of the sun, watching its rays through a couple of gray clouds. I listened to the birds in the trees, and saw a few excited kids ride on their bikes with their friends. The air was buzzing with end of school energy.

It made me remember my excitement, and my sadness on the last day of high school. It had been surprising that I had somewhat felt sad that it was all over. I was admittedly scared about the future; having wanted to go to college, as well as take care of Gracelynn. She'd been a baby then, and I knew next to nothing about how to raise a child.

I did it though. I had a little help from my family of course, but I took on a lot of responsibility. I never regretted my decision to raise her, it was hard, but it was also so very worth it. I am proud of who she is, and who she will become.

I stopped and giggled to myself as I looked around. As lost in thought as I was, I almost walked right past the house. I unlocked the door and stepped inside. With everything almost all packed, it looked so different.

I walked to the kitchen and grabbed a small bottle of juice from the fridge. I had begun craving orange juice almost daily, so Bobby made it a point to keep it on hand. Almost as soon as he came to mind, I heard the truck pull up. I smiled and greeted him by the door.

He walked in, grabbed my waist and pulled me to him for a deep kiss. When he pulled back I was shocked and somewhat breathless.

"Well hello to you, too," I giggled.

"Hello, beautiful," he said, and then he got on his knees and kissed my growing belly. I had a feeling I was going to get big, because at almost three months there was already a noticeable roundness to my middle.

My stomach fluttered with nerves as I felt his hot breath caress my skin. I closed my eyes and gripped his shoulders to steady myself.

"Mmmm hot Momma!" he whispered huskily, standing back up to give me another sound kiss on the lips.

"Where's our girl?" he asked, glancing around the room.

"She is spending the night with Lilly. Didn't I tell you that the other day?" I asked, not really remembering if I had.

"You may have," he looked lost in thought for a moment before he shrugged. "So we have the house to ourselves then."

He kissed me again, his fingers in my hair, his muscles taut, and I sighed leaning into him, into his promising kisses. All plans of more packing fled out the window for a while.

Later, we sat on the porch. Bobby grabbed my hand and we snuggled close, watching the sun dip lower and lower in the sky. My mind raced with thoughts of Beth as the sun went down. It was a strange feeling, getting closer to someone that was no longer around. She was with me in spirit, and in my heart, but our friendship was so deeply missed. I closed my eyes for a moment, and I opened them to Bobby's hand caressing my cheek.

"You okay love?" he asked, kissing my forehead.

I nodded and offered a small smile. "I was just thinking about life, the move, everything." I shrugged.

"I love you," he said as he held a hand out to help me up. I grabbed his hand, and kissed his cheek, feeling the soft stubble of hair growth on his face against my lips.

"I love you too. I love you so much," I said, clinging to him. He smoothed my hair back and kissed my forehead again before I reluctantly let him go and we went back inside.

"Are you hungry?" I asked and laughed as he nipped at my ear.

"Mmhmm." His breath was hot on my neck and it tickled. I laughed again, playfully shooing him away.

We went to the kitchen together to search for something to eat, but nothing looked good to me, and as I watched him twitch his lips from side to side I smiled.

"Wanna go out to eat?" he offered.

I nodded. "I'd like that."

I asked him for a couple of moments while I got out of my "grungy clothes" and he scoffed. "You'd look good in a paper sack!"

I laughed as I changed into a pair of jeans and a loose top, it was a warm evening and I didn't want to feel sticky. After running a brush through my hair, I was ready to go.

Bobby patiently waited on the couch and he whistled at me when I walked in. "You are such a beautiful woman!" he said, giving me a once over.

"I thought you said I'd look good in a paper sack," I said, giving him a sly grin. Bobby pinched me on the behind and chuckled as I yipped in surprise.

"You always look good."

I felt myself blush, it amazed me that he could still make me blush after so many years together. We had been apart in college, but we had always kept in touch. We called and texted every day, and we would visit one another on breaks too. We never drifted, despite how busy and new everything had been.

Bobby has been the one constant in my life. I took his hand as we walked outside and he opened the truck door for me.

"I feel like a teenage girl again," I laughed as I got inside his truck.

"My feelings for you have only gotten stronger since then," Bobby said seriously as he got in.

I felt a lump forming in my throat at his sweet words. *Dang hormones!* He turned on the radio and drove us to town. At the stoplight he placed a hand on my stomach. "What does my baby want?"

I laughed and put a finger to my chin in thought. "Hmmm I think I want some pasta," I said after a moment. He wiggled his eyebrows and drove us to the local Italian Garden.

"Mmm, excellent choice babe! We haven't been here in a while." He chuckled. "I thought you'd enjoy this."

Turning off the truck, Bobby got out and opened the door for me. He always had such manners. Hand in hand we walked into the restaurant.

Smells of garlic and butter filled the air and I inhaled deeply. My stomach rumbled loudly and with heated cheeks I looked down at it as Bobby and I both chuckled. Once we were seated I ordered an iced tea, and he got himself a soda. We looked at the menu for a little while, and when the waitress came up to us we didn't quite know what we wanted yet.

I noted how the waitress' eyes drifted to Bobby, almost seductively. I felt a little ping of jealousy. *What if he didn't find me attractive when I got bigger?* I thought. I quickly told myself I was being silly. As if to prove my point, Bobby gave her a half smile, one that clearly stated he wasn't at all interested in her. "My wife and I will make up our minds in a minute," he said rather dismissively.

She walked off almost in a huff, and I smiled slightly to myself. However, she was nothing but manners the rest of the evening, making sure to refill our drinks and clear off empty plates. I gave her a nice tip when we had finished, and we took our dessert to go.

Bobby drove us to the park, and we ate our dessert together under the stars, making small talk as we ate. We laughed about old times, and talked of the new. He expressed his excitement to begin our new life, and he discussed his concern for Gracelynn.

"She will be okay. I know this move will be different and a little hard on her at first. But I know she will make friends quickly, and it is going to be so nice to be closer to our families," I told him as we finished our walk around the park. Bobby's lips touched mine softly, and we simply enjoyed the moment embracing one another.

After some time, the bugs got thick so we headed home. I decided I was ready to do a little bit of work so Bobby turned on the music, and together we did some packing. We didn't have much left to do by the time we were finished for the night. With only two more days left before the move, all that was left were the necessities and the big furniture, which we could put in the small U-haul we had on reserve.

I sat down on the sofa and took a long drink of the glass of water Bobby had brought to me. Tired from the events of the day, we enjoyed the silence together. I leaned my head on Bobby's shoulder and he ran his fingers lazily through my hair.

"Hmmm, that feels good. You might put me to sleep," I told him as I yawned.

Bobby chuckled softly—the sound making my stomach flutter. "I love your hair, it's so soft, like a curtain of silk," he said quietly.

A smile tugged at the corner of my mouth at his sweet words. "Thank you,," I mumbled into his shoulder. My eyes closed as his fingers continued to comb through my hair. Soft as a whisper, I could feel tiny goosebumps raise on my arms.

"I love you Katie," Bobby whispered. His whisper seemed loud in the quiet of the room. My eyes popped open and I sat up, I was going to fall asleep if we continued this activity.

I turned toward him and smiled. "I love you too," I told him. My lashes fell as he stroked my cheek with smooth fingers, and I leaned my face into his palm before kissing it.

"Thank you for today," I told him, eyes still closed. His touch sent an electric current down my spine, making my heart kick up a notch.

"Of course! I love spending time with you, I always have. You're like…my best friend."

I looked at his face then, his eyes so intense I felt a little breathless. "You're my best friend too."

After a while, we went off to bed. Content with snuggling, my body relaxed, and it wasn't long until sleep found us both.

Seventeen

I dropped Gracelynn off at my mom's before making my way to the farm. We'd just begun unpacking, having the last bit of stuff emptied out of the house. I had thanked the empty home before we left. It had been our home for the last six years. I would miss it there, and I knew Gracelynn was going to miss it as well.

When I pulled up at the farm, I smiled as warm memories filled my mind. Bobby had brought me several times, and each time was dear to me. I opened the door, grinning as I heard Bobby's voice. He was talking with a friend helping us move the heavy furniture. He happened to be telling his friend that he was excited about the baby when I walked into the room.

My cheeks warmed and I instinctively placed a hand on my stomach. They both greeted me with a smile, and Bobby blew me a kiss before they moved the furniture around the room. There were boxes everywhere, in each room, and though I felt overwhelmed, I was truly excited.

The farmhouse had tons of space for all of us, and the new baby when he or she came into the world. I also loved that we would have a big yard and farm animals. Chickens, and a couple horses, and cows. They were dairy cows, and I looked forward to fresh milk, and of course I was thankful for the laying hens. There were a couple of dogs too, though they rarely came up to the house. I also loved the idea of having a nice-sized garden. I'd always liked flowers, and I'd always wanted to grow vegetables too. It would be fun for Gracelynn and I to tend a garden together.

My favorite part was that it was surrounded by trees, and there was a pond a little ways from the house. It would be nice to plant some more plants and flowers around the pond, and sit out with a good book. *First though,* I thought as I looked around the room, *we have to get settled in.*

My mom had offered to keep Gracelynn for the week so that we could get a good start on the house. Though I missed her already having just dropped her off, I was thankful that we could focus on the house. We had so much to do.

Besides, I planned on working on Gracelynn's room first, to make sure it was ready for her when she came home. I just prayed she would feel like she was home, moving had been pretty hard on her. She'd cried after we'd packed the last of it. I'd held her in my arms and just let her cry.

I headed up to Gracelynn's room and sighed with a smile as I noticed her bed had already been set up, along with her dresser, mirror, and her nightstand, they were all covered in plastic. The paint that Gracelynn had picked out, as well as all the supplies, was sitting on top of the plastic covering the floor.

I opened the paint, doing my best to ignore the strong and unpleasant odor that followed. I opened a couple of windows to allow some ventilation in the room while I worked. I put on some music from my phone, and immediately got started.

Gracelynn had chosen a beautiful periwinkle color for her walls, and wanted to keep the woodwork as is. The color went over the white walls with ease. After a time I stopped to rest my aching arm. I put a hand on my hip and looked around the room at the progress

I'd made. The fresh wet paint twinkled in the sun streaming through the windows, the color equally calming and welcoming.

I yawned as I walked down the stairs and into the kitchen. The guys were still hard at work getting furniture into place. I grabbed a glass out of a box and filled it with cold water, swallowing it down in quick long gulps, feeling relieved as the cold liquid made its way down my dry throat. I filled the glass up again before I headed back to Gracelynn's room. I set it on the windowsill away from the paint, and got back to work.

By the time I had the first coat complete, I was hot, tired, and hungry. I cleaned up my mess, and headed downstairs to let Bobby know that it was way past time for a break. When I got into the living room he was saying bye to his friend that helped us move. He shut the door and leaned against it, obviously tired. I walked up to him, and he grinned down at me as I put my head on his chest.

"Are you ready to find some food?" he asked, as if reading my mind.

"Mmhmmm!" I said, nodding against his chest. He kissed the top of my head.

"Well, I have to get cleaned up so I can take you out for some food! There is no way we are going to locate dishes right now in that mess of a kitchen," he said with a chuckle.

I sighed, picking my head up to look at him. "That means I'd better get cleaned up too. Probably have paint everywhere."

He made a show of inspecting me. "Yep, you my dear, need a shower too," he said. I laughed as he tickled my sides, wiggling out of his reach and toward our master bedroom and into our bathroom. Thankfully, everything we needed was put in a good location. The towels and soap were easy to find, as the boxes had been placed in the bathroom.

I turned on the faucet, testing it until it reached the desired temperature and stepped in, welcoming the massaging stream of water. I washed my body, and realized that not only was I obviously pregnant, but my breasts seemed larger, more sensitive. I had some stretch marks forming on my chest, as well as my thighs. I was also getting acne, something that I personally hadn't had to worry about since puberty! I made a mental note to pick up some acne treatment.

When I was done, I wrapped myself in the towel and as Bobby got ready for his shower he caressed my skin, and for a moment, I tugged my towel closer to myself suddenly hyper aware of my changing body and also weirdly sensitive about it. Bobby frowned, noting my distance.

I left the bathroom, feeling confused, stupid, and sad. I'd always been beautiful to him. *Why would I feel like this?*

Trying desperately not to cry, I chose a pair of loose fitting jeans that were at the top of my suitcase, and pulled on a random t-shirt. I was putting on my socks and shoes when Bobby entered the room. He was covered from the waist down, and I watched as a drop of water dripped slowly down his muscled back before he shoved his arms through a shirt he found in a box.

He quietly sat down beside me, and tucked a wet strand of hair behind my ear. I inhaled his clean scent and noticed his eyes were sad and questioning as he looked at me. I felt my throat constrict as he pulled me close, and I silently cried against his shoulder.

"It's okay love," he murmured, stroking my hair.

When I finally calmed down I glanced guiltily at him, wiping a tear off my cheek. "No it's not…I'm so sorry!" I croaked.

"You don't have to hide your body from me sweetheart," he said softly.

I nodded and bit my lip, ran a hand through my hair and sighed loudly. "I don't know what that was, I just felt really self-conscious. I don't know how to explain it."

"Your body is changing, quickly. It's probably completely normal to feel the way you are feeling. Baby, I don't want you to ever think that I could find you unattractive. You are beautiful to me, you always have been. Not just on the outside, but in here." He placed a hand against his chest.

My chin quivered and I lunged forward, embracing him. I was truly blessed. "I love you so much."

"I love you too, now let's go get some food," he said gruffly. I sniffled and then we both laughed as my stomach gave a loud rumble.

As we drove toward town Bobby gazed at me with a smile. "What sounds good?"

My stomach rumbled again and I shrugged. "I think I would be fine with just about anything right now, I'm so hungry!"

Bobby pulled up to the Chinese buffet place and I nodded before he even had to ask if I would be okay with it. He shut off the truck and then immediately went to my side to open my door. I took his hand with an appreciative smile.

The best thing about a buffet? There was no waiting! You could order your drink and get right to making your plate! When I was satisfied with my first plate I got back to our table. Not able to wait for Bobby to join me, I began eating. It had been way too long since I'd eaten and it was almost as if the baby were complaining, because I couldn't seem to shove the food in fast enough.

When Bobby joined me, he sipped his coffee before he began working through a large portion of chicken fried rice. I ate a couple of stuffed mushrooms and ate a good-sized portion of lo-mein before I finally slowed down.

Bobby caressed the top of my hand with a finger and I looked up into his eyes. "Feeling better?" he asked quietly.

I nodded with a smile, and thanked him before eating a piece of honey chicken. When I was finished with my first plate, the nice waitress took it for me and I went back up for a bowl of salad and a side of chocolate mousse for dessert.

By the time we left, I was stuffed and tired, but Bobby didn't drive us straight home. I raised an eyebrow in question and he grinned mischievously. When he turned down a familiar path, my stomach flopped with excitement and I gasped in surprise.

Noting my obvious exuberance Bobby chuckled. "We haven't been here in forever!" he said as we parked. We got out at the same time, I couldn't wait for him to open the door for me.

"Oh my goodness" I said as I glanced around us. The sun was beginning to set in the sky, the horizon a beautiful violet and indigo blue. The wildflowers were blooming all around us and I walked ahead of Bobby. So many memories and emotions. I closed my eyes feeling nostalgic as Bobby's arms went around my waist, and he pulled me close.

"This is where I told you I loved you for the first time," he said, kissing my ear. I shivered as his warm breath brushed my neck.

"So many beautiful memories here, love," I agreed, my voice barely above a whisper in the quiet evening. We walked together, his hand warm in mine.

"We will have to bring Gracey here sometime," Bobby said, breaking the silence after a time. I smiled up at him and we watched the sunset together.

"She would absolutely love it here, all these flowers, this open space," I said wistfully.

"Let's go home," Bobby said, kissing my cheek. "It's getting late and it's been a long day. You need some rest."

We walked toward the truck and I glanced back at the small meadow before we headed back home, reliving that first night that Bobby had told me he loved me.

It had been a long and busy day, but it had also been really good. When we got back to the farm, I dressed in my favorite pajamas and it wasn't long before Bobby joined me in our bed.

We were surrounded by boxes, but Bobby had made sure to keep a safe and open path for me so that I wouldn't trip over anything should I need to get up in the middle of the night.

I watched the moonlight filter through the window. The old house creaked and groaned in the silence, and it took some time to get my mind quieted enough to relax. It has never been easy for me to fall asleep in a new environment, especially in old houses that made so much noise at night. I stared up at the ceiling for quite some time before I finally closed my eyes.

The days were growing long, and the nights even longer. It had only been three days since we dropped Gracelynn off with my parents, but I was missing her fiercely and it felt like much longer than just three days. I had finished painting her room, and it was drying when Bobby suggested we go over to see her and visit with my parents.

I was probably driving him nuts worrying over Gracelynn. Of course, with my parents she was in terrific hands. I am really not used to being away from her for very long. Calling wasn't enough, I needed to see her.

We wasted no time getting ready and heading over to Mom's, I was practically bouncing in my seat by the time we arrived. I squealed in excitement when Gracelynn opened the door and ran up to me. I was so happy to see that she was glad to see me too, and I wasn't just being crazy.

Gracelynn held my hand as we walked up the steps and then gently patted my stomach when I sat down. "I think the baby is growing, you look bigger," she said honestly. Her eyes wide and her cute little nose wrinkled as she studied my stomach.

I nodded with a laugh. "Yeah, I think you're right." We talked in the living room for a while before Mom insisted on making at least some sandwiches for lunch. I helped Mom in the kitchen, we talked about how the unpacking was going, and how I was feeling.

My eyes kept darting to the other room where I could hear Gracelynn laughing, and Bobby's chuckle following. I felt a smile tug at my mouth, and when I turned I noticed mom regarding me with a grin.

"You appear to be so happy, honey. I'm proud of you!" she said, shoving several triangle-shaped sandwiches onto a single plate. It was only the four of us, my eyes widened at the stack.

"Thank you mom! You really didn't have to make so much," I told her when she grabbed two bags of unopened chips from the cabinet.

Mom placed a hand on her hip, and gave me "the look." I knew I had lost the argument before I commented further. I smiled my gratitude, and helped her by bringing plates to the table after she had insisted on doing everything herself.

Once we were all settled at the table, we made small talk as we ate. Gracelynn didn't stay at the table once she was finished, asking to excuse herself so that she could finish watching a movie.

When Dad opened the door I stood and half ran up to him for a hug. I felt a lump form in my throat as his arms wrapped around me. "Hey, Pickle!" he said.

"Hi, Dad! It's been a while. How have you been?" I asked, letting him go long enough to get a look at him while taking in new wrinkles and graying hair.

"Busy as always, your mom's trying to get me to retire. I probably should, " he said with a small chuckle as we walked into the dining room.

We sat at the table again, Dad had a couple sandwiches and we all talked. After a while when we had our fill, I helped Mom clean up, and Bobby joined my dad in the den. I assumed they were going to talk or watch sports. Bobby isn't much of a sports fan, but I knew he was just giving me time to visit with my mom.

As soon as the men left the room, Mom instantly started talking about the baby, and asking if I had an OBGYN yet or not. She was not thrilled that I hadn't been in to do that, but I reminded her that we'd been so busy with the move, and promised that as soon as we were more settled in, I would get everything set up.

We spent a couple of hours catching up, and then I spent an

hour with Gracelynn in my old bedroom. It was almost exactly the same. I enjoyed Gracelynn's company and listening to her talk about her time with her grandparents, and how excited she was to go home with us in four more days.

"I can't wait to see my new room!" Gracelynn said with a huge grin. I smiled, I knew that she would love it, and I told her as much. I let her know the paint she picked out was perfect, because I could tell she was curious about it.

I didn't tell her though, that her room was completely ready. Bobby had helped me move the furniture around, and I had gotten her a really cute mushroom lamp for her new desk. She had a new computer waiting for her on that desk, as well. She was pretty responsible for her age, and I felt confident that she'd take care of it.

These days kids have to have a computer for school anyway, and I knew that the school would supply a computer, but this way she would have one of her own to work on homework, and to keep in touch with Lilly through emails.

We had a wonderful visit, and I hugged Gracelynn fiercely before leaving. I promised her again that she would love her bedroom. I watched out the rearview mirror as we drove away and waved until I couldn't see Mom or Gracey on the porch any longer.

Eighteen

Gracelynn stood shocked still in the doorway to her new bedroom. Her eyes searched, and a smile lit her face as she took it all in. She stepped into the room slowly, and before I could ask if she liked it, she stood in the middle of the room and spun in a huge circle before leaping toward me for a hug.

I embraced her with a soft laugh. "I take it that you're happy." I kissed the top of her head.

"It's so beautiful! Thank you for the new stuff, I have my own computer?" she asked as she glanced back down at the baby blue laptop on her desk.

"We thought it would be nice for you to be able to do homework, and to keep in touch with Lilly too."

Gracelynn hugged me again before walking around to inspect everything. "Thank you so much! I love it!" she said happily.

I left Gracelynn to get acquainted with her new space, and walked downstairs to the kitchen for a cup of water. Summer weather was quickly approaching, I wiped a small bead of sweat off of my forehead with the back of my hand.

Now that we were getting more settled, I made a mental note

to head to town to the hospital and get myself an OBGYN, and family doctor.

"Why don't you sit down for a while," my mom said, as she sat at the island in the kitchen. I sat beside her, taking another big gulp of water.

"Sounds like Gracelynn is happy with her room, I could hear her excitement from down here," Mom said with a laugh.

"Yeah, she really loves it. She picked a pretty color, and Bobby helped me get everything ready of course," I said before she could tell me that I was overdoing myself.

"I will be sure to go up and have a peek," Mom said as she patted my arm and looked around. "You guys have made great progress already though, I'm so happy you're closer to home. Especially now that you're pregnant."

I did nothing to hide my prideful smile. With the nausea mostly passed, pregnancy had been enjoyable. To my relief I could also eat tomatoes again without getting sick. I thought about a doctor's visit. I was looking forward to my ultrasound, I was ready to see my baby, and to feel him or her growing inside me. Scared as I was, I couldn't seem to help but be excited.

"I plan to get myself to the hospital next week, get a family doctor, and to get an OBGYN of course," I told my mom.

She nodded, and smiled a smile that lit her soft brown eyes. "I can't wait to see this little one," she said, placing a hand on my protruding stomach.

"Yeah, me too. Gracelynn is really excited. I think she is hoping for a sister," I said with a small laugh. It became quiet, as I thought back to the letter for Gracelynn in Beth's diary.

"What are you thinking about?" my mom asked.

I couldn't see any reason not to tell her. "Beth wrote Gracelynn a letter." Mom studied me, her head tilted to the side in question.

I shrugged. "Even though I'm scared of what she may think or how she may feel…I can't read it, it's not my place. Once she gets settled, I plan to give it to her."

Emotion filled my voice, making it hard to swallow, and Mom wrapped an arm around me. I lay my head on her shoulder. "She wrote me a letter too," I confided.

Mom kissed my forehead and tucked a stray hair behind my ear as she had when I was a child.

"It will be okay, sweetheart. Gracelynn is a strong little girl, and you've done such a beautiful job raising her. You and Bobby both have. Beth would be so proud." Her voice broke, and I felt my chin quiver just before my eyes pricked with tears.

"What's wrong?" Mom and I both turned to see Gracelynn standing behind us with concerned eyes.

"Nothing sweetheart, we're just pretty happy," my mom said reassuringly.

Gracelynn put a hand to her hip. "Why do you look so sad?" she asked me.

"I'm fine honey, I promise. It's been a busy week and I feel tired, but I'm so very happy."

Gracelynn studied me for a moment before she said "Okay," and tapped her grandma on the shoulder. "Wanna come see my room?"

They headed upstairs, and I could hear the enthusiasm from where I sat. Her excitement was contagious and I couldn't help but smile as I listened to the giggles and animated chatter.

Mom helped unpack several boxes, even though I had told her that she didn't need to. I knew that it would do me no good trying to persuade her otherwise.

After a while, I nodded wide-eyed and excited. "Thank you for helping Mom. It does feel good seeing this room start to come together."

Mom waved me off. "Well, I'm getting hungry. How about we go to the kitchen and see what we can whip up?" she offered. I laughed before following her toward the kitchen. *I could eat.*

Mom shoved some chicken nuggets onto a cookie sheet and put them in the oven. As they started to bake, I worked on a cold spaghetti salad with juicy tomato, cucumber, purple onion, and sweet red and yellow bell peppers that needed to be used up, then I splashed in some Italian dressing.

Mom whipped up a cheap box of pudding, then set the table.

Of course, there was way too much food for the three of us. We sat with Gracelynn at the table for lunch, and to my surprise Gracelynn made herself another plate of pasta.

"I never thought I'd like cold spaghetti," she said as she slurped a long noodle into her mouth.

"It really is super good!" my mom said after she swallowed.

I thanked them both with a smile as I slowly worked on eating my lunch. It was a bit warm and I didn't really feel too hungry, but I knew I needed to try anyway.

Bobby came home early, and helped himself to a plate after he changed his clothes and gave me a swift peck on the cheek. He also complimented me on the pasta salad, and I made a mental note to make them off and on through the summer. They were quick, easy, could be made with any kind of veggie, and it was apparently a big hit.

Mom helped me clean up after lunch, visiting a little longer, and after saying her goodbyes I watched her drive away.

I enjoyed the visit, and the productivity of the day, but I also felt completely and undeniably exhausted. We all enjoyed a movie, and then Bobby and I relaxed by sitting outside while Gracelynn ran around in the wide open space of her new yard.

I had wanted to do some more unpacking, but I didn't want to push myself too hard. I knew I was needing to slow down. My body told me as much when I climbed in bed that night. Bobby massaged my back. I felt my body relax in the softness of our bed and fell quickly to sleep.

The next morning, I woke earlier than planned and slipped my robe on. Bobby had already gotten up to get to work on the farm. When I made it to the kitchen I smiled to see there was fresh coffee waiting for me. I made myself a small mug and welcomed the silence of the living room. I gazed out of the bay window to see the sun just beginning to rise.

When 8:00 am rolled around and the house was still silent, I went upstairs to check on Gracelynn. I found her slung across her bed sleeping peacefully. I pulled her sheet over her before heading back downstairs.

I could see Bobby out by the barn with some of the farm hands, hard at work. I decided to eat some leftover pasta salad. An interesting breakfast choice, but I didn't feel up to cooking. I ate quicker than usual, realizing I was hungrier than I'd thought. After I finished, I rinsed out my dish and began working on the living room.

There were only four boxes left to unpack, so that didn't take me all too long. There were knick knacks, some cushions for the couch, and a box of movies. I was thankful it was all easy stuff to put away. All that was left for the living room was to hang up the family photos, and I wouldn't do that until Gracelynn was awake.

When I got dressed after my shower, Gracelynn was at the table with a heaping bowl of cereal.

"Well good morning sleepy head." I said as I towel dried my hair.

"Morning," she said sleepily. Her ebony hair was a chaos of curls, her eyes still heavy with sleep.

"Did you sleep well?" I asked her as I sat myself down with a glass of orange juice.

Gracelynn nodded with a yawn. "Yeah, it was weird though cause I kinda forgot where I was for a second," she said with a laugh.

"I understand, I did the same thing!"

She gaped at me with wide eyes. "You did?" she asked in disbelief.

"Sure did! So did Dad!" I said with a laugh, and Gracelynn

giggled, shaking her head. "I would have liked to see that!" she stated before stuffing her mouth with a big spoonful of cereal.

Gracelynn finished her breakfast, and ran upstairs to change her clothes, stating that she wanted to go outside to play on the tire swing, so the house was quiet once again.

Feeling cool and refreshed after my shower, I put my damp hair up in a ponytail and started hanging the photos in the living room. I worked slowly, so that I wouldn't end up hurting myself, or overworking myself too quickly because I planned on getting more done for the day. I didn't think I could stand looking at these boxes much longer.

When I was done, I nodded as I looked around the finished room feeling excited and pleased with my work. I cleaned up my mess, and broke down the boxes to take them to the recycle bin.

While outside, I walked slowly to the recycle, taking in the warm sun on my skin and smiling as I heard Gracelynn's laughter. I peeked over at her, still on the swing and having a blast.

When I got back in, I unpacked and placed the old china dishes and small knick knacks in the curio cabinet. I inspected them all to be sure they weren't chipped or broken. Then, I hung the few photos that belonged in the dining room. I moved the table slowly toward the center of the room, unpacking the small box that contained the centerpiece for the table. It was a three piece candle set that my mom had gotten me. Once the table was clean and pretty, I broke down the few boxes and placed them by the back door to take out later.

I turned on the radio, and grabbed the broom and dustpan so that I could sweep the two finished rooms. When I was satisfied, I stood between the rooms and took in all of the progress. I glanced at the clock, it had only been two hours of fairly steady paced work. I decided to sit on the sofa, embracing the moment with my eyes closed. Now that I'd made some good progress, I was feeling some stress lift off of my shoulders. I opened my eyes remembering I still needed to get to the hospital.

I offered to take Gracelynn with me, and she nodded enthusiastically. I headed out into the sun to locate Bobby to let him know we were headed out.

She didn't take long changing her clothes and joining me in the car. I turned on the radio and half listened to the music while I drove to town with Gracelynn. She was in a good mood, bobbing her head to the beat of the song. Her good mood was contagious and I turned up the volume, enjoying the music with her.

When we made it to the hospital, I sat unmoving, staring at the building for a bit longer than necessary.

"Are you okay?" Gracelynn asked, bringing me out of thoughts that had drifted to the past.

"I'm fine sweetheart, I really don't like hospitals." I told her honestly.

Gracelynn nodded before unbuckling her seatbelt. "Well, we may as well get it over with, right?" She encouraged me.

I twisted in my seat and gave her a small smile. "I suppose you're right." I got out, my stomach flopping as we walked toward the building. When the automatic doors opened, the smell hit my face and I swallowed hard. It's amazing how memories can be so overwhelming.

As if sensing my discomfort, Gracelynn put her small hand in mine and gave it a light squeeze. I looked down at her, and into her brilliant green eyes. She gave me a smile and patted my arm. I felt a little ridiculous acting so scared in front of her.

"It's okay to be scared, you know what I do?"

I raised my eyebrows at her and with a grin I said "what do you do?"

Gracelynn looked into my eyes, her expression rather serious. "Well, I think of somewhere else. Like the zoo, or a rainforest or something like that. Maybe you can think of a place you like to be. If you use your imagination, maybe it will help calm you down. It always works for me." She said, tucking a stray hair behind her ear as I contemplated her words.

"You know what?" I asked.

"What?"

"You are so smart, and I love you!"

Gracelynn gave a soft giggle that filled me with pride and joy. "I love you, too. Let's go." She tugged my hand a little, we walked into the hospital, I spoke to the receptionist, and then we waited.

Nineteen

When Dr. Ray walked into the little room Gracelynn and I were put in, she gave me a kind-hearted smile, and a hug.

"Katie! It is wonderful to see you again, I can't believe it's already been nine years!" She turned then to see Gracelynn sitting beside me, and I watched as her eyes grew wide.

"Oh my goodness! Look at you!" she said kindly, stooping down to Gracelynn's eye level.

"Hi." Gracelynn said it quietly, a hint of nervousness in her voice.

"Honey, this is Dr. Ray. She was your momma's doctor, and she helped bring you into this world."

Gracelynn studied Dr. Ray with wide, searching eyes. I felt a lump in my throat as Gracelynn's lip trembled, and she gave the doctor a hug.

"I have always wanted to meet you," she said politely before sitting back down.

"It's very nice to meet you, Gracelynn." Dr. Ray returned, a hand on her heart in sincerity.

Dr. Ray took her seat on the black roller stool as she went through some paperwork.

"Okay, so you're transferring to my care," she said with a smile before continuing to peruse the file. "I see you haven't had your ultrasound. Let's get that taken care of, shall we? You haven't recently gone to the restroom?" she asked me softly.

"Uh no, ma'am, I was hoping that I would be able to have an ultrasound today!" My throat tightened with emotion as together we walked to another exam room. The equipment setting me even more on edge.

I lay there with Gracelynn sitting sweetly by my side, holding my hand like I held hers when she had doctor appointments. I felt a little sad because Bobby wasn't here for this.

The gel that Dr. Ray splattered on my stomach was so cold that I jumped with a surprised gasp. Gracelynn giggled, and Dr. Ray apologized. I closed my eyes, and took a deep breath. My heart was racing wildly. *Why was I so nervous? Breathe…breathe.*

"You ready?" Dr. Ray's voice broke through my quick meditation.

I swallowed past a lump in my throat and nodded, forcing my eyes to open, I turned to peer at the screen. I stole a glance at Gracelynn, she was sitting with her hand still in mine, her eyes focused on the screen beside us. I wondered what she was thinking, if she was scared like I was.

Dr. Ray moved the probe around and then pressed a few buttons on the keyboard, she moved the probe again, and zoomed in on the image. After what felt like a long stretch of silence, pointing to the small image on the screen, she said "there."

The baby is around two inches long, Gracelynn pointed and smiled back at me. "Look! Can we see if it's a girl?" Gracelynn asked.

Dr. Ray gave her a kind smile. "I can usually tell the sex around the fourth month, so we will have you guys come back to find out, okay?"

Gracelynn didn't seem too pleased with having to wait, but she nodded, barely taking her eyes off of the screen. My eyes were full of tears, and I couldn't help but to smile.

After I got dressed Dr. Ray scheduled the next appointment, she printed my ultrasound photo, handed it to me, and sent me on my way. As Gracelynn and I headed toward the exit doors someone said my name.

I turned, glancing around the waiting room when I saw her. She stood and squealed, rushing over to us. "Lane?" I squeaked in disbelief as she came closer. She looked like she had in high school, except her hair was long, past her shoulders and pulled back in a neat braid. Behind her stood a boy Gracelynn's age, and my eyes widened as I realized it was Malachi. I'd been in the delivery room with her when she'd had him. He gave a shy half smile, and a wave. Gracelynn smiled back.

"My God, girl! Look at you!" Lane said as she hugged me. Then glancing at Gracelynn, her lip pulled into a pout. "Look at her! She's so beautiful! She looks exactly like her mother!" She said the last softly, so that only I heard.

I hugged Lane back, tears brimmed my eyes. "You look exactly the same!" I laughed. "And Malachi! Gosh, it's been so long!" We pulled away from one another, giggling like a couple of school girls in the middle of the hospital.

Lane got called in for her appointment, so we didn't have time to talk. We did take a moment to exchange phone numbers.

As we walked out of the hospital Gracelynn chatted about Lane, she was curious about her.

"We used to be in school together, Lane was popular. The kind of girl that didn't hang out with someone like me…Things changed when she got pregnant and became friends with your mom. Lane and I became really good friends, and I learned that just because someone is popular, doesn't mean they aren't a good person. People can surprise you Gracey, remember that."

Gracelynn buckled up as we headed out of the parking lot. She looked wistful, she gave me a smile. "I'm happy that you got to see Lane, she's nice and she's really pretty, like a princess!"

I nodded with a smile of my own. "She's always been really pretty, I'm happy to have gotten to see her too. Maybe we will see more of her, and her son."

Gracelynn didn't say more as we made our way to the grocery store. Once we were in, I took my time enjoying the air conditioning. I slowly grabbed the things I needed on the list I'd made, and I allowed Gracelynn to get a few things that she wanted.

When we made it to the register, the clerk checked us out, and I let Gracelynn hand her the cash. Gracelynn thanked the lady, and we left.

"I like paying for groceries." Gracelynn said.

"Yeah? What do you like about it?" I asked, bracing the paper bag on my hip while I unlocked the car.

"Well, I like that it makes me feel older!" She was looking at me with a beaming smile. I couldn't help but to grin back. She really was growing up too quickly!

"I love that you enjoy some responsibility, sweetheart! I just don't want you to feel like you have to be grown up so fast. I want you to enjoy being young," I said as I started the car.

"I do enjoy being my age, because I have good friends but I can't wait to grow up, because when you're an adult you get to have a job, and go shopping, you can stay up as long as you want, and get a boyfriend, and it just sounds like a lot of fun!" She talked so fast, and had that adorable sparkle in her eyes.

I felt emotional, but I offered a smile. "Being an adult can be fun, yes, but I hope you enjoy your childhood as much as possible, before you have to become an adult. It happens quickly sweetheart. I want you to enjoy it all."

Gracelynn nodded and gazed out the window with a dreamy smile on her face. I was sure she was busy thinking of her future. "Did you just say you wanted a boyfriend?" I asked, breaking the silence. Gracelynn looked at me with huge eyes.

"Well not right now, Momma Katie! But someday. I'm too young for boys right now!" she said with a laugh. Her nose wrinkled as she talked. I laughed with her, feeling pleased that she wasn't ready to have that discussion just yet. I knew though, that soon enough I'd have to get prepared to have "the talk."

I remembered when my mom had "the talk" with me. I'd been so mortified, but Mom had been simple about it. I remember her telling me "your first time should be with someone you love, someone who values you for all that you are."

I also remembered when I'd been having such crazy hormones, and hadn't really wanted to talk to my mom about it. I'd actually talked to my boss, back when I worked at the diner. She had talked about being ready, and marriage… back then of course I'd been too young to think about marriage, but a very large part of me hoped I would always be with Bobby.

I smiled as I thought about my husband. It had indeed always been Bobby. I felt lucky that even when we had gone to different colleges we still stayed together. It had been hard, the distance a living heartache. We made time for one another, our relationship continually blooming, we never let the distance come between us.

I remembered our wedding day as if it were yesterday. We had been engaged for a year before we'd gotten married after college. We didn't move in together until we were married, Bobby had wanted to do everything "right." Our wedding had been simple but also the most beautiful day of my life, our wedding night had been magical too.

A small sigh escaped my lips as I parked the car in the driveway. Gracelynn got out and grabbed a bag of groceries, running inside while I grabbed the other bag and locked the car. Bobby whistled at me from the barn. I turned to see him shirtless, sweaty, and sexy as ever leaning against the barn. I felt my heart skip a beat as his eyes swept over me.

I'm not sure how it's possible to have this reaction to him after so many years together, but I love that man with all my heart. He sauntered over to me and drew me in for a kiss, taking the bag of groceries from my arms in the process, before slapping my behind and walking away.

"Hey!" I protested and giggled as he ran ahead of me. I walked into the house, the air hit my heated skin. Being pregnant in the summer was rough business. I headed into the kitchen and watched Bobby put away the groceries.

"More avocados," Bobby sighed, as he placed them in the basket where we kept the fruit. I laughed at his disgusted expression.

"Gracey is crazy about them." I said as I rubbed my growing stomach.

"Are you hungry?" Bobby asked as he finished putting things away.

"Not really, just hot," I replied with a sigh.

Bobby made a glass of ice water and handed it to me. I thanked him and took a long drink, closing my eyes as I enjoyed the refreshment.

"Well, tonight I want you to relax. I'm gonna make dinner!" he stated as he joined me at the island. I leaned against his shoulder, suddenly feeling exhausted.

"How was your appointment?" Bobby asked against my hair. I opened my mouth with a gasp. *How could I forget the sonogram?*

I walked to the couch, pulled the sonogram out of my purse, and joined Bobby back in the kitchen. His eyebrow arched in question of the item in my hand and I handed it to him with a grin I could not control.

Bobby studied the sonogram, I couldn't describe the expression on his face as he studied it.

He looked at me then, tears in his eyes and pulled me toward him. We studied the photo together. He tilted my chin up to meet his gaze.

"Our little nugget! I love you so much!" he said, my face in his palm.

"I love you, too!" I replied softly, and his lips brushed mine.

I heard a giggle before a little voice said "eeew," Bobby and I turned to see Gracelynn standing in the doorway of the kitchen, watching us.

"Eeew?" Bobby exclaimed, he jumped off the chair and ran toward her. Gracelynn squealed and tried to get away, but laughed as Bobby caught her and peppered kisses on her cheeks.

"Aaaah Daaad!" she said as she laughed and wiped her face with her shirt sleeve. I couldn't control my own laughter as I watched them. Gracelynn squirmed out of Bobby's arms, successfully getting away from him and running toward me.

"Save me!" she giggled as she threw her arms around my neck.

Bobby gave a look of pretend defeat and sat on the chair beside us with an exaggerated pout, making Gracelynn and I both laugh again.

"Can we watch a movie?" Gracelynn asked after a few minutes of silence.

"That sounds like a great idea, you two watch a movie, I'm going to shower and work on dinner," Bobby offered.

Once Gracelynn picked a movie, I put it in for her and she snuggled up on the couch with her head in my lap. I ran my hand through her hair as we watched the movie "Princess Diaries." We'd seen it several times, but Gracelynn loved it. I watched the movie, laughing along with Gracelynn at the funny parts, enjoying the moment with her. I knew it wouldn't be long before these moments would be few and far between.

I woke to a light touch on my cheek and I gazed sleepily into Bobby's eyes. Gracelynn was asleep with her arms around my waist. It had been a long time since she'd fallen asleep on me like this.

Bobby and I both smiled down at her. "Dinner will be done soon, love." I looked at the time. It was almost six p.m! Gracelynn rose and yawned. "I don't remember being tired, I missed the rest of the movie!" she groaned.

Bobby smiled at her and turned on the T.V.

"I knew you'd want to finish it, so I paused it when you fell asleep." He clicked play, and I stood stretching before following him into the kitchen as Gracelynn finished her movie.

I refilled my glass of water and stood beside the sink while I took a drink, watching Bobby chop vegetables and slide them into the skillet. *Why is everything he does so sexy?* I wondered, and then giggled at my train of thought. *This pregnancy must really be messing with my hormones.*

"What's so funny?" Bobby asked as he stirred the pot of noodles. I nibbled my bottom lip as I looked at him, smiling as his eyes dropped to my mouth.

"I like watching you cook."

"Well I love cooking for you," he said, winking at me before turning his attention back to the stove.

I drank my water, and decided I'd better let him focus on dinner. I placed my now empty glass of water on the counter beside the sink and decided to go into the room that was now considered the library/office.

I loved this room with its light peach walls and gray accents. A few bookcases lined a wall, books on every shelf, a beautiful oak desk in the corner had my computer on it, a huge neon pink bean bag chair had been placed in the far corner, and a small round table was in the middle of the room with a couple cushioned chairs around it. A few hanging plants added to the beauty and comfort of the room.

I made myself comfortable at the desk and opened my laptop. I hadn't been on my computer in a very long time. I checked my email from my phone those days. I opened the laptop with a sigh as I looked at the lock screen photo. It was Beth and I, a long time ago. We were just kids, standing on a pier holding hands as we faced toward the lake. It was one of my favorite photos of us as children. I typed my password, and the photo faded and was replaced with a picture from my wedding day; Bobby and I looking down at a younger Gracelynn as she smiled up at us with beautiful white flowers in her hair.

Twenty

I jumped slightly as I felt warm air tickle the back of my neck. "Did I scare you?" he asked against my heated skin.

"I didn't hear you come in." I let out an audible sigh as I closed my laptop.

"I don't get to see what's had your attention for the past few days?" Bobby asked.

"I'm not sure what it even is yet," I admitted with a laugh as he nibbled my neck. My heart was doing that familiar little pitter patter in my chest as I turned to look at him.

"It is getting late, do you want to go to bed?" His tone suggested more than sleep. I felt goosebumps on my arms as I gazed into his eyes.

"Yeah, I'll be done shortly." He kissed my cheek and walked out. I had been in here longer than I'd planned. I opened up my computer again, continuing where I'd left off. I'm not sure how it happened, but as I peered at the words of the story I was writing, I felt like I'd started something quite magical.

I typed for a while longer, and sighed as I glanced at the clock. It really was getting late. I saved my document and closed my laptop gently. I stood, stretched, rotating my shoulders. I'd been sitting in the same position for too long and my body was complaining about it.

I closed the door after shutting off the light, and made my way to Gracelynn's room. I gently opened the door to see her sleeping peacefully. A book was resting by her head. I set it on her bedside table and kissed her forehead before heading into our bedroom.

Bobby was sitting on the edge of the bed when I came in. He was in his favorite pair of pajama pants despite how warm I thought it was. "Hi honey," I said in the doorway.

Bobby looked up and smiled at me, standing up to kiss my cheek and then my lips and neck. My hormones were going wild by the time he pulled back, but I felt sticky and really needed to cool off.

"Hold onto that thought?" I asked. Bobby nodded with a grin as I went to our bathroom.

I had to take a shower, we kept the house cool, but it felt stifling to me. I bent my head, staring at my growing belly before I rubbed it. "Summertime will be gone before we know it, little one," I said softly. *Not soon enough!* I thought to myself, as it hadn't even really begun yet. I wanted Gracelynn to enjoy this summer, but I was already so tired of the heat. The shower was quick, but wonderful. I shut the water off and dried myself off with a large cotton towel.

Bobby was still sitting on the edge of the bed. He looked to be in deep thought. He leaned his head against my belly as I stood in front of him, his hands on my hips.

"Feel better?" he asked, gazing up at me. I smiled down at him.

"Yeah, a little. I can't seem to cool off." He laughed and rubbed my belly.

"You're making it hard for your mommy already," he said to my stomach. I smiled, I loved when he talked to our baby.

"Listen, it hasn't been that hot yet so I need you to try to be nicer okay?" He kissed my stomach.

Bobby looked at me with a wicked grin. "What I want to do definitely would not cool you off," he said as he stood he pressed his body against mine, and I no longer thought about the temperature.

"Bobby, I'm sorry I've been kind of distant."

"I'm about to remedy that, baby," he growled playfully.

My eyes widened in surprise as Bobby picked me up and pressed me lightly into the mattress. When his lips touched mine, it was as if I were truly lost in the heat of his gaze. I felt so loved.

Much later I fell asleep in Bobby's arms and I sat up with a gasp. *Beth! Beth!* Glancing around the room, I realized *it was only a dream*. I wiped the tears from my face, *only a dream*. I didn't normally have bad dreams and couldn't help but wonder if they might be a common part of pregnancy. I hoped not! I got up, careful not to disturb Bobby's sleep, and padded into the bathroom, quietly closing the door behind me.

I splashed cool water on my face and braced myself against the counter. I peered at myself in the mirror, my tired brown eyes stared back at me. I blotted my face with a towel and made my way to the kitchen. There was no way I was getting back to sleep anytime soon.

I took a drink of water from the sink before stepping outside. It was nice out, a slight chill in the air. There were so many stars glittering brightly in the sky. I loved that about being in the country. In town we didn't have anything close to this good of a view. The trees swayed in the cool breeze, crickets sang, and owls were hooting softly in the distance. I plopped down on the porch swing and put a hand on my stomach before I began rocking myself back and forth.

When I heard the screen door squeak I looked up to see Bobby stepping out. He joined me on the swing and wrapped an arm around me. His hair was tousled from sleep, and he was wearing a pair of sweats.

"What's wrong, love?" He asked.

"Bad dream." I shrugged, a lump forming in my throat.

"Would you like to talk about it?" he offered.

Not really. I thought to myself, but instead I snuggled in close to him and put my head on his shoulder. "I had a dream about Beth, we were talking and laughing like old times." I felt a small smile on my lips remembering the only pleasant part of the dream. I swallowed hard. "Then all the sudden it was so dark, I was searching for her, but couldn't find her. I could hear her calling for me, but her voice got so quiet, distant, until she was just…gone, and I was all alone." I wiped a tear from my cheek and Bobby lifted my chin to meet his eyes.

"I'm so sorry, love." He wiped my cheeks with his thumbs. His hands were smooth, cool and strong, everything I needed. I held his hand in mine and sniffed, wiping away a few more tears.

"It's okay baby," Bobby soothed.

"I didn't mean to wake you," I said as I shook my head, feeling like a child.

"It's nice out here," Bobby replied, not seeming to mind as he gazed at the night sky.

Bobby held my hand and together we looked out into the night. "I love being out here, we never get to see this many stars in town," his voice a mere whisper, echoing my own thoughts. We sat like that for some time, and I slowly felt myself beginning to get tired again. After a while we went inside, and back to bed. I nestled in close and prayed I wouldn't slide back into that terrible dream.

The following morning I looked across the table at Lane. She and Malachi had decided to surprise me with a visit. The kids were quick friends, Gracelynn eagerly showed Malachi around while Lane and I enjoyed a cup of coffee and caught up.

I read that it wasn't good to drink too much caffeine when you are pregnant, so I didn't have much coffee anymore. *I don't think two cups would hurt, would it?* I shrugged the thought off as I smiled at Lane. She really had changed since high school. Not so much in her looks, but her overall personality. She was calmer, not as edgy, and she seemed happy. Very happy.

"So what brings you back to town?" I asked Lane after she'd told me that she had been in New York.

"I really couldn't stand it!" she said with a laugh and a shrug. "At first I loved it, I loved all the noise, the crowds of people, the shops, oh God all the shops! And the energy…but as time wore on, it all just got really exhausting! Malachi didn't like his school, I wanted to be back home, and I really felt like it would do him a lot of good too."

Lane sighed heavily, her eyes suddenly sad. "Mal was diagnosed with asthma. He got really sick, Kate. I was terrified I'd lose him. He was in the hospital NICU for almost a week, poor little thing! I stayed by his side the whole time. Anyway, a while after that we came back home. Big city doctors kind of suck, they weren't very nice and they didn't explain things to me very well either. Now he has a great doctor, and I have a great OBGYN."

"I'm so happy he is okay! How terrifying!" I swallowed a hard lump in my throat. I couldn't imagine how hard it had been for her. Just the thought of Gracelynn going through something like that was enough to chill me to the core. It had been fortunate that Gracelynn had fantastic health.

"So what else is new with you?" I asked as I stood and rinsed my cup in the sink. I grabbed a glass of water before sitting back down.

Lane regarded me with a smile. "Well, I'm pregnant, hence the OBGYN. Almost four months now…" My eyes widened as I gave her a once over. She didn't look pregnant!

"Four months! I can't even tell! Look at me!" I exclaimed, gesturing at my stomach.

Lane snorted. "Some women just don't show as soon as others," she said, staring pointedly at my growing bump.

I couldn't help but smile, and my hand instinctively came to rest on my belly. Lane grinned, glancing around. "You have a really nice home, Katie. I'm happy for you, and still with Bobby!" she smiled widely.

I cocked my head to the side as I looked at her, wondering if she had someone but not sure how to ask. "It's always been him," I said with a small shrug of my shoulders.

Lane nodded. "Yeah, I know." She tucked a stray hair behind her ear. "It took me a long time to find someone that made me happy, as happy as Bobby makes you," she said. I was surprised to see tears in her eyes.

"That's great Lane, you deserve to be happy," I told her honestly.

"Thanks. Justin is pretty amazing, and way different from any kind of guy I used to hang out with." She rolled her eyes as if recalling her past, and I couldn't help but laugh.

"He is tall, dark, and handsome of course, but he is also really smart, in kind of a cute nerdy way. He makes me laugh…" Her voice trailed and her cheeks flushed a pretty pink.

"I am so happy for you, Lane," I told her, but then thought about her son. "So what about Drake? Is he still in the picture at all?" I asked, wondering about Malachi's dad. They had been together off and on through highschool.

Lane sighed, "Drake is a very touchy subject," she said, her eyes dropping toward the floor. I reached across and touched her arm gently.

"Hey, it's okay if you don't feel like talking about it," I reassured her. Lane gave me a small smile, and with a deep breath she began.

"Drake didn't hang around very long after I got into college. He would take care of Mal, after I'd begged and begged, just so that I could focus on my classes." She swallowed. "I went over to his apartment one day with Mal, I was going to surprise him with a day together. When I got to his apartment, he didn't answer the door but it wasn't locked. Anyway, I put Mal down in the living room, and I found him in bed with another girl."

I gasped, feeling terrible for her. "Oh Lane, I'm so sorry! That's awful!" Lane took a deliberate breath. "It's okay, it was a long time ago. He pays child support, and sees Mal once in a while. Mostly just for big holidays. They don't have the greatest relationship."

"I'm sorry," I said softly, not sure what else I could possibly say to comfort her.

"It's okay. Things are better with Justin. He's the sweetest guy I've ever met." She twirled a loose strand of hair around her finger and giggled, like a schoolgirl.

"That's amazing Lane, and if he takes care of you and Mal…" My voice trailed.

"Oh he does, he takes great care of us. He's super excited about the baby too, and we are getting married in like two months," she said with a smile.

"Congratulations! That's so exciting!" I grinned at her.

"We are keeping it small, just family and a couple close friends."

"There's nothing wrong with a small wedding," I encouraged.

"Will you be my bridesmaid?" she blurted.

"Of course! I'd love to. Thank you so much!" I got off my stool and hugged her, feeling giddy to be included in her wedding.

We both turned our heads when the kids entered the room. "We're getting hungry." Malachi said.

"Are you ready to go?" Lane asked.

Malachi shrugged his little shoulders and glanced at Gracelynn. "Not really," he said after a moment.

"You guys could stay here for lunch if you'd like? I have plenty of sandwich stuff," I offered.

The kids lit up with huge smiles on their faces. I was happy they were getting along.

"If you're sure it's no trouble," Lane said with a perfectly arched brow.

I slid off the stool. "No trouble at all!" I headed to the fridge and began taking lunch meat and cheese out of the fridge, along with a fresh head of lettuce and a juicy red tomato.

We sat at the table together, eating our sandwiches and talking. I glanced over at Gracelynn, it was good to see her having such a great time. After they were finished, Gracelynn asked if they could watch T.V. We each gave them the "okay," and we giggled quietly as they skipped hand in hand to the living room.

"Seems like they are getting along great!" I said with a smile.

"I'm so happy! Mal doesn't have very many friends," Lane said as she made herself another sandwich. I stood to make myself a second as well, but this time I had just tomato and mayo with a little salt and pepper.

Lane was stuffing her sandwich with chips and I laughed. "Is that good?" I asked curiously.

"Oh yes!" she said, taking a huge bite. I could hear the crunch of chips. I laughed again and took a bite of my own sandwich. *Delicious!*

While the kids watched T.V. Lane peered over at me as if she wanted to say something.

"What's up?" I asked after a moment.

"She looks so much like Beth. Is it ever hard to look at her?" she asked softly, leaning her head on her hand.

I ran a hand through my hair. "For a while it really was, and honestly her birthday has always been bittersweet," I admitted.

"I could understand that. Welcoming a child into the world on the same day as losing your best friend… well." She cleared her throat and looked away, but not before I noticed the tears in her eyes.

"I found her diary," I blurted out. I just felt like I needed to tell her.

Lane glanced up at me with wide eyes, her mouth gaping open a little. "Wow! I bet that was hard!"

"It really was. She wrote me a letter too. I found it in the back of the diary, along with one to Gracey," I said, keeping my voice low.

"Did you read them?" She asked curiously.

"I read mine, and I cried like a baby! I didn't read Gracelynn's.

I feel guilty for not giving it to her yet. I won't read it though, not unless she wants me to."

Lane smiled but it didn't quite reach her eyes. "I can't imagine how hard it was to come across that, and reading a letter from her." She swallowed hard. I knew she was trying not to cry, so I changed the subject.

It felt so good to catch up with Lane, getting to know her again. We talked as we cleaned the kitchen together. I insisted that I could do it all later, but she wouldn't take no for an answer. We'd talked and laughed about old times, and enjoyed a hot cup of tea while we rested after cleaning up the kitchen.

Lane and Mal left after we'd checked on the kids and saw they had fallen asleep in the living room. We whispered our goodbyes to one another and she left, Malachi walking sleepily beside her. I closed the door softly so I didn't wake Gracelynn.

It had been a great visit, but I was drowsy after my not-so-good night's sleep. I sat on the recliner beside the couch where Gracelynn slumbered, and pushed the button on the side to recline and relax, leaving the T.V on for white noise. I closed my eyes and drifted off.

Twenty-One

Bobby held my hand in the doctor's office, my shirt was pulled up and Dr. Ray slipped the probe around my stomach. Bobby anxiously watched the screen, I swore I could hear his heartbeat from where I lay.

We heard the beautiful rhythmic sound once Dr. Ray turned a knob on the machine. "Well there's the heartbeat. Everything is looking great! Do you want to know the sex?" she asked with a smile. My eyes were closed as I listened to the healthy beat of the baby's heart, then I glanced at Bobby.

He swallowed, hard. "Uh, yeah, yeah." *He's nervous and it's adorable!* We stared at our little peanut on the screen, the baby was growing, and healthy. I drew in a deep breath as Dr. Ray fumbled with the probe while seemingly tapping a dozen buttons.

"Being just a little difficult here…" her voice trailed off as she moved the probe, twisted a dial and then she smiled "Ah! There we are!" Dr. Ray pointed to the screen. "Congratulations, you're having a girl!"

I looked over at Bobby to find huge tears streaming down his face. He grabbed my hand in both of his and brought it to his lips. I could feel his tears on my fingers. *Oh honey don't cry.* I thought, my lip trembled.

He smiled at me and gave a nervous laugh. "We're gonna have a girl!" he said proudly. I felt so happy, and so scared all at once. *We are having a baby girl!* I wiped at my tears that fell freely and watched the screen again while Dr. Ray pressed a button, announcing that she would be right back with the sonogram photos.

Bobby and I stared at the screen in companionable silence while we waited for Dr. Ray. "What do you want to name her?" he asked, breaking the silence.

I turned to him with a smile, and crinkled my nose. "I don't know yet!"

Bobby gave my hand a small squeeze. "Well, we still have about four months to figure it out." My eyes widened at the thought. *Four months, only four more months!*

Bobby kissed my cheek and I glanced at him. "I guess we should start working on the nursery!"

He laughed and nodded, "Can't wait! Our moms are going to go wild! This baby girl is going to be so spoiled!" he said through a chuckle as he placed a kiss on my forehead and I couldn't help but to laugh. I knew he was right. She would be so loved, and probably a little spoiled. Dr. Ray cleaned the jelly off of my stomach and Bobby helped me into a seated position. Then, she whisked out of the room. Bobby and I smiled happily at one another. *A girl!* Dr. Ray entered the room as quickly as she'd left, and handed me the sonogram photos with a smile.

We left the hospital after I went to the bathroom, and I got in the truck with Bobby's assistance. I was excited and I couldn't wait till we got back to my mom's to share the news. *What would Gracelynn think?* I knew that she was happy about the baby, but what if she felt like she was left out or something? I never want to make her feel like that. I placed a hand on my stomach and tried to take a calming breath.

"Hey, you okay?" Bobby's voice broke through my tormented thoughts.

"Yeah, I'm okay. Just nervous," I said, not being completely honest. I didn't want him to worry.

"Babe, what is it?" He asked at the stop light.

Of course he would know I wasn't being completely honest with him. He knew me too well. "I'm really okay honey, I just worry that Gracelynn might feel left out or something."

"Oh baby, Gracelynn will be fine. We've talked about this…" his voice trailed off, ending on a long sigh, he held my hand in his. "We would never leave her out. She's as much ours as this little one," he said softly.

I knew he was right, and I love that he has always thought of Gracelynn as his own. He'd always been there for the both of us. He'd fallen in love with Gracelynn almost as quickly as I had, she had us both wrapped around her little finger.

We pulled up at my parents' house, and I blinked in surprise. That had been a quick trip. I blew out a quick breath and took Bobby's hand as he opened the door for me.

"Shall we?"

Gracelynn greeted us first, hugging us both as if it had been days since she'd seen us instead of a couple hours. I hugged her back just as fiercely with my hand against her curls.

"Well, let them come in sweetie," Mom said behind Gracelynn with a laugh.

"How was it?" Mom asked the moment Gracelynn was out of my arms.

I giggled, and put my purse down. "Is dad here?" I asked glancing around, and smiled when he walked into the room.

He threw his arms around me. "Hey, pickle!" I hugged him tightly and for reasons I didn't really understand I felt like crying. When he pulled back he wiped his thumb over my cheek. I guess I was already crying.

"Let's sit down and talk," he said as he ushered me toward a chair, making sure I sat before he took a seat. He had been excited to hear about the baby, but apparently he was going to be a worry-wart. I smiled at my parents, and chose the seat next to Bobby. Gracelynn wedged herself between us.

I pulled the sonogram from my purse and passed the envelope to my mom. She grabbed it greedily and after a moment she let out a soft cry. "Oh honey!" she said as she passed the photo to my dad and came to me for a hug.

I stood and hugged both of my now crying parents. Gracelynn suddenly stood with a hand on her hip and said "Well, what about me?" I smiled widely and handed her the photo.

Gracelynn studied it with a frown, I could tell she didn't really understand what she was looking at. She began reading it and smiled widely. "I'm going to have a sister!" she let out a loud "Yippee!" and the room erupted in laughter.

We ate dinner with my parents. My mom made her delicious Swiss chicken with garlic herbed potatoes and a baby green salad. It was mouthwatering, and I ate more than enough. After we cleaned up, Bobby and my dad went to the den, while Mom and I sat at the table. Gracelynn was in her room getting her stuff so that we could get ready to go.

Paul came in with a girl at his arm. This was a different girl than the last, but at least this girl had more clothes on and a genuine smile. They actually looked really cute together. Paul gave me a hug and introduced us to his new friend. "Guys, this is Sadie," he said with a smile. She shook our hands. *Oh, and she had manners!*

"So what brings you here, sis?" Paul asked as he plopped himself on the couch, he patted the spot next to him and Sadie shyly sat down.

"We just found out the baby is a girl!" I told him, not able to contain my excitement. He gave me a hug, congratulating me, and to my surprise so did his girlfriend. *I like her!*

We left after a while, it was beginning to get dark and Gracelynn was tired. After the busy day I'd had, I was exhausted as well and ready to get my aching feet propped up. Gracelynn fell asleep on the way home, and Bobby carried her into the house and easily up the stairs to her bed.

I breathed in the quiet. It felt so good to be home. I slipped out of my shoes with a sigh of relief and grabbed a glass of water, sitting myself at the table. I left the lights off, and watched the sun set on the horizon from the window. I was so mesmerized by the vibrant yellows, reds, and oranges that graced the sky that I didn't hear Bobby come up behind me.

I gasped when I felt his breath on my neck. "Sorry love, didn't mean to scare you," he said softly and kissed my cheek before joining me at the table.

"You really need to walk louder or something." I giggled, nudging Bobby with an elbow. My eyes wandered back up to the sky. "It's so beautiful."

"Very beautiful," Bobby agreed, slipping his hand in mine. "And I will try to make more noise so I don't keep scaring you," he said with a laugh, it was a sound that I loved so much.

We enjoyed the sunset together, I wanted to be outside but it was too sticky. Summer had arrived with a vengeance. The heat made my nausea almost unbearable. I didn't like taking anything unless I had to, but I made a mental note to pick up some Dramamine when I went to the store again. I recalled them helping Beth with her morning sickness. The medicine I'd been prescribed at the doctor's hadn't helped in the least.

"Are you ready for bed, love?" Bobby asked, jerking me from my thoughts.

"Mmhmm, but I'm going to shower." A shower would surely cool me down before bed.

Bobby held his hand out to help me out of the chair, even

though I was totally capable of handling it myself for now. *I wasn't THAT big yet. Why did I feel so snappy?* I sighed, accepting his help. *Stupid hormones, Chill!* I berated myself.

"You okay?" Bobby asked, a slight frown on his brow.

"I'm fine, just hot. A little irritable I guess." I shrugged and went to our bathroom to stand happily under a stream of tepid water. I stood under the water for quite some time, easing the tension in my shoulders, and my mood began to shift, thankfully. *How is him helping me up from a chair different from helping me from the truck?*

I rubbed my stomach in thought after drying off and dressed for bed in a long, soft, cotton t-shirt. I laid down beside Bobby, and because I'd just cooled off, I kept the comforter from touching any part of my skin. He rolled over to his side, facing me. He nuzzled my neck making me giggle. "You smell good. Feel better?" he asked.

"Thank you, and yes I do. I'm tired of feeling hot and sticky all the time," I whined. Bobby kissed my cheek, and then gently glided his fingertips over my belly. I sighed, allowing his soothing touch to calm my nerves and felt myself relax.

Hey, how are you doing today?

The text from Lane made me smile, pulling me out of thoughts.

I'm okay I think…how are you?

I pressed send and waited, absentmindedly twirling a strand of my hair around my finger. I knew Lane would know something was up, but I wasn't sure I wanted to talk about it.

What's up? You know you can talk to me if you need to, right? Also, I hate this heat! Boobsweat strikes again! I'm okay otherwise.

I laughed out loud. She had always had quite a way with words. I bit my lip and took a moment before replying.

LOL! It is definitely very hot! I do know I can talk to you, and thank you. I really appreciate it. I gave Gracelynn the letter from Beth yesterday. She took it to her room, and she hasn't said anything about it. I don't know if she's read it, or what…it's just that she's been awfully quiet, and I'm worried. I don't want to pry. I don't know what to do. She's so distant…Bobby says she will come around, and I'm sure she will, I can't help but to worry. I mean, I can't even begin to imagine how Gracey must be feeling.

I got up and occupied myself by cleaning the kitchen. It was already clean, but I needed to do something other than wait for Lane's response. Gracelynn was in her room, I could hear her footsteps, and I wished she would talk to me. When I heard my phone ping, I threw the rag and rushed back to my phone.

Yikes!! I wish I knew how to help! I'm sure she will come around though, maybe just give her some time. I am sure she knows she can talk to you about everything, anyone that knows you knows that. You are a great person Kate, take a deep breath, I have total faith that she will open up when she's ready.

My bottom lip quivered, and I was crying before I could stop it. I wiped at my tears and tried to collect myself before responding.

Cue the waterworks! Thank you so much Lane, I really appreciate you, and likewise! You are a great friend. I am sure you're right, I'm just not used to her not talking to me. We talk about everything. Maybe I waited too long to give her the letter. I told her that I'd had it for a while. I wanted to give it to her at a good time, and during the move definitely wasn't the right time. Moving away from friends is hard, and I didn't want to overwhelm her with so much at once.

I pressed send, and wrung out the rag that had landed in the sink with a loud thud. I went to the living room with my phone and a glass of water and sat down on the couch with a soft plop.

Hey, I think you did the right thing by waiting. During the move would have been too much for her. Have faith, she will come around. I think that deep down you know that she will. My honest opinion, I think you're scared of her being mad at you.

I read her message, and then reread it. Lane had always been straightforward with her opinion, and I appreciated her for that. It didn't make seeing it any easier. I knew that she was right though.

Of course I'm scared! I hate it when she's mad at me. It hasn't happened often and I feel so bad when she is. Worse now, because I kept this from her…as much as I didn't want to, I had to give her the letter. I just hate not knowing if she's okay! She is barely speaking to me Lane…I don't know how to handle that.

I cleared my throat and placed the phone down, taking a long drink of my water. I needed to calm down, I was starting to feel sick to my stomach. As usual, whenever I felt emotional I felt sick.

Girl, I get it! Mal has been mad at me more times than I can count! It got worse after I got with Justin! He was so mad, later I realized he had been scared. His father basically walked out of his life, and he was afraid Justin would do the same. I know this doesn't really compare to that, Try to take a deep breath and relax, have some ice cream or something lil momma! This will be behind you soon, I'm sure of it!

I rubbed my grumbling stomach with a smile. Ice cream did sound pretty good. I looked at the clock, I hadn't had lunch yet. Maybe I'd make lunch, and have ice cream with Gracelynn.

Thank you Lane, for everything. I'm sorry that Mal was mad at you, about Justin, but I appreciate you. I'm sure you're right. I will wait for her to come around, and in the meantime, ice cream sounds like a great idea. I hope you stay cool!

I got up and went back to the kitchen, busying myself with a platter of sandwiches. I'd make sandwiches for Gracey and myself, as well as for Bobby and the crew. They were hard at work out in that heat. I was sure they would appreciate something to eat, and some ice cold lemonade.

Over a half loaf of bread later, I was sure that there would be plenty of sandwiches, so I called for Gracelynn and she helped me with taking them and the lemonade outside. I was right, the men were all very grateful and thankful for lunch. Bobby gave me a kiss, thanked both Gracey and myself, and let me know they would be done within another couple of hours.

When Gracelynn and I were sitting at the table, she smiled but it didn't reach her eyes. I bit into my tomato and mayo sandwich and briefly closed my eyes with loud appreciation, "mmmm."

Gracelynn covered her mouth with a giggle, a sound that went straight to my heart. I smiled, feeling hopeful.

"Are you doing okay?" I asked quietly. I didn't want to pry, but I had to ask.

Gracelynn shrugged before taking a bite of her sandwich. I could tell she wasn't ready to talk, and I didn't want her to feel pressured into talking before she was ready.

"What would you like to do today?" I just wanted her to talk to me.

Gracelynn shrugged again, but finally said "I think I'm going to go back to my room, and send a message to Lilly, clean my closet."

I felt a little deflated, but nodded with a forced smile. "Sounds like a good plan, I'm sure Lilly will be very happy to hear from you."

"Yeah. I miss her a lot, maybe I can spend the night over there soon?" she asked. She looked so sad, and I wanted nothing more than to make everything better.

"I'm sure that would be fine, I'll call her mom so we can pick a good day," I assured her. Gracelynn finished her sandwich, the silence stretched on. She excused herself, rinsed her plate in the kitchen, and went back up to her room. *So much for ice cream together*, I thought blandly.

I stretched, and got up to clean up after our lunch and decided to sit outside on the porch. Only for a little while, I knew it was too hot for me to stay out for very long. I didn't want my stomach to get upset again.

I took in the bright blue sky and the birds singing a cheerful tune in nearby trees before closing my eyes. The air smelled like freshly mowed grass and soil. I was getting used to the smell of the farm animals so it didn't bother me as much as it had at first. I slowly rocked myself on the swing. My eyes popped open when I heard a whistle, and I saw Bobby leaning against the barn with his cowboy hat on, watching me. *Why was he so dang cute!?*

I whistled back at him with a smile, earning a laugh from the farm hands. I felt my cheeks heat in embarrassment. I hadn't meant to create a scene. Bobby shook his head, and waved them on getting himself back to work. I went back inside, it was getting too hot, and I was obviously being a bit of a distraction.

Deciding I would go to the office/library I turned on the light and breathed in the welcoming smell of books on the shelves. I had always loved the smell of books, and enjoyed the energy in the room. As I opened up my laptop and placed my fingers on the keys, I felt my mood shift exponentially. I was writing before I knew it, and was transported to a whole realm of possibility on the blank pages.

Twenty-Two

I sat up in bed quickly. I glanced over to see Bobby sleeping peacefully, and I tried not to wake him. *I know I felt something,* I thought as I rubbed the sleep from my eyes.

Maybe I had been dreaming? With a soft sigh I leaned back against my pillow and rubbed my stomach, closing my eyes again. It was early, and I didn't really want to get up.

There it was again! I kept my hand steady on my stomach. "Bobby!" I said, and grimaced, I hadn't meant to be so loud!

Bobby jolted awake looking at me with concern. "Are you alright?" he asked, blinking in the light now beginning to stream through the window. I grabbed his hand and without a word, I placed it on my stomach.

It felt like we sat there forever in silence. *Kick!* Bobby gasped in surprise. "Oh my God!" He sat up in bed, his eyes wide, full of wonder and joy and love.

"She's kicking!" he said with a smile. He wiped his thumb over my cheek, I hadn't realized I was crying. I'd been waiting for this day for so long, waiting to feel the life I knew was growing inside of me. Dr. Ray had said sometimes it wasn't until around the fifth month that you felt the baby start moving. Today put me at exactly five months. I smiled widely at Bobby.

"This is so cool!" I said, feeling incredibly giddy.

We lay there together for a while until we heard Gracelynn moving around, I got up eagerly, I couldn't wait for her to feel the baby moving! *What if she was still mad at me? What if she didn't want to feel the baby move?* I tried to ignore my unpleasant thoughts.

Bobby looked as excited as I felt. I moved quickly to the kitchen, and grabbed a glass of water trying to be patient while we waited for Gracelynn to come down.

"Good morning sweetie!" I said brightly as Gracelynn walked down the stairs and into the kitchen. She gave me a sleepy-eyed half smile, I poured her a glass of orange juice and set it beside her.

"What would you like for breakfast?" I asked.

Gracelynn gave me a shrug and took a small drink of her juice. "I'm not really hungry," she said. Bobby frowned at the same time that I did. It was an off day when Gracelynn didn't want any breakfast. She almost always woke with an appetite, in fact, the last time I remembered Gracelynn not wanting breakfast she had gotten a bad stomach bug and had been sick for a week.

I shuffled over to her and placed a hand on her forehead. "Honey, she feels hot to me!" Bobby left the room quickly, to locate the thermometer.

"Alright, let's check you out here sweetheart," he said softly.

Gracelynn sighed loudly. "I'm not a baby, and I'm fine! I'm just not hungry." I frowned at her tone, I'd never heard her talk like that before.

Bobby bent to her level. "We are just going to check your temperature to make sure you don't have a fever like last time, okay?" Gracelynn rolled her eyes. *She rolled her eyes!?*

She yanked the thermometer from Bobby's hand and stuck it in her mouth, crossing her arms over her chest. Was she actually pouting? Gracelynn hadn't pouted since she was maybe four years old.

When the thermometer beeped Bobby took it out of her mouth. "99.7, a mild fever, but we are going to keep an eye on it alright?"

Gracelynn got up and poured the barely touched juice down the drain, walked past us, marched upstairs, slamming her door with a loud bang.

"That was not how I was expecting this morning to go!" I said, and felt even more irritated when my bottom lip quivered. I swallowed the lump in my throat. *I do not want to start crying!* I pleaded with myself to stay calm.

"It's okay honey," Bobby said softly, kissing my forehead.

I leaned into him with my eyes closed and sighed. "I've never seen her like this, where did that attitude come from? I'd better go see if I can talk to her," I said. I stayed put for a moment, enjoying his arms around my waist, he was always so comforting.

I made my way upstairs and tapped on Gracelynn's door. "Can I come in?" I asked through the door.

For a while there was no sound, and then I heard a sniffle. "I guess," came a rather irritated reply. I felt my lip quiver again and cleared my throat before walking in. I didn't know what to do with this kind of behavior from Gracelynn.

My eyes rose in shock, Gracelynn's room was a disaster! She had clothes and things strung all over the place. I tried my best not to show my irritation, and made my way to the edge of her bed.

"Honey, I've been so worried, and this morning with that attitude?" I paused, placing a hand on her back. "I know you're not feeling very good, I think you would probably feel better if you tried to talk about what's bothering you." My voice was small, almost a whisper.

Gracelynn turned toward me, her tear-streaked face making my shoulders sag. I wasn't used to seeing her like this, I didn't like it. I felt powerless. I wanted to make everything better for her.

"What's bothering me?" she repeated, rolling her eyes at me. I didn't like this attitude! After a moment, she dropped her eyes to the floor, picking at her fingernails before she finally started talking "I'm just so mad!" Gracelynn wiped at her face angrily. I did my best to sit still, remain quiet, and give her the time she needed to continue. With a shaky breath she sat up, not looking at me while she spoke.

"I read the letter, I read it three times, and I'm mad at you for not giving it to me sooner!" Gracelynn paused and her tears began in earnest. "I'm mad at you for giving it to me too, and I'm mad because I didn't ever get to meet her, and I can't tell her that I'm angry at her, and I am so mad that I'm angry at her! I'm scared about you having a baby, what if I lose you too? Cause I don't think I can deal with that." Her shoulders shook hard, and before I could stop myself I scooped her into my arms.

Gracelynn clung to my neck as she sobbed. I stroked her back softly, as I used to when she was much younger and upset, which wasn't really often, and never like this. I held her and rocked gently from side to side as she cried against my shoulder. It was hot, and she was getting heavy but I didn't care. *She needs me!*

After some time Gracelynn's crying began to quiet down, and finally reduced to tiny hiccups and sniffles. "I'm so sorry sweetie, I'm so sorry," I murmured softly. Gracelynn nodded, gazing up at me. Her face nearly broke my heart, I was trying so hard not to cry.

"I don't know if I want you to read it yet, is that okay?" she asked, wiping her nose across her sleeve.

"Oh sweetheart, it's okay. You don't have to ever let me see it if you don't want to. That letter was written for you, not for me. I only waited because when I found it we had just moved, and everything was so crazy and new. I didn't want to overwhelm you. Gracey, I'm sorry I didn't give it to you sooner."

Gracelynn nodded and her lips twitched. "Well, we did have a lot going on… is there anything else I need to know?" she asked, her eyes fixed on mine. I felt almost intimidated.

I nodded slowly and began. "I read your mom's diary. I found it in a box of some things your grandma found. I'm not sure you are ready to read that diary, about the things that are in there, but if you want to, I will not stop you."

Gracelynn let out a pent up breath and shook her head, her bottom lip trembled. "I don't want to read it. Not now." I hugged her again and smoothed her hair off of her face and neck.

"I'm sorry I got so mad," Gracelynn said a little while later. We were still sitting together on her bed. She had calmed down, and after checking her temperature and seeing that it was still low grade I felt better.

"Sometimes, bottling things up like that can make you sick," I told Gracelynn as I brushed and braided her hair for her. It had been a while since I'd put her hair up, I'd almost forgotten how thick it was.

"Maybe that's why I'm not feeling good, I didn't feel good yesterday and I just felt so mad I didn't want to talk to anyone." She shrugged.

"I know," I told her. Gracelynn frowned, waiting for me to continue. "Well, you have never been so distant as you have been lately and I could tell you were thinking hard yesterday. I didn't want to pressure you honey, I wanted you to know that you could talk to me. You can always talk to me."

Gracelynn nodded and gave me a small smile. "Thank you, I know. I just didn't know how to talk about all that, I feel really bad for acting like I did. I'd better apologize to dad, I was kinda mean," she said as she looked at her hands. I could tell she was sincere.

"Hey, everyone gets mad sometimes. We just want you to know that you can always talk to us, about anything. Try not to bottle everything up okay? It's not good for you, I learned that the hard way too," I told her honestly.

"Thank you, Mom. I'm sorry I was mad at you" Gracelynn

placed a small kiss on my cheek. We left her room together to find Bobby. He was easy to find, I only had to follow my nose. He had the coffee ready, and it smelled heavenly.

I sat down as Bobby made Gracelynn some toast after she apologized to him for her attitude. She also promised to clean her room after she was done eating. I smiled, the morning was finally getting better.

Gracelynn didn't eat much of her toast, but said that she was feeling a little better. Bobby checked her temperature, it was only a smidge higher than last time.

"I'm going to keep an eye on that fever sweetie, make sure to let me know if you start feeling worse okay?" I asked.

My stomach twitched and I smiled at Gracelynn. "Hey, come here."

Gracelynn came over to me and I put her hand on my stomach, the baby kicked right under her hand and Gracelynn's surprised eyes shot up to mine. "She's moving!" she squealed, placing both hands around my bump.

Kick

Kick

It felt weird and beautiful at the same time. I closed my eyes, recalling that day when Gracelynn had kicked for the first time. Beth had been filled with such delight, and fear. Now I got it, I understood how she had felt. I wanted to cry suddenly, I wished so much that she was by my side to share this with me. Tears pooled in my eyes and I cleared my throat. Gracelynn gave me a hug and went back to her room, sensing somehow that I needed a moment. Bobby came to sit beside me, his hand making soothing circles along my back. I closed my eyes, and allowed myself to feel sad, and also to feel supported.

The morning had been emotionally charged, and the tears rolled slowly down my face. I didn't try to stop them. Besides, hadn't I just told Gracelynn not to bottle her emotions?

I should start taking my own advice. I thought.

The day moved slowly. With Gracelynn not feeling well, and still feverish, I made homemade chicken noodle soup for her, even though it was summertime. It was my mom's recipe, and mom's homemade chicken noodle soup had always made me feel better.

After the soup was finished, I dished a small amount in a soup cup and placed a few crackers on the plate. I hadn't heard a peep from Gracelynn and figured she probably fell asleep. I brought the soup carefully up to her room, moving slowly so that I wouldn't spill any of the hot soup on myself or on the stairs. Then, with a small tap on her door I walked in.

Gracelynn was asleep when I made my way to her night stand. I put the plate down and sat carefully beside her. I moved a strand of hair from her face, and froze. She had big pink blooms on her cheeks, I used the back of my hand to check her forehead, her skin was sweaty and terribly hot! I got up and scurried to the bathroom cabinet to find another thermometer. Practically running back to the bed, I woke her to check her temperature. Gracelynn mumbled something incoherently and began to cry.

"It's okay sweetheart," I murmured, making circling motions against her back. I pulled the thermometer out of her mouth and my eyes widened. 101.9. I went back to the bathroom, ran a clean soft washcloth under cool water and rang it out before running back to place it against Gracelynn's forehead."Mom? It hurts!" she groaned in her pillow.

"What hurts baby?" My heart began pounding in my chest. *What's happening to my girl?*

"My tummy," she said with a cry.

"Okay honey, okay," I soothed. "Can you show me where it hurts?"

She pointed toward her belly button. My brow furrowed. I kissed her forehead and told her to stay still and that I'd be right back. She barely gave me a nod as she slid back to sleep.

I nearly ran downstairs, a hand on my belly. The baby seemed to be kicking in protest to the unexpected motion. I ran outside once I was off the stairs.

"Bobby!" I yelled.

A couple of the farm hands peeked out and I waved frantically. One of them yelled toward the barn and Bobby came running toward me. He was covered in straw and dirt. He tried to dust off his clothes as he ran.

"Katie, what is it?" he asked as he made his way to the porch.

"It's Gracey!"

Bobby ran in the house and quickly removed his dirty shirt and jeans, getting a clean outfit on in a hurry. He ran up the stairs with me trailing not far behind him while I explained.

"It's okay, baby girl!" he murmured as he rubbed Gracelynn's back. She was nuzzled into his chest, her arms wrapped around his neck tightly as she cried. "We need to get her to the hospital," he said, glancing at me. I nodded, my heart racing.

Bobby carried her down the stairs while I grabbed my purse and slipped into a pair of flip-flops. Gracelynn was shivering so I grabbed my powder-soft throw blanket that I kept on the back of the couch. She cuddled into Bobby's chest and hummed as she felt the warmth of the blanket.

My nerves were on edge the entire ride to the hospital, it felt like an eternity to get there. I watched him swallow hard as he looked at her in the rearview mirror. He grabbed my hand that was white knuckling the seat and caressed the skin there, giving me one of his secret smiles—the one that said *everything will be okay.* With a prayer in my heart I closed my eyes. *Please let her be okay.*

When we finally made it to the hospital we checked Gracelynn into the E.R and Bobby called our parents. My mother was there in less than twenty minutes, holding my hand, trying to comfort me. It took me to a time long ago when I had worriedly waited for my best friend to have her baby. A sob tore from my throat, and Mom embraced me in a hug. Bobby was at my side in an instant.

"Mr. and Mrs. Farris?" a young doctor came out of the ER. We all stood, waiting for news of our girl.

"Gracelynn is okay, she is in surgery."

My heart stuttered and my lip trembled. "Oh my god! What happened?" I asked, gripping Bobby's hand tightly. *Surgery? I promised I'd never let anything happen to her. I promised I'd keep her safe…oh God, what's wrong with Gracey?*

"Her appendix almost ruptured, you guys made a good call rushing her in when you did. She should be in a recovery room within an hour."

I slumped against my husband, his scent enveloped me and I inhaled deeply. I had always hated the smell of hospitals. My mom rubbed circles on my back and pushed my hair off of my neck. "We'll see her soon?" she asked politely.

"Immediate family, yes," he replied.

"I'm her grandmother, young man," she said with an arched brow and a hand on her hip. I could see the doctor move back an inch. *Yep, no one says no to my mom,* I thought, trying to hide a smile.

"Yes ma'am," he said, "you all will be welcome to see her as soon as she is out of surgery. We will keep you updated," he said. Then he walked off, leaving us standing there.

"Oh my God!" I sighed as I plopped down into a chair. "What if we hadn't gotten here in time Bobby?" I cried.

"Baby, it's okay. She's going to be alright. She's safe," he said with a kiss on my forehead. One hand was in my hair, the other was protectively on my stomach. "Let me get you some water, okay?" he offered.

I nodded quickly and my mom sat down beside me as he left, taking my hand in hers. "Honey it's alright. She will be just fine. You hear me? You heard the doctor, she's going to be just fine," she said again, patting my hand. Her vanilla scent engulfed me, I tried to focus on nothing but that comforting scent.

Bobby was back in no time. I grabbed the bottle of water that he handed me and drank on it slowly. *She's okay, she's going to be fine.* I allowed the soothing words to calm my nerves as we waited. It felt like we'd been sitting there for hours, waiting.

What is it about hospitals! I sighed audibly. It had been an hour already, did something happen? Just as that thought entered my mind, the young doctor appeared again.

"We ready?" he asked softly, giving my mom a look. I almost laughed, he was obviously a little intimidated.

I was the first to jump up, and I followed quickly behind him. He moved fast, I felt like I needed to jog to keep up. We went down the hall quietly. The silence was so loud. I glanced behind me, offering a nervous smile at my mom and Bobby close behind.

Finally, we came to a dead stop. I almost ran into the doctor's back. He cleared his throat and apologized before addressing us. "She's probably still asleep, and will be tired for a while. We've made sure she's comfortable."

I had my doubts that my girl was comfortable in that hospital bed right after having surgery. She must have been so scared. I gathered a breath and nodded as the doctor opened the door. Gracelynn was on the bed, she looked so small and helpless, attached to an IV, but she seemed better. Her color was back and she was sleeping. I walked over to her and lightly touched her cheek.

"Mmm," she mumbled, her eyes slowly opening. "Can I go home?" she asked.

"Not yet sweetheart. They probably want to make sure you can eat and stuff before they let you go home." Gracelynn's lower lip quivered and I kissed her forehead.

"You did very well, Gracelynn," the doctor told her. "You were very brave, and if you are able to eat dinner, and then breakfast, we may let you go home in the morning," he told her with a smile.

"I have to stay the night here?" she asked, her eyes wide. I held her hand.

"It would probably be best sweetheart, to make sure that you're okay," I offered. She sighed loudly and then nodded.

"Well, at least there's a T.V." she said moodily. The room erupted in smiles. "Are you going to stay here?" she asked me.

"Of course sweetie, I'm not going anywhere." I couldn't bear the thought of leaving her by herself at the hospital.

Mom and Bobby left after a while. Bobby assured me that he would be coming back with an overnight bag for me, and something to eat later. I thanked him with a soft kiss and rested beside Gracelynn, watching her slip in and out of sleep. The T.V. was on but I didn't really watch it. I was tired after the day that I'd had, and being so worried about Gracelynn. I began drifting to sleep when there was a knock on the door.

A young nurse with kind blue eyes checked Gracelynn's vitals. She told me quietly that the surgery site looked good. After letting me know that dinner would be served in about half an hour, she shuffled out of the room as quickly and quietly as she'd come.

I must have fallen asleep because when I came to, the smell of cafeteria food permeated the air. There was a nurse talking to a wide awake and alert Gracelynn, she was uncovering a plate of food for her. I peeked at the plate. It appeared to be chicken noodle soup in a small plastic bowl, with a roll, some crackers, and a small container of jello. They even brought her fresh ice water in a giant cup, and a can of lemon lime soda. "Would you like us to bring you a plate?" the nurse asked me. I smiled, and shook my head.

"My husband is coming with dinner for me," I said kindly, thanking her for the offer. Besides, hospital food is terrible! I thought, my nose wrinkling as Gracelynn took a bite of the soup.

The nurse left again and it was just me and Gracey, she was watching cartoons, seeming to enjoy the meal. She must be hungry though, she hadn't really had much of anything all day. *Too bad she couldn't have had the soup I'd made her instead.* "Taste okay?" I asked as she put the empty bowl down after she'd slurped all the broth.

"Yours is better, but I was hungry," she said honestly. I smiled.

"I'm just so happy you're feeling better!"

"Do you want my soda?" she asked sweetly.

"Oh that's alright, you go on and drink it." She opened the can and took a long drink before settling back down. She picked at the rest of her food, and ended up falling asleep again by the time Bobby showed up with my dinner.

"How is our girl?" he asked quietly, handing me one of the bags he was holding.

"She's doing so well. Ate almost all of her dinner before she fell back to sleep."

I opened the bag and inhaled deeply. He'd gotten me a sub sandwich with a chocolate chip cookie. *Delicious!* I unwrapped my sandwich. A yummy toasted turkey, cheese, lettuce, tomato, and pickle. He even remembered my favorite sweet onion and mayo sauce. "Hmmm thank you love," I said, taking a large bite. I was starving!

Bobby ate dinner with me and we talked quietly as we ate. He stayed for a little over two hours before he needed to get back home. I didn't want him to go but I understood. Gracelynn had stayed asleep throughout his visit, plus two checks from her nurse. I'd asked if it was normal for her to be sleeping this much. They informed me that she was on some good pain meds.

After Bobby left, I snuggled in on the reclining chair beside Gracelynn. One of the nurses gave me a heated blanket. It was a little chilly in the room. I watched the T.V. for a while, not really interested in whatever it was. I felt myself getting sleepy, it was already 9pm.

I kept the T.V. on, knowing it would be a comfort to Gracelynn, and with one more look at her, I turned off the overhead light, and closed my eyes.

Twenty-Three

We fell into an easy routine after Gracelynn spent the first week at home taking it very easy post-surgery. She assured me that she felt fine, and her energy was back in full. There was barely even a whisper of a mark. The hospital did a great job taking care of our girl.

Lane had brought Malachi over the day after we came home from the hospital. Gracelynn had proudly showed off the angry red site. Malachi had commented "cooool!" before they entertained themselves on his portable video game, leaving the two of us to talk. We had a wonderful visit, comparing our baby weight, of course I looked more pregnant than she. Even though we are right around the same due date!

Bobby merely chuckled and shook his head in disagreement while I'd groaned about it not being fair that she looked so much better pregnant than I. "You are beautiful, glowing, and growing with our baby," he'd said, and had been reminding me of that every day.

The days are long and hot, the late June heat keeping me indoors. I get out in the mornings for a little walk, and once in a while I sit by the pond and read. It's nice and cool, and quiet in the early morning. I also tend to the garden, with Gracelynn's help. We have been growing tomatoes, cucumbers, squash, onions, and broccoli. We also have chives, cilantro, basil, and sweet peppermint growing in a small herb garden to the side of the veggies.

On the days that it is too warm and I want to do something creative, I find myself writing more and more often. I feel at peace when I write, it's kind of an escape from everything. I've been writing about Beth, about her diary. How I felt when she had passed, and how I feel when Gracey is missing the connection that she didn't ever get to have.

Writing is helping me heal, and I wish I'd taken it up sooner. *Better late than never.* A voice in my mind reminded me as I finished up another page. I have kept a journal for many years, but I've not done anything like this…I realized just the other day, I'm writing a book.

I've always enjoyed writing, so I wonder why I hadn't thought of doing this before, but it was all coming and flowing so naturally. Of course, it helps that I am basically telling my story, and writing about my friendship/sisterhood with Beth. At first, it was really hard to write about her, but now it feels good recalling all of the memories—some sad, some beautiful.

Bobby is proud that I am writing, he hovers sometimes, excited to see what I'm working on. He mostly gives me quick kisses that serve as little reminders that he's here for me. It means the world to me to have his support in all that I do and all that I desire.

A tap at my door brings me out of my thoughts. "Yeah?" I ask in the quiet room. Bobby opened the door and gave me his sweet smile.

"I'm going to take Gracelynn to the store, do you want to come along?" he asked.

I stretched and rotated my neck. I had been sitting there for a while, and could use a break. "Sure, let me get changed."

Bobby fetched my flip-flops, they are the most comfortable to wear. My feet were beginning to swell along with my stomach and behind. *Hopefully I will not retain too much baby weight,* I thought as I glanced in the mirror. I chose to wear my new favorite jumper, I got it from Lane as a gift. She didn't like the way it fit her, she'd said. It's pretty, deep navy blue, loose around my stomach, and the fabric is buttery soft.

"You're so beautiful," Bobby said with a quick kiss on my neck, and a hand on my stomach. The baby instantly began to kick.

"I think we are going to have a daddy's girl on our hands!" I laughed as I grabbed my purse.

"She's gonna be Gracey's girl!" Gracelynn said behind me with an arm around my waist.

"She will love you to pieces!" I assured her, smiling widely. I thought about how much I loved our little family and how ready I was to meet our little angel.

We all walked to the truck and got in, Bobby assisting me up. A while ago, that would have been a little annoying, but I appreciate his help now that I'm getting much bigger. I'd gained almost twenty pounds already! Dr. Ray says the baby is growing perfectly, and the weight just comes with the territory. She assures me every visit that we are both absolutely healthy.

Bobby comes to most of my appointments, and Gracey has seen every sonogram, she doesn't want to miss a single opportunity to see how her baby sister is growing. She's so very excited.

"Mom?" Gracelynn pulled me out of my thoughts.

"Yeah?" I asked, turning slightly in my seat so I could give her my attention.

"Would you name the baby Elizabeth?"

Her question surprised me and Bobby's hand gripped my thigh. I clasped his hand in mine and swallowed. "Maybe her middle name could be," I told her after a moment.

Gracelynn smiled. "I'd like that. I think she would like it too," she said, peering back out her window with wistful eyes. Then she looked back at me. "What will her first name be?" she asked curiously.

I giggled at her excitement, and Bobby glanced over at me as we stopped at the redlight. His eyes were huge and excited. *Is he ready to name the baby?* I wondered. Then I asked him. "Have you any ideas?"

Bobby smiled widely. "We have just over three more months," he began, with a quick hand through his hair. *He looks nervous,* I thought. "I was thinking we should pick something unique, a name that we don't hear often." He paused, lost in thought before he continued. " Like Devlyn, Ember, Danika, or we could call her Leia…" He finished with a shrug. He only said it because he'd seen Star Wars recently.

"Like the princess in that one movie?" Gracelynn piped up from the back seat. Bobby confirmed that's exactly what he'd been thinking. Gracelynn shook her head and laughed.

"I don't think so, Dad. But I guess it's an idea," she said with a shrug.

I smiled while Bobby and Gracelynn talked about the movie. I hadn't realized he'd been giving it much thought. I gazed out my window, up into the bright blue sky. Thinking back to all of those years ago when Beth and I had happily compared lists of baby names. *How I wish she were here.*

I swallowed back a lump in my throat, and stroked my stomach. My hand stilled, and I closed my eyes. I wanted something different too, something unique and beautiful. A small smile played on my lips as a name entered my mind. "Those are all beautiful names. I don't think I want to name her after a character in a movie though," I said looking at him with a smile. He grinned widely at me.

"Well what do you think?" he asked.

"How about Everly?" I suggested.

Bobby clasped my hand in his and gave me the most genuine smile, Gracelynn gasped in the backseat bringing my attention to her. "Everly," she said, trying it out. "Everly Elizabeth Farris." She said louder. "That's so pretty!" she exclaimed. I couldn't help but to smile in response to her excitement.

"What do you think?" I asked Bobby.

"Everly…" He pulled into the parking lot of the store. "I think Everly is a truly beautiful and unique name, a bit of a mouthful, but I kinda love it!" He leaned his forehead against mine as he helped me out of the truck. I laced my arms around his neck and sighed against him as he pulled me down and onto the pavement. He smelled of pure sunshine, and radiated joy.

Hand in hand we walked into the A/C, I closed my eyes as the blast cooled my heated skin. "You okay?" Gracelynn asked, grabbing my hand.

"I'm okay sweetie, I just don't like the heat very much right now."

"It is hot." Bobby and Gracelynn said it at the same time.

We took our time going down the aisles, Gracelynn loved to shop, and I honestly wasn't in a hurry to get out of the air conditioned building. We grabbed hotdogs, hamburgers, buns, and condiments, for the upcoming fourth of July celebration. We invited our parents, Lane and her family, Gracelynn invited Lilly, and I even invited Beck, but she said she wasn't able to come down. She had been keeping touch with Gracelynn via email though, which I am happy for. The farm hands and their families were welcome as well.

I grabbed the fixings for potato salad and deviled eggs. My parents were supplying the fruit and vegetable plates, and his parents were bringing chips, juice, and soda. Lane offered to come prepared with paper plates, napkins, and plastic silverware to minimize cleanup. I felt like it was going to be a great get-together, and I looked forward to having everyone over.

We planned to have the majority of the party outdoors, so I made sure to grab sunscreen and insect repellent before we made our way to the registers. There was a long line, and I had to pee so badly I was beginning to do a dance.

"Honey, I'm going to go to the ladies room. I'll be right back." Bobby nodded, and Gracelynn went with me.

While we washed our hands, I splashed some cool water on my

face. Gracelynn cocked her head at me in the mirror and I smiled at her reflection. "Are you having one of those hot flash thingies?" she asked. I breathed out a sigh, and nodded, feeling my stomach curdle as another hot flash took me. *Please don't get sick, please don't get sick!* I chanted to myself, trying desperately to drive the nausea away. Gracelynn, sensing my discomfort, rubbed my back softly.

"Are you gonna be sick?" she asked, concern showing in her eyes.

The question made me feel even more like hurling the moment she asked. I leaned against the sink splashing more water on my face, neck, and arms. The prickling began to stop, and I let out a sigh of relief as my heart rate slowed.

"I think I'm okay," I told her, once I felt like I wouldn't be getting sick.

When we came out of the restroom, Bobby had paid and was waiting on a bench beside the grocery cart. He jumped up when he saw us and offered me a concerned smile as we approached.

"She had one of them hot flashes again," Gracelynn told him sympathetically.

Bobby rubbed my back as we walked together out into the heat. "I'm okay," I assured them both, but they stared intently at me as I helped put groceries in the truck. Once we were all loaded up, Gracelynn pushed the cart happily to the cart return that we parked beside, and Bobby helped me into the truck. As soon as Gracelynn was in, he turned on the A/C and we headed home.

I leaned my head against the seat. *Hot flashes are definitely not my favorite part of pregnancy.* The baby kicked around in my stomach forcefully and I smiled. Sometimes those little kicks hurt, but it was a beautiful reminder that she was growing and healthy.

Seeing my stomach move, Bobby placed a hand on the protruded globe and smiled widely. "She's so active!" he said in awe. I nodded with my eyes closed, enjoying the cool air on my face, and the comforting weight of his hand on my stomach.

"Wow! I can see your belly moving a lot!" Gracelynn giggled from her seat in the back. Bobby and I both chuckled with her.

"She definitely kicks a lot more now," I admitted.

"Does it hurt?" Gracelynn asked.

"Most of the time, no. Sometimes though, when she gets my ribs, or my bladder, that can hurt."

Gracelynn made a face and then shrugged. "I bet it would suck total balls!" she said after a moment. My eyes widened and I whipped my head around to look at her. I could see Bobby trying to stifle a smile.

"Where did that language come from?" I asked, and there was this childish part of me that wanted to laugh, but I felt that I needed to be stern.

"Malachi says it all the time, I've even heard you say balls." She shrugged and arched a brow, looking so much like Beth. *Lord have mercy!* I thought as I cleared my throat.

"Sweetheart, just because you hear it, doesn't mean you should say it," I told her softly.

Gracelynn glanced at me and then her eyes dropped from mine, as they do when she feels she's in trouble—which doesn't happen often at all.

"Sorry," she said solemnly.

"It's alright, I will try not to talk like that, too."

Saying balls really isn't that bad compared to some of the things children say these days, I thought to myself as we pulled up to the house.

"I mean, it's not really a bad word though," Gracelynn said as she grabbed two light weight bags to carry inside.

"No, it isn't," I conceded. "But it's the context in which you said it, that made it sound bad."

I watched as Gracelynn pondered this, practically seeing the wheels turning. "Oh, you mean like when we were talking about Hell that one time?"

"Yes, kinda like that. Hell isn't a bad word by itself, it's just the way some people say it that makes it not sound very nice."

Gracelynn nodded her head as we walked toward the house with our bags, leaving Bobby to finish grabbing the heavier ones.

"I understand. Sorry, Mom," she said to me as we worked on putting groceries in the cabinets and fridge.

"It's okay, thank you for talking about this with me. It's important to me that you understand what you are saying before you say it."

After we finished getting everything put away, I grabbed a glass of ice water and sat down. Gracelynn went off to play in her bedroom after making sure I didn't need any help with anything. Seeing that I was settled, Bobby changed clothes and went out to the barn.

That evening, as Gracelynn was getting ready for bed, I leaned my head back and soaked up the silence. *In just three months we will have our baby girl.* My heart swelled with pride and gratitude as I thought about the future, I could easily picture Gracey with her new baby sister.

I knew that she would be such a good sister. I just hoped that she wouldn't ever feel like I loved her less. Gracelynn is Beth's daughter, but I am her mom in every sense of the word. I have learned that being a mother goes further than blood, and I prayed dearly that Gracelynn knew that too.

I wiped at the unexpected tear sweeping down my cheek and drew in a deep breath.

"What's wrong?" Bobby asked as he opened the door to find me sitting with tearfilled eyes.

"Stupid hormones." I shrugged, wiping at my cheeks.

Bobby sat down beside me and rubbed my back. "Anything you want to talk about?" He offered softly. I felt again so grateful for his love and affection, he was my constant, my forever. I let out a slow breath and closed my eyes against his touch, feeling comforted and safe.

"I feel scared as the time draws closer," I began, I folded my legs and faced him. "I just don't ever want Gracey to feel like she's not as important and loved as our little one." I placed a hand on my belly, instantly feeling our daughter kick hard, it felt like she was trying to climb my ribs in there. *Ouch!* I winced and applied slight pressure on the area in hopes that she would move.

"Baby, we've talked about this." Bobby held my hand in his and rubbed the skin there gently. He hates when I'm worried. "Gracelynn knows that we love her so much. We would never treat her any differently once the baby is here."

"It's been the three of us for so long, and I'm just concerned." I choked back another lump in my throat, willing myself not to cry again.

"I get it, love. I'm scared too," Bobby confided. He leaned his forehead against mine and I breathed in his scent. "One day at a time, sweetheart," he soothed.

I knew that he was right, and once again I was filled with such gratitude for him. "Thank you," I said softly, kissing his forehead, both cheeks, and then soundly on the lips. Bobby chuckled against my mouth, and then placed a hand on my stomach.

"The only thing that is changing is that we are going to have another girl to love with all our hearts," he said happily.

As he caressed my stomach, it felt like our daughter was following his hands. He moved to the left, she went to the left, then to the right, kick, kick, kick. We laughed watching my stomach bounce around.

"This weekend, I want to start working on that nursery," Bobby said.

"We really do need to get that done soon, we only have just a few short months before she will be here, and I know our moms will want to help us decorate," I replied with a grin.

Bobby gave me a wide smile. "Should we go to Baby Land this weekend?" I couldn't contain my excitement.

"Yes! We can create a registry for the baby shower, you know our moms are planning to throw me one soon. I know anything we get is going to be wonderful, but I think it would be a good idea for the things we definitely want."

"That's a great idea!" Bobby agreed.

That being settled, I headed for the kitchen to fix dinner and Bobby went upstairs to get Gracelynn. We sat at the table and enjoyed sandwiches and chips. After the table was cleaned off, Gracelynn requested Monopoly for family time. It had been a while since we'd played and Bobby and I laughed as Gracelynn eagerly bought up property after property. She was always pretty competitive.

After Gracelynn won the very long but enjoyable game, we packed it away and got ready for bed. It had been a long day, and would be a busy weekend! The fourth of July celebration with our family, plus a trip to the mall to go shopping for the baby! *I'm going to need my rest!* I thought as I took my pajamas with me to the bathroom.

Once I showered, I peeked in on Gracelynn to see her sleeping soundly. Her curls were spread out over her pillow. I pulled her comforter up and kissed her forehead softly. Shutting off lights as I walked through the house, I joined Bobby in bed and I was asleep not long after my head hit the pillow.

Twenty-Four

The 4th of July celebration was a huge success. We were surrounded by family and friends, food and laughter. The kids had a wonderful time and we all enjoyed the fireworks in the yard that evening. We ladies stretched out on lawn chairs while the kids laid down on picnic blankets. I smiled as I watched Gracelynn and Lilly run around with Malachi. Tracey's husband had brought Lilly over and was catching up with Bobby.

Lane and I conversed quietly with each other. She had confided that she and Justin were planning to elope and have a big celebration after having the baby, saying that neither one of them really wanted a huge wedding. And while I had been looking forward to seeing her walk down the aisle and say her vows, I respected her decision and offered to help decorate for their celebration.

We left the lighting of the fireworks to the men. We all erupted in "Ooh"s and "Ahh"s as we watched from our seats. The sky was rich with color as the fireworks exploded in the velvet night.

Our parents helped with the cleanup in the yard. The men cleaned up the mess of all the explosives, and everyone began to leave. It was well past time for bed, so Bobby carried a sleeping

Gracelynn into the house and up to her room. We said our goodbyes and went inside, my ears ringing in the sudden silence.

It had been a great time and it was an honor to have everyone there. I smiled at the house lovingly, it was wonderful to be able to invite everyone down for a celebration…our other house wasn't big enough to be able to host gatherings like this one, and once again I felt truly thankful for the space of our farm home.

I was exhausted but in a good way, and looked forward to the rest of the weekend. I was so excited to go to Baby Land with Bobby! I slunk off to our master bedroom, where I gathered my night clothes before heading to our bathroom and starting a bubble bath. I wanted nothing more than to soak and relax in the tub after such a busy day.

The next morning greeted us with a bright sun. I dressed in a simple, but comfortable sundress and flip-flops. Then, I piled my hair into a bun to get it off of my neck, securing it in place with a few clips. We left the house early, in hopes that we could enjoy some of the cooler part of the morning. With it being as hot as it had been, I was so ready for autumn!

Gracelynn whistled happily in the back seat. I'd asked Tracey the week before if Gracelynn and Lilly could have a playdate. She said yes, and offered to keep Gracelynn overnight.

"EEEE!" Gracelynn giggled in the backseat as we reached our first destination. She practically threw herself out of the truck before I could even unbuckle my seatbelt.

"Hold your horses," I laughed as I grabbed her overnight bag and slung it over my shoulder. Bobby hopped out to help me.

I walked Gracelynn up to the porch and she rang the doorbell, jumping from one foot to the other impatiently. When Lilly opened the door they grabbed each other's hands and erupted in loud and joyous squeals, as if they hadn't just seen one another. Tracey and I laughed as we watched them run off together. "Thank you so much for doing this, Gracelynn is so happy to spend more time with Lilly." I smiled.

"Not a problem, look at you!" Tracey smiled pointedly at my globe of a belly.

"Yeah, I've gotten huge!" I returned with a laugh.

"I'm so happy for you all! You guys enjoy your day."

I thanked Tracey once more and walked slowly toward Bobby, who was waiting by the truck to help me back in. He reached for my hand "ready?" I nodded and got in with a little boost. After closing my door, he got in, buckled up, and we were off. I couldn't help but feel excited as we drove to the mall. I hadn't been in quite some time.

Bobby parked in a shaded area once we reached the mall. I was nearly bouncing in my seat, I couldn't wait to start looking at baby clothes! Bobby took my hand in his, and together we walked into the bustling building.

At first, we took our time toward our destination, but once I caught a glimpse of the sign I picked up my pace. Bobby chuckled softly, easily keeping up with me. "I'm so happy you're excited!" Bobby said with a small squeeze of my hand.

"I really am!" I admitted, my smile wide. When we entered the store, I immediately thought back to all of those years ago when I'd come here with my mom, and Beth. Her excitement, and eagerness. I remembered how I'd felt so lost, not knowing what in the world I would get for a baby.

As I glanced around the store with Bobby by my side I placed a hand on my stomach protectively. There were many other mothers in here as well, and we smiled knowingly at one another in passing.

"Hi! Do you need any help finding anything?" A chipper voice asked. We turned to see a young woman, looking roughly my age, standing not far from us with kind gray eyes.

"Hi, thank you! I actually want to do a registry," I said politely.

"Right this way, I'll get you started!"

We walked up with her, and after a few questions and filling out a form, we were both handed a couple of scanners and told to "have a great time."

And that we did!

Bobby was as thrilled as I as we both found things we wanted for the nursery. I took my time amongst so many clothes, and once I found a perfect outfit to bring her home in, I showed Bobby. He smiled widely at the adorable light violet outfit and wrapped me in a hug. He closed his eyes, leaning his forehead against mine. "I can't wait to welcome our little girl into this world," he said. His eyes filled with tears.

I could feel people were watching us, and once Bobby pulled away I held his hand in mine and gave it a good squeeze. We both had a lot of things on our registry by the time we were finished, and we made a couple of purchases before we left.

Next, we went out to eat. He stopped at our favorite Mexican restaurant for fried tacos, and then we hit the hardware store.

"I can't wait to pick out paint for the nursery!" I beamed.

"Any ideas what color you want?" he asked.

"Not really… Gracelynn mentioned the other day that she thought neon pinks and greens would be awesome."

Bobby chuckled. "We might work that in somehow," he said with a shrug before cutting the engine and helping me out of the truck. I slid down and took his hand happily. I was getting a little hot, and a little bit tired, but I was having such a great time! From the smile on Bobby's face I could see that he was also enjoying himself. It felt so good to have this time together, and I vowed to myself not to complain about the heat.

Once we got started looking at paint, it felt like we were there forever. So many colors and color combinations to choose from! In the end, I really wanted to incorporate a little bit of pink and green in the decor, so I ended up looking at the lighter, more neutral tones for the walls. Bobby and I finally agreed to a pearly white satin finish.

We left the hardware store with all the necessary items we needed and two gallons of paint. Before we headed home, Bobby pulled into the ice cream shop. "Feels like a good day for some ice cream," he said with a wink.

We sat at a booth and ate our double scoop cones, giggling like we were kids. Once we were on the road home I leaned back against the seat feeling equal parts giddy and exhausted. "Looks like naptime," Bobby said, glancing at me. I yawned and nodded sleepily.

"Thank you for today."

Bobby gave my thigh a small squeeze as he drove, and kept his hand resting there. I placed one hand on his, and the other on top of my full belly, rubbing slow lazy circles. We made it home in no time, and I helped Bobby with a few bags. After I sat down, he grabbed the rest and put it away. I then grabbed my cell phone and decided to text my mom about the registry at Baby Land.

How exciting! I can't wait to start shopping! Mom replied quickly. I couldn't help but laugh. Mom did love to shop!

We picked out her first outfit, and a couple other things, and we got the paint picked out! I typed happily.

I can't wait to see it! I love you all!

We love you too, Mom! We will be starting next week! I put my phone down to take a long drink of ice water.

Mom and I texted back and forth for a little longer, and then I stretched out on the sofa, bringing my arm up over my head, feeling drained after such a busy day. Bobby came back inside and smiled at me, placing a hand on my stomach. "I think I'm going to start painting," he said.

His palpable excitement made me smile. "I could join," I said lazily. Bobby chuckled and pressed his lips against my forehead.

"Get some rest. If you're feeling up to it you can join me later," he said, and then he headed upstairs with supplies.

The baby would be sleeping in her bassinet close by for a while, but I could understand why he wanted to get the room ready. They sure don't stay that little for long. I allowed my eyes to close as I thought about Gracelynn. How fast those years had passed, how big she'd gotten, how lovely she was, and how lucky I was to have her.

I woke up feeling refreshed after my nap. I got up and drank a tall glass of water, and then walked upstairs to join Bobby. He was painting away, seemingly lost in his own world. The pearlescent white paint gleamed like silver in the sunlit space.

I walked up behind him, wrapping my arms around his waist and putting my head on his back. He sighed, leaning into me slightly, and I snuggled in with a grin. "Have a good nap?" he asked.

"Yes, thank you. I was more tired than I thought. Didn't mean to nap for so long," I admitted. I'd slept for almost two hours.

Bobby moved to set his roller down and turned around to face me. "If you're not up to helping it's okay, I don't want you to feel like you have to," he said with a press of lips to my forehead.

"I'm okay, and I definitely want to help," I assured him.

Bobby and I painted in companionable silence for a while before I turned on the radio for some added motivation and energy. After over an hour, we decided to take a break with some fresh brewed iced tea. Bobby massaged my feet, which were beginning to swell, and we both laughed when my stomach jiggled as the baby began to kick and stretch. We talked of the future, and of the baby. We talked about the farm, and how much we both loved being here.

After our break, we got back to work, and finished the first coat of paint. We would be putting on the second coat and doing the trim later. Bobby and I carried the paint tools downstairs and he took them outside to clean them until their next use.

While he washed the brushes I decided to take a shower. I

scrubbed at my paint-speckled arms, taking care to get around and under my nails. I stood in the shower for a while rotating my neck and stretching tired muscles. After dressing in shorts and an over-sized t-shirt, I headed to the kitchen to decide on dinner.

I pondered the fridge for a while, twitching my lips from side to side. We still had some leftovers from the fourth of July to get eaten. I took them out and placed them on the table. I warmed up two hamburgers and the last of the hotdogs in the microwave and added them to the table. Then, I grabbed a couple of paper plates, plastic forks, and poured two glasses of iced water.

Bobby was out of his shower in no time, we fixed our plates and sat together to enjoy our dinner. Afterward, Bobby and I cleaned up the table and kitchen. He took out the trash while I did the few dishes. Then, we cozied up on the sofa with our legs kicked up and enjoyed a movie before bed.

Later as we lay in bed, Bobby gently caressed my swollen belly, chuckling as the baby kicked right where his hand traced. "Already a Daddy's girl and not even here yet," I said with a soft smile as I watched my stomach ripple. It seemed like forever before I was able to fall asleep, I hummed in content when she finally settled down.

Twenty-Five

Gracelynn started her first day of school. Though she had been nervous, she had come home in a great mood. She said her first day had been awesome, and she was in the same class as Malachi. I was thankful that she had a friend from the start! We celebrated her first day of school by taking her out to eat, her choice. We ended up at Sweeties, the cafe I used to work in so many years ago!

I smiled warmly as my old boss told me that if I wanted the job I could have it. I had happily gazed at my stomach telling her it would be a while. She had been excited for the both of us, it was great catching up. She had helped me so much when I was a teenager, going through all of those crazy new hormones, and then everything that had happened with Beth. She had not only been a great boss, but she had also been a good supportive friend and had made me feel safe.

It was hard at first when Gracelynn started school again. After a long and enjoyable summer, I wasn't used to her being gone most of the day, and had to come up with ways to spend my days. I filled most of my time by doing little things here and there around the house, and enjoying some time in the library/office working on my story.

After the first week of school we fell into an easy routine. Gracelynn took the bus, she left around 6:30 in the morning and then didn't get home until around 4:00pm. If she had homework she was good about jumping right into it when she came home. Occasionally we would play cards or board games, and sometimes watch a movie together before bed.

It was still hot out, being mid August. I looked forward to autumn with its crisp temperatures and beautiful colors. I didn't much care for the time change however, *did we really need to set our clocks back an hour?* I never did like losing sunlight so early in the evening. Still, I couldn't complain because I was so over the heat!

"Keep them closed!" Gracelynn hollered for the fourth time as Bobby helped me up my parents' front porch steps. It was the weekend, and Gracelynn had been excited for this all week.

"They're closed, sweetheart," I assured her.

"Promise you won't peek?"

I couldn't help but laugh. "I promise!" I already knew what was going on, though Gracelynn had tried very hard not to spoil any surprises. I didn't want to be a party pooper—even if I was tired, had swollen ankles, was hot, and just feeling altogether irritable.

When I made it up the steps, Bobby helped me into the room. It was weirdly quiet, but I smelled food and my stomach gave a loud grumble. I thought I heard someone snickering. I sighed and tried to keep my eyes squeezed shut as I heard Gracelynn call out for my mom.

"SURPRISE!!!!" The room erupted, I opened my eyes wide, blinking in the sudden bright light and beaming faces. The living room was transformed. There were gifts everywhere, and some were not even wrapped because they were too big!

"Oh my goodness," I gushed, as my mom wrapped me up in a hug. Then she stepped back and rubbed my mountain of a belly. "You get bigger each time I see you!"

"Don't remind me," I groaned. The guests laughed again, and mom stood aside so that I could begin saying hi to everyone. There were a few faces that I didn't really recognize at first, they were from my old youth group! There were years of catching up to do!

Once I got done with the greetings I gazed around the room. They had outdone themselves. Everything was bright pink and green, per Gracelynn's request. There were silver streamers and glitter balloons. There was even a bright pink banner stretched between the living room and dining room that proudly stated "It's A Girl!"

We crowded in the living room with snacks on colorful plates and visited for a while. Bobby had joined my dad in the den, away from the baby shower. Gracelynn had gone upstairs with Malachi to play, but informed us that she must be back down for present time. I promised that I wouldn't start without her. Lane sat close to me, her own stomach bulging proudly. She was positively glowing!

I stuffed another mini sandwich in my mouth, and laughed as Lane helped herself to yet another pickle. It was her fifth. "This baby loves pickles!" she said with a shrug.

"You really don't want to know what you're having?" I asked her again for probably the millionth time. Lane laughed and shook her head.

"I don't know how you can stand not knowing!" Bonnie said. Bonnie used to be in youth group with me, we hadn't been close, but she was always nice.

"We want to be surprised. We love our little nugget no matter what," Lane said with a dismissive shrug and took a huge bite out of her pickle with a loud CRUNCH.

"I couldn't wait to know!" I said with a laugh. "Though I always thought I'd have a girl," I admitted, setting my plate down.

I finally felt like I'd gotten enough to eat for now. I was eight months pregnant to the day, and everything was looking good. The baby was healthy, and my weight normal, Dr. Ray had assured. I felt like a cow! Dr. Ray had stressed that I be careful with the type of foods I was eating because the baby gained more in the last month of pregnancy.

"I am so ready to hold my granddaughter!" my mom gushed, jolting me out of my thoughts as she placed a gentle hand on my belly. The baby kicked, and it felt like she did some summersaults, too.

"I think she's ready to meet you too!" I said with a laugh as my stomach bounced about.

"Just one more month!" Mom said wistfully.

I felt my throat tighten. One more month! These months had been flying by, and as I inched nearer to my due date I couldn't help but to feel a bit scared.

After playing a few games of charades and pin the tail on the donkey, Mom suggested presents. Once Gracey was downstairs, I was placed in the middle of the room, Lane and Mom sitting closest to me, and the gifts began.

It felt like Christmas! There were so many cards to read. *Why must everyone wish me to read them out loud?* There were bottles, diapers, formula, blankets, shoes, socks, and so many clothes. A beautiful diaper bag, stuffed animals, and a collection of baby books. Some people had put money in their cards for the things we might need.

Mom abruptly stood and brought out several bags from the other room and placed them in front of Lane. "SURPRISE!" she hollered. Lane sat wide eyed as she peered at the gifts in front of her.

"You didn't think you were leaving empty handed, did you?" Mom asked with a hand on her hip.

Lane stood and enveloped my mom in a hug. "Thank you so much Anne, you didn't have to do this!" She wiped tears from her eyes and took her seat, eagerly opening her first gift. For a while we opened our presents together. Both of us were extremely excited and enthusiastic over the adorable baby items.

Since mom didn't know what Lane was having, the clothes that she had gotten her were in yellows and whites with tiny paw prints. She also had gotten Lane a bath set, and some scented candles. "A little something for you too," she told Lane with a wink. I had gotten Lane a baby mobile, she'd mentioned needing one still. It had little frogs on it. It was too cute to pass up, and I knew Lane would love it. She'd cried and hugged me when I'd given it to her.

Mom then stood and pointed to the baby swing, addressing me. "Your dad and Paul got this for you," and then she pointed to the carseat "this is from me!" she said happily. They were both from Baby Land, and I felt my eyes water. They were exactly the ones Bobby and I had wanted.

Just when I thought I was almost done she brought out another huge bag and placed it down in front of my feet.

"Mom!" I exclaimed. "This is too much!" I was beginning to feel overwhelmed.

"Honey, hush!" she said with a dismissive wave of her hand.

I opened the big gift bag and smiled. Inside was a luxury pink sea salt bath set for me and a deep blue shirt that said "lil momma" on it, that I proudly showed off. There was a gift card for my favorite Italian place, with enough on it for Bobby and I to have a couple date nights. There was a beautiful card, that I of course read out loud while trying not to cry, and a one hundred dollar bill with the instructions that I was only to buy something for myself with it.

"Just a little something for you sweetheart, as a reminder to take care of yourself," Mom had said.

After tons of thank you hugs, great conversation, and yes, more food, the party was over and the guests began to leave. I thanked everyone again individually, earning more hugs and multiple belly rubs. *Why must everyone touch me?* I thought sourly. I knew I was just getting tired.

Later when Lane was ready to leave, I gave her a big hug and thanked her again for coming, and for the adorable dress she got the baby. Unexpectedly, Malachi gave me a hug and placed a sweet kiss on my belly, making tears brim my eyes once more.

After the guests were all gone, Bobby and Dad came in to clean up. I protested when they all told me to sit down and let them handle the mess. My ears were ringing in the sudden silence of the room. After some coaxing I was at least allowed to help bring food back into the kitchen and put it away.

A few hours later, they all took several trips to get the gifts loaded up. Bobby helped me into the truck after I hugged and thanked both of my parents once again. I was the perfect kind of exhausted as I leaned my head against the seat and closed my eyes with a smile. It had been a wonderful day despite my mood earlier. I felt nothing but peace as we made our way back home.

Once home, the farm hands gladly helped Bobby unload the truck and bring the gifts up to the nursery to be put away later. I made my way to the couch to lie down, not really in the mood to do anything else except that. Gracelynn walked in and got on her knees beside me. Her eyes full of concern.

"Are you okay?" She asked sweetly as she tucked a stray hair behind my ear, as I do with her when she is sad or doesn't feel well. Pretty sure my heart melted, I gave her a smile and nodded.

"I'm okay honey, just feeling a little tired is all," I told her honestly.

"Well, we did have a busy day!" she said, her eyes wide and face expressive.

"Yes we did. Thank you so much for the beautiful surprise. I know you helped your grandma a lot."

"It was so much fun!" she exclaimed. "I got to help decorate and even blow up the balloons! Well, I am going to go to my room so you can rest." With a kiss on my forehead she left and bounded upstairs and into her room where she closed her door softly behind her.

I laid back with a contented sigh, closing my heavy eyes. It felt good to be home with my swollen feet up. I opened one eye when I felt Bobby's hand on my stomach, and gave him a small smile.

"Get some rest baby, I'm going to get to work," he said. I mumbled my thanks for the day, before slipping off to sleep.

I woke up with a small tap on my shoulder, I turned, sleepy-eyed into Gracelynn's bright green gaze.

"What's up sweetheart?" I asked, my voice barely more than a croak from sleep. I sat up and rubbed sleep out of my eyes, yawning widely. *How long was I out?* I wondered.

"Dad says dinner is almost ready." Gracelynn smiled. "You were sleeping a long time." She came to sit beside me. "Are you feeling okay?"

"Oh, I'm okay. I must have been more tired than I thought. I didn't plan to sleep all day!" I stretched and stood, feeling well rested. "Wow, I was asleep for almost four hours!?" I stared at the clock, astonished.

"Yep, you just looked really tired so I stayed quiet so you could sleep."

I gave Gracelynn a hug and thanked her, then followed my nose to the kitchen. Bobby was just placing sauce into the steaming pot of noodles when I walked in. "Well hey there sleepy head," he greeted me with a kiss on the cheek, before returning to the spaghetti.

"I invited some of the guys for dinner, I hope that's alright," he said as he began to toss various seasonings into the pot. Garlic and pepper assaulted my nose and I abruptly sneezed, making Gracelynn laugh.

"Bless you," she said.

"Thank you. That's a lot of food, so I am glad we have guests coming to help us eat it." I laughed as I pointed to the enormous amount of spaghetti. Gracelynn opened the fridge and got out a bowl of pre-made salad and put it on the table, before walking back into the kitchen and grabbing the pitcher of iced tea.

After helping Gracelynn set the table, I took a shower before guests arrived for dinner. I felt much better and wide awake after my spectacular nap. I also couldn't wait to start putting away the gifts I had received at my baby shower. I planned to leave the baby swing downstairs in the living room, and the car seat of course, so that we could get it secured in the back seat of the car.

Once the table was set, we put the food in the middle so that guests could easily grab what they wanted. Stan and Billy came first, and then George shortly after. Gracelynn and I ate quietly while the men discussed work, and after a while they left and Bobby and I did the dishes together. Gracelynn did her part by cleaning the table, and taking out the trash.

We played a game of Go Fish together, and then I decided to head upstairs to work on putting stuff away. Bobby made sure I was settled before going back downstairs. He really was so sweet— always making sure to help me up the stairs and staying to see if I needed any help. After taking the tags off the clothes, Bobby took them downstairs and began the washer once I assured him again that I wouldn't do anything strenuous.

I put things away slowly, smiling as I did so—enjoying my time in the nursery and picturing our baby girl there. I soaked in the silence as I gazed around the room. Of course, she wouldn't be in the room until she was sleeping through the night.

Once everything was put away, I sat in the rocking chair that Bobby had gotten for me and rocked gently, cradling my enormous belly.

"Soon sweetheart," I crooned. As if responding, she kicked me soundly in the ribs.

"Well you can't kick your way right through." I laughed as she did a few more turns, watching my stomach wiggle wildly.

The nursery was all done! It was so beautiful with its pearly walls, and soft yellow trim. Splashes of pinks and greens in the decor gave it a fun and playful feel.

Gracelynn had gotten to pick out some stuffed toys, and the first blanket. Her eyes lit up when she'd come across this neon pink and green fleece blanket with asymmetrical shapes. She was officially obsessed with bright radical colors, it reminded me of Beth. Beth had always loved bold colors as well.

Bobby came back upstairs to find me relaxing and smiled. He held a basket of fresh clean baby clothes. I hadn't realized I'd been up here that long, time had gotten away from me. He walked over and put the basket down, looking around the room. "We did a good job. And our parents helped so much with setting up the baby furniture and arranging it," he said.

I stood and placed a hand on his chest. "I really love this room. Thank you for everything." I rested against my husband for a moment, before bending over to grab the basket.

"Oh no you don't!" Bobby swooped up the basket before I even bent down all the way to grab it.

"Honey, it's not even heavy," I whined.

"Yeah, but you don't need to be bending down like that," he said with a worried brow.

I sighed with a shrug, defeated. "Thank you." He was about as bad as my mom when it came to me doing anything. I began folding and putting clothes away slowly, inhaling the fabric softener, enjoying the calm and repetitive activity. The tiny socks, little dresses, onesies, and tiny shoes, it all made me so giddy for the baby's arrival.

After I was finished, I turned off the light and shut the door softly behind me. I then walked to Gracelynn's room and tapped on her door. She was sitting at her desk, typing away on her computer. *Wow! She is really good at typing!* I thought as I watched her fingers move over the keys. Gracelynn smiled as I entered her room. She finished what she was working on and closed her computer.

"I hope I'm not interrupting anything," I said as I stepped in. Her room was nice and clean. "It looks so good in here," I complimented her.

"Thank you, and you didn't interrupt me. I was just sending a message to Lilly and Aunt Beck about school. Lilly says she doesn't like being there without me, but she likes it other than that. I basically told her the same thing. Only I told her about Malachi."

I was pretty sure I saw her blush. *Oh no! She's much too young for boyfriends!* I thought as I listened to Gracelynn talk. Gracelynn and I chatted about various things and then I left her to get ready for bed, heading back downstairs slowly. I wasn't even down halfway when Bobby came to assist. I leaned on him slightly, remembering that I needed to be thankful for his help.

Twenty-Six

I woke up with a groan and slapped the off button on the alarm clock. I yawned widely and sat up to stretch, my breath hitching as my stomach tightened uncomfortably. Bobby jolted awake looking at me wide eyed. "What's wrong?" his eyes riveted on my hand clutching my stomach.

"I don't know, love. Feels really tight." I leaned back with a sigh of relief as it subsided.

Bobby rubbed my stomach tenderly. "Should we go to the doctor?"

I groaned, not really wanting to go. "How about I call her and see what she says?" I offered. I could tell he didn't like the idea but he nodded.

"Please, let's see what she thinks." Bobby pleaded.

I got up carefully, used the bathroom, splashed my face with cool water, and pulled on my sweats before going to the living room to find my cell phone. I had Dr. Ray on speed dial, and was waiting for her to answer as I paced the living room floor, my right hand clutching my phone, while my left cradled my huge abdomen.

Bobby got Gracelynn up and ready for school and I could hear him reassuring her that I was okay while he fixed her breakfast.

"Hi, Dr. Ray, it's Katie Farris." My heart felt like it was going to jump out of my throat. I was scared, what if she wanted us to come in and they found something wrong? I still had a month to go!

She asked what was happening. I sucked in a breath, forcing myself to calm down, and tried to speak as calm as I possibly could. "I woke up this morning with just this really tight sensation in my stomach, there was a stabbing pain first though."

Dr. Ray was quick to say "It is probably Braxton Hicks, they are just little contractions you get around this time in the pregnancy, but I would like for you to go ahead and come in just in case. I have a free spot in about an hour."

Taking in a rush of air I swallowed and nodded, "Okay, we will be on our way." Bobby was by my side in a moment, eyebrows arched, waiting.

"She wants us to go ahead and come in, but she seems sure it's Braxton Hicks."

Gracelynn gave me a big hug and patted my stomach gently before she ran down the driveway and into the waiting school bus.

After Bobby was showered and dressed he brought my flip flops to me to slide my feet into. I didn't bother changing out of my sweats, it would take me too long to decide what to throw on, nothing fit right anymore anyway! After grabbing the keys and my purse, Bobby helped me down the porch steps and to the truck. I was indeed thankful for his help, it was getting more difficult for me to get around these days with all this extra weight I'd gained. Stairs were the worst, and I felt like a waddling duck.

We were pulling up to the hospital parking lot in no time, Bobby helped me out and we walked hand-in-hand through the doors into the cool building. We made our way to the floor we needed and after checking in at the desk, we sat in the waiting room, we were a little early.

Dr. Ray came out for us herself, making small talk as she led the way to a dark room with a single bed, two stools, a monitor, and some other important-looking equipment. I sat carefully on the bed as we began again to talk about what kind of pain I had experienced. She asked if I had any bleeding, that answer was a no. Also, no dizziness or anything like that.

She had me lie down and lift my shirt over my belly, the room burst into laughter as my stomach rippled with movement. "Well she is certainly active, that's a good sign," Dr. Ray said as she prepared the sonogram machine. She squirted the gel, and I was amazed by how warm it was.

"Wow, that is nice," I couldn't help but to say.

"I thought you'd like that!" Dr. Ray said with a smile as she applied the probe to my abdomen. With slight pushes and gentle nudges, she got the baby in position for a good look. Bobby held my hand, his eyes fixed on the screen with a huge grin plastered on his face.

"Well, we are just fine! I want you to start coming in once a week now that you are closer to term," she said as she took a few photos before putting the probe down and wiping the goop off of my stomach with multiple paper towels.

She helped me sit up, and I rolled my shirt back down as she handed me the photos from the sonogram. "Katie, soon here she will begin to move less. You will be in your nesting period. You remember what to expect?" She asked with an arch of her brow.

I nodded with a smile. "I remember. Plus, Bobby and my mom have been so much help." I assured her.

"Good, I want you to remember to take it easy as well. No overdoing yourself, so you won't go into early labor. We want this little girl to make it to term, but I do encourage you to take little walks maybe ten minutes long twice a day. Nothing too crazy, but a little exercise is very good for you. Also, you are a little dehydrated. Please make sure you are drinking plenty of fluids."

I nodded as Bobby helped me off of the bed, with Dr. Ray's assistance. "Thank you." I said, smoothing out the wrinkles in my shirt.

"You take care, and I will see you in a week."

We said our goodbyes, and made our way to the receptionist's desk to get our next appointment scheduled, then we were on our way out the door. My stomach rumbled, reminding me that I hadn't had any breakfast.

"Time for some grub?" Bobby asked.

I nodded enthusiastically. "I'm starving!"

"Do you want to dine somewhere, or hit a drive through?" Bobby asked.

I didn't feel much up to getting in and out of the truck again, so I opted for a drive through…we ended up at McDonalds for breakfast burritos. With as hungry as I felt, I didn't care, I just needed some calories!

As Bobby drove, he ate one-handed while I devoured my breakfast happily beside him. After two burritos I felt much better. I took a long drink of my orange juice, enjoying the cool liquid as it traveled down my throat. Satisfied, I wiped my mouth with my napkin. "Thank you! We feel much better." I sighed as I rubbed my stomach, gazing at Bobby.

At the stop light, Bobby tucked a strand of hair behind my ear. My body responded of its own accord, practically melting under his gentle affection. *I could never grow tired of this.* I thought, as he gently stroked the skin of my cheek with the back of his fingers.

We made it home in no time, and with a moan I plopped gently onto the sofa. The morning activities seeming to have worn me out, I allowed my eyes to close for a moment, soaking up the silence. Bobby sank down beside me, a hand covering my abdomen. "Feels like she's settled down."

"Mmmm," I hummed.

"Gonna take a nap?" Bobby asked.

I felt my lips twitch and I opened my eyes to gaze at him. "I'm just so happy everything is okay. Honey, I was really scared," I confided.

"Me too." He ran his fingers through my hair and again my eyes fluttered closed, appreciating the sensation.

I opened my eyes to study him. He still looked a lot like he had as a teenager, but there were laugh lines around his eyes. I toyed with the stubble on his chin, liking the way it tickled my fingers.

"I really need to shave," he grunted

"I dunno…. it's kinda sexy," I told him with a sly grin.

Bobby crinkled his nose. "Really?"

"Mmhmm." I scooted closer and placed a kiss on his cheek feeling the stubble tickle my lips.

"Well enjoy it while you can, cause I'm gonna shave it off," he said with a laugh.

We sat together enjoying one another's company. After a while Bobby decided to get up and head out to the barn to check on the cattle as well as the hens, since he didn't want me going out there to do it.

I got up and waddled off to the kitchen for a glass of water, and made my way to my office. I made up a to-do list before the baby was born.

Car seat in car
Emergency hospital bag
Diaper bag packed and ready to go
Bassinet set up in bedroom
Breast pump handy
Baby bottles cleaned and sanitized

Once I felt satisfied with the list, I shut down my computer and made my way to the dining room. I wiped down the table and lit a tealight candle in the oil warmer. The room was soon filled with the spicy/sweet scent of amber and patchouli. It had become my favorite out of the collection of oils I'd gotten last Christmas from my mom. There were other great scents too, such as cedar, vanilla, lavender, and tea tree. I also had eucalyptus, peppermint, and cinnamon, I used those mostly in the colder seasons.

Not wanting to sit back down just yet, I swept the floor. I was doing that when Bobby came back in with a few eggs from the coop. "I hope you aren't overdoing it," he said, giving me "the look." *Ah yes, I know that look.*

I placed a hand on my hip while holding the broom with the other. "I'm fine babe, I needed to do something. I am going slow, and I will sit if I need to. Besides, you heard Dr. Ray, A bit of exercise is good for us." I waved a hand at my large stomach for emphasis.

Bobby smiled and swiftly pecked my cheek. "As long as you're being careful." He shuffled off to the kitchen to rinse and put away the eggs. He gave me a playful wink before heading back outside.

"Your dad is as much of a worrier as your grandma," I said out loud to Everly. Then, with a shrug I finished sweeping the floor, humming a little tune. After I was done with that, I put the broom back in its closet and sat myself at the kitchen island with a cold glass of water.

The day was spent doing small tasks until I felt satisfied. I also spent some time talking with my mom on the phone, and texting back and forth with Lane, who had also begun having contractions. She had shared that when she had them with Malachi she upped her water intake and they would subside. I remembered Dr. Ray said that I was dehydrated too, so I thought they must be connected. I grabbed a bottle of Gatorade for electrolytes and rested on the front porch swing.

The air smelled a little like cattle, but I was getting used to it. The breeze felt amazing! It was only around 80 degrees and the trees swayed gently. I closed my eyes and sighed with gratitude. It would be nice and cool very soon with autumn on its way, and I was thankful for it.

Being pregnant in the sweltering heat was brutal, I wouldn't wish it on anyone! Hearing footsteps moving toward me, I opened my eyes to see Bobby. He was covered in dirt, mud, and I didn't want to know what else. He stood a respectable distance, tipping his hat at me.

"Well hey, cowboy!" I said playfully.

Bobby let out a chuckle. "Hey yourself, you doing okay?" He eyed my belly. I grinned, nodding.

"Yep, just fine thank you. It feels good out here, I thought I could use a little fresh air."

"Well, I'll get outta here so it will be a little bit fresher," he said, turning on his heel. I couldn't help but laugh. Bobby glanced back at me with an answering smile before disappearing back into the barn.

Out of habit I laid a hand on my stomach, and gazed out. There was so much wide open space out here. I loved it, being around all of these trees surrounded by nature. It was peaceful to feel truly at home.

Dust on the road brought me out of my thoughts and I smiled. Gracelynn was just coming home, it would be time to start dinner soon. When the bus pulled to a stop at the end of the driveway, it opened and Gracelynn jogged down after waving at some of her friends. When she spotted me, she broke into a run with a huge smile on her face.

She was red and panting by the time she made it to the porch. "Hi Mom," she said, greeting me before sitting down beside me on the swing. It groaned under our weight. I wrapped an arm around her shoulder.

"Hi sweetie, how was your day today?" I asked

"It was great! We got extra recess, and I played soccer, and I won!" Gracelynn's enthusiasm was contagious and I couldn't help but smile.

"Are you feeling better than this morning?" she asked. My heart warmed at her thoughtfulness.

"I do feel better honey, thank you. So, you won the game?" I asked, happy for her.

Gracelynn nodded, her curls bouncing against her back and shoulders. "Yeah! I won against the boys!" she laughed as she held her hand up for a high-five. Our hands slapped together and she hugged me before going inside.

I was just about to get up to go in, when Gracelynn came back out with a glass of water and handed it to me before sitting back down. "Is this for me?" I asked, glancing at the cup.

"Yeah, I saw your bottle was empty," she said, looking at the empty Gatorade bottle.

"Thank you sweetheart, you're so thoughtful!" I complimented her.

"You're welcome. Do I have time to send Lilly a message before dinner?" she asked.

"Yes, you do," I said with a nod. Truth be told, I didn't even know what I wanted to fix yet.

Gracelynn left me on the porch again to go to her room, and after drinking the water, I got up and walked back into the house. I felt temporarily blind as I made my way to the dark kitchen, seeing big spots of yellow as I blinked, trying to adjust my eyes to the light. I put the glass on the counter, and began surfing the fridge and cabinets for dinner options.

Deciding I wanted tacos, I began searching specifically for the things I'd need. *Dang, no tortillas!* I put a finger on my lip in thought. "OH!" I said out loud, as I opened up the snack cabinet remembering that we had just recently gotten a bag of corn chips. We could have taco salad instead of making a special trip to town for tortilla shells.

With a satisfied smile, I began humming a little tune as I got the hamburger and chopped onions sizzling on the stove. It smelled amazing, and my stomach rumbled greatly with the expectation of dinner.

Twenty-Seven

Ugh! I am so tired of having my lady parts poked and prodded! I thought
bitterly as I lay on the exam room bed. I could only see the top
of Dr. Ray's head over my gigantic belly. After she was finished
checking me, she helped me to a sitting position. I breathed heavily
as I readjusted my sweater. It was finally getting cooler out, and I
was thankful!

After my appointment was over, and I made another for the
following week, I met Lane in the waiting room. Bobby had gone
to visit his parents, and Gracelynn was at school. Just so I wouldn't
have to be alone, Lane had brought me. She stood when she saw me,
her own stomach protruding hugely.

"Look at us!" Lane said, laughing as we made our way out to her
van. She was almost as big as me, *almost*. Dr. Ray had said I was carrying a lot of water. She also calmed me down by giving me another
sonogram to prove that I was indeed not having twins, after I'd had a
crazy dream. "The dreams are completely normal, many first moms
experience them," she'd said.

"We are quite the pair!" I said to Lane with a laugh as we both
buckled our seatbelts.

I studied the sonogram, and Lane leaned over to peek. "Aww, look! She is going to be so beautiful!" Lane said, her eyes watering.

I felt my lip tremble. "Don't cry, you're going to make me cry!" I pouted, but the tears began to brim my eyes and spill over before I could stop them. Lane rubbed my shoulder sympathetically and then we were on the road.

"Want some ice cream?" she offered. We both giggled as my stomach gave an involuntary rumble.

"I'm always hungry!" I said. It was true though, it seemed all I wanted to do anymore was eat, and sleep too! *This baby girl is going to be big enough without me eating all day long!* I thought.

Lane pulled up to the ice cream shop and we both got out and made our way in.

We spent a lot of time ordering, neither of us sure what we really wanted. In the end, I chose peanut butter ripple, and she had gotten a scoop of strawberry, and a scoop of cookies and cream. It didn't look really appetizing, but I knew better than to question a pregnant woman's food choice. I savored my ice cream slowly, listening as Lane talked about her last appointment.

"I am so excited to get this baby out of me! " she said, as she took a huge bite.

"Girl, me too! I feel like I've been pregnant forever!" I confided.

Lane gave me a knowing look and smiled. "Yeah, I know what you mean. But, you have done so good! You hardly complained, not like I did when I was pregnant with Mal."

"You were still very young when you had him though, it was scary and you had the right to complain what with everything that had been going on," I replied.

Lane's parents hadn't been supportive at all, they were gone most of the time and really wanted nothing to do with her pregnancy. Her high school boyfriend, Drake, had been a complete airhead, but at least he had been there for her when she'd had Mal.

I smiled as I recalled sitting with her, holding her hand in the delivery room. I'd been scared shitless! It was also one of the most beautiful things I'd ever witnessed in that time of my life, and it made me sad realizing that what I had now was everything I had hoped for for Beth.

"I'm so thankful for you for being there when I had Mal," Lane said, breaking me out of thoughts of the past.

"You know, I was just thinking the same thing," I told her with a smile. I took another bite of my ice cream.

Lane finished hers and wiped her mouth as she leaned back against the booth while I finished my own treat. "I think we are going to have the Justice of the Peace perform our marriage next week."

My eyes grew wide as I smiled. "I am very happy for you both!" I told her honestly. Her fiancé was such a nice guy, Lane was happy, and he treated Malachi like his own. I grabbed her hand that was resting on the table. "You deserve to be happy, Lane. I am so happy for you!" I told her with a smile.

Lane beamed. "Thank you. I really am happy, and Malachi is accepting Justin now. They were playing video games together just the other day, and Mal called him 'Dad'! I hadn't said anything, because I didn't want to make a big deal out of it, you know? It really warmed my heart," she confided, her eyes bright with unshed tears.

Once we were finished, we carefully slid out of the booths and made our way back to the van. I snuggled into my sweater. It was a chilly day for early September, Lane rubbed her arms when she got in and shut the door. "I should have worn a jacket!" she said as she turned the heat on in the van.

On our way back to the farm, we were soon nice and toasty. The sky suddenly darkened and it began raining heavily. I offered for Lane to stay until it slowed down. She happily agreed as we made our way inside. We removed our wet slippers at the door and headed to the living room. I went to the bedroom, grabbing an oversized sweater. I brought it out for Lane. "Oh my gosh, thank you!" she exclaimed, shoving her head and arms in quickly.

"Would you like some hot tea?" I asked. Lane nodded, "That would be wonderful." As I turned, Lane followed me to the kitchen. I filled up the kettle and put it on the stove to boil. Soon, it let out a whistle and I filled two nice-sized coffee cups with the hot water, and brought out my container full of various flavors of tea.

"Mmm fancy! Lots of choices, and caffeine-free too!" Lane said, fingering them until she found one she wanted to try. Her excitement amused me, and I bit back a laugh as she smelled the tea bag before putting it in her steaming water.

I put my raspberry and mint tea bag into my cup and allowed it to seep for a few minutes. "That smells good!" Lane said pointing to my cup.

"You choose lemon and peppermint?" I asked.

"I did, I love peppermint tea. Do you have any sugar?" she asked as she dunked her tea bag several times.

I stood and grabbed the sugar dish off of the counter before sitting back down beside her. She plopped two teaspoons full in her cup, stirred, and sipped. "Ahh that is so good!" she said, closing her eyes in obvious delight.

"You don't take yours with sugar?" she asked as I took my first sip.

I shook my head, sitting the cup down. "Nope, I never really liked sugar in my hot tea."

"Hmmm. Well thank you, this is delicious," she hummed with contentment as she took another sip. We sat in silence for a while, enjoying our hot beverages.

"Want to see the nursery?" I asked after some time.

"Oh yes! I have been really wanting to see it since you were talking to me about it! You could have sent photos, you know?" she said, lifting a perfect brow.

"Sorry, I really wanted to show you in person." I grinned, hoping that she wasn't truly upset with me for not sending photos.

I led the way, walking very slowly, holding the handrail as I went up, glancing back at Lane every few steps to make sure she was doing okay. When we both made it up we were gasping for air. "Phew, that's a lot of stairs! I hope you plan to have her downstairs for a while!" Lane said with a groan.

I placed a hand on my belly and tried to catch my breath. "Yeah there are a lot of stairs, and I will definitely be keeping her downstairs at least until she starts sleeping through the night. We have her bassinet in the bedroom, still need to get it set up."

"Well good, you are going to be way too sore and tired to carry her up and down these stairs."

Lane followed me into the nursery and gave a great gasp when I turned on the light. "Oh my God!" she exclaimed as she began looking around the room in awe. "It's so beautiful!" She placed a hand on her chest.

"Justin won't let me see the nursery yet! It is a surprise he says!" Lane rolled her eyes and I couldn't help but laugh.

"I'm sure it will be beautiful and worth the wait," I told her as I gazed at the nursery. It really was gorgeous. "Gracey helped a lot!" I told Lane as we walked around the room.

"I love this neon pink and green!" Lane said as she held out the baby blanket.

I smiled, running my fingers over the softness. "Gracey picked it out, the pink and green was all her!"

"She's got great taste!" Lane complimented as she folded the blanket back up and put it down.

"She comes by it naturally," I told her.

We looked around in silence for a little longer, before heading back downstairs. I clutched the baby blanket to me as I walked down slowly. I'd be wanting the blanket when we brought her home.

After another hour or so, the rain finally stopped and Lane got ready to leave. "I had such a great day today, thank you!" she said, stepping out. She had tried to offer the sweater back to me, but I told her she could give it to me on our next visit.

"Thank you for spending the day with me! For taking me to the appointment. It was nice not to have to go by myself," I said. She gave me an awkward hug, our bulging bellies touching. I watched as she got back into her van. We waved at one another, and I stood there until I couldn't see the vehicle anymore.

Once inside, I shut the door and shivered. It really was chilly, with a high reaching 58 degrees. I went to the kitchen and rinsed out the mugs, setting them in the sink. Then, I poured myself a glass of water. After a satisfying gulp, I went to the living room and sat down. I let out a sigh, the silence was deafening. The only sound to be heard was the ticking of the clock on the wall.

I twitched my lips from side to side, trying to decide what I wanted to do. Most days I could occupy myself quite well, others… not so much. In the end, I decided to flip through the channels on the television. I didn't need to clean anything, nor did I really have the energy to do so. It felt good to kick my feet up, and wrap myself in my soft throw as I surfed the T.V. guide. I decided to watch Beethoven; laughing at the antics of the Saint Bernard, and wishing Gracelynn were around to snuggle up with me. I hadn't seen the movie in quite some time, and Gracelynn had only watched it once.

Once that was over, I got up and stretched, taking myself to the kitchen for another glass of water. While in there, I grabbed a couple of chocolate chip cookies, plopped myself back down on the couch and found another movie to watch. *I may as well enjoy the day,* I thought. *What better way than movies and cookies?*

I yawned and stretched my arms above my shoulders. I must have fallen asleep! I rubbed my eyes, taking in the light streaming through the curtains. I glanced at the clock, I'd only been asleep for about an hour. I felt nice and refreshed, and hungry! I hadn't technically had any lunch yet. *Cookies didn't really count as lunch.* I made my way to the kitchen and opened the fridge. I didn't really feel like having a sandwich, so I closed the door and then opened up the cabinet. "Hmm vegetable soup?" I asked myself out loud. My stomach rumbled and I laughed. "I know sweetheart, I'm on it!" I said rubbing it gently.

I opened the can and dumped it in a small pot, sitting it on the flame of the stove. *Soup is great on a day like this!* I thought as I grabbed a half teaspoon of butter, and then tossed in some garlic seasoning and pepper. *I have to liven it up somehow,* I thought blandly. Once it came to a boil, I left it to simmer while I located some crackers. I crunched some up into my favorite soup cup, and then returned to the stove. I brought the pan up and carefully poured, so that I wouldn't splash either myself or the counter.

At the table, I gave it a slow stir, scooped up a bite and blew on it. I noticed that the butter and garlic helped take out some of that can flavor.

Once the soup was gone, I felt satisfied and warmed from the inside out. I rinsed my dishes off in the sink before putting them in the dishwasher, and made my way to the office/library. Instead of staring at another screen, I decided I'd read a book. I scanned the shelves with a twitch of my lips, I didn't really know what I wanted to read so I grabbed at random, ending up with a Nicholas Sparks novel. I knew I'd probably end up crying, but I did enjoy his writing style.

I curled myself back up on the couch, rearranging a pillow behind my back, and a pillow against my stomach. *Ah there we go, so comfy!* I thought with a deep sigh of appreciation. I opened the book and began to read a story about young love. As I read, my lips turned up in a smile as I recalled falling in love with Bobby. I'd had such a crush on him in school, but I'd thought that he didn't really ever notice me. Boy was I surprised to realize that he had indeed noticed me. He had confided that he had a crush on me too!

Another smile came to my lips, remembering the sweet way he had asked me out. Written on a napkin were the words "Do you like me Katie?" with the words 'Yes' and 'No' on it. I giggled as I shook my head at the delightful memory, and brought my focus back to the book. *Oh but it does feel good to reminisce!*

Time seemed to stretch on, and I was positively elated when Gracelynn got home from school. Shortly after, Bobby pulled up. We sat around the table at dinner and each talked about our day. Gracelynn talked of school, and how she wanted to join the girls soccer team. She talked about loving her English class and teacher because she made the class expand their minds. I was beyond thrilled, English had also been my favorite subject throughout school. Bobby talked about his time with his parents, and how he'd helped his mom rearrange the living room. Gracelynn and I were both laughing as he explained how they'd moved it around three times before she was happy with it.

I talked about my appointment, how everything was on track. How Lane and I enjoyed our time together, and that yes I had indeed had a very good day filled with relaxing, reading, even a little bit of writing, and eating—of course. But mostly, I was so pleased for them both to be home.

After dinner we played Monopoly together at the dining room table. Bobby won the game, and Gracelynn showed she was a good sport by giving him a handshake saying "good game, Dad." Afterward, we watched a movie together. Bobby ended up falling asleep during the movie, his head nestled in my lap, and my fingers playing in the soft strands of his hair. These little moments were my favorite. Each sweet hug, each gentle kiss, any time we got to spend together, no matter what we were doing, I truly treasured.

When the movie was over I leaned forward slightly to grab the remote, and Bobby's eyes met mine. He gave me a sleepy smile, and kissed my stomach before sitting up and stretching.

"Sorry love, I didn't mean to fall asleep." He yawned.

"It's okay. I didn't mean to wake you, but now that you're awake, let's get ready for bed."

"Wake up, it's time for bed, eh?" Bobby asked with a chuckle. I couldn't help but laugh.

"Gracelynn already go to bed?" he asked.

I nodded. "Yeah, she was falling asleep so I sent her on up to bed. It is a little after ten." I yawned and stretched, my muscles pulling sorely as if punishing me for sitting in the same position for so long.

That night I lay my head on Bobby's chest as it gently rose and fell with each breath. I studied the stars through the window, feeling thankful and blessed for this life. I closed my eyes, and was soon fast asleep dreaming dreams of past, present, and future.

Twenty-Eight

I woke to the sound of the phone, and rubbed the sleep from my eyes. *Who the hell is calling at five am!?* I groaned and sat up. Bobby mumbled something in his sleep and I quietly got up and went to the living room as fast as my legs would allow. I felt wobbly as I made my way through the room. Thankfully I made it in time so the answering machine didn't pick it up.

"Hello?" My voice croaky from sleep.

"Katie?" it's Justin, Lane just went into labor! We are at the hospital now."

"Oh, oh! But she isn't due for another three weeks!" I gasped. My eyes wide and awake, my heart picked up tempo as I leaned against the sofa for support. I felt adrenaline pumping through my veins.

"Yeah I know, she seems okay. She asked me to call you."

"Okay, thank you so much, I will be there as soon as I can! Stay with Lane!" I practically shouted.

I didn't hear what he said afterward, I slammed the phone down and shuffled off to the bedroom. I flipped on the light "Honey! Honey, wake up! Lane is having her baby!" I said, shaking Bobby lightly.

"Wha? What? You're having the baby?" Bobby quickly sat up, eyes wide.

"Honey, Lane is in labor! I have to get to the hospital!" I said, my heart racing wildly.

Bobby rushed around helping me get ready. I didn't bother searching for suitable clothes, I put on my pajama pants, and shoved my arms into the hoodie Bobby handed me. "You're sure she's in labor? She still has what? Three or four more weeks?"

"Yeah she's in labor, oh I have to get there!" I said, feeling a lump in my throat.

"Calm down baby. How are you feeling?" he asked, resting a hand on my shoulder and the other on my huge stomach.

I took a calming breath and nodded. "I'm fine, I'm really worried about Lane." My lip trembled. Bobby cupped my cheek and I allowed myself to breathe and calm down. Bobby called my mom, and let me know that she was on the way to watch over Gracelynn while we went to the hospital.

He quickly went upstairs to check in on Gracelynn before we left. "Still sleeping peacefully," he confirmed as we walked out the door, leaving it unlocked for my mom. She would be there soon, and being out here I wasn't too worried about leaving Gracey by herself for a little bit.

As we were pulling out, George was pulling in to begin work. Bobby rolled down his window and told him the situation. George said he'd keep an eye on the house till my mom got there. We thanked him and then we were off.

We made it to the hospital in good time, Bobby helped me out of the truck and to the building. We went up to the maternity floor and I went straight to the nurses' station to ask about Lane.

The receptionist on duty glanced at me with kind brown eyes and a sympathetic smile. "I will let Mrs. Fields know you are here." Lane and Justin had gotten married by the Justice of the Peace, but instead of taking his surname, he had taken hers. She confided that she never understood why women always had to change their name, and he didn't seem to mind taking hers. Lane hadn't ever really followed the rules, and besides why would it matter if he took her last name? I thought it was kind of sweet.

Lane's husband came into the waiting room, sweat coated his forehead as he walked toward us. My heart fluttered in my chest, seemingly in my throat. *Oh Lane please be okay!* I said a silent prayer. "She's asking for you," he said, giving my shoulder a small squeeze. Bobby waited in the waiting room, and a nurse I didn't recognize followed Justin and I.

"Are you family? Only family can be in there!"

"My wife wants her in there!" he practically roared.

To my astonishment the lady nodded, but then said "Very well, I'll just talk to her doctor about this!" I got the feeling he didn't care because soon, we were in Lane's delivery room where Lane was working through a contraction.

"Oh Lane!" I cried, rushing toward her.

"It's early, it's too soon!" she wailed and then whimpered as another contraction came.

The doctor came in, and I felt myself tense, assuming he would kick me out. "Alright Lane, let me see how we are doing." He sat between her legs on his stool.

"How the hell do you think I'm doing!" Lane shrieked.

I held her hand tightly as the doctor prodded at her cervix. "Well my dear, looks like we are almost ready to push," he said with a smile.

"But, it's too soon, and what is with this *WE?*" she cried.

"You just breathe and start pushing as soon as this next contraction hits," he replied, completely unaffected.

"Oh Lane, we've got you!" I said as I pushed her hair away from her sweaty face. Her husband was on the other side, holding her hand and saying encouraging things like "You've got this baby! I'm right here, you can do it!"

"Katie it hurts, God it hurts so bad!" she said with a sob. I felt a lump form in my throat and forced myself to breathe through it. *She needed me to be calm, she needed to know she could handle this!*

"Lane hey, you can do this! You did it before and you'll do it again!" I spoke slowly and softly, but with determination. Lane nodded, and then with a glance at her husband she sat up and began pushing with a contraction.

A lot of commotion happened at once, followed by an adorable wail that filled the room and my heart. "It's a girl!" The doctor hooted. The baby was wrapped in a soft blanket and laid on Lane's chest as he began taking care of Lane.

The tears fell freely as I studied the baby. "You did it Lane, and she's beautiful!"

"Alright let's get this baby girl cleaned up for you," the young nurse said. Lane nodded, tears pouring down her face. Her husband followed the nurse, unable to keep his eyes off of the bundle.

"Oh Lane, she's absolutely beautiful," I crooned, kissing Lane's forehead.

"Thank you Katie, thank you for being here," she said through tears.

A while later, I left Lane with her little family and went to the waiting room where Bobby sat flipping through a magazine. His eyes shot up as he spotted me, he put the magazine down and crossed the room to me. "Is she okay? Are you okay?" he asked.

I nodded my head and sniffed, my eyes watering anew. "She had a baby girl. Her name is Ella, and she's beautiful!" Bobby wrapped me in a hug and pressed a kiss on my neck. I leaned against his chest feeling tired after the morning's activity. "I'd better call Mom," I said, reluctantly moving out of Bobby's comforting embrace.

"I'm sure she'd appreciate that."

I fished my cell phone out of my purse that I'd left with Bobby and called my mom. It didn't ring more than once before she picked up.

"Hi Mom, everything's okay. Yes, Lane's doing great." She barely gave me a moment to talk. "Yes Mom, I'm okay too." I sighed and sat down.

We talked about the baby for a while, and I gave her an update on Lane—she was doing well, asleep now. Once we hung up I let Justin know that we'd be back soon. Bobby drove us straight home after I'd confirmed I wasn't ready for breakfast yet.

Once inside, I sighed in the silence, and then frowned as I glanced around the room. Mom had been cleaning. "Mom?" I called into the silent house. She whisked into the room, drying her hands on a tea towel.

"Oh you're here!" she said and gave me a hug, taking a minute to place both hands on my protruding stomach to say hi to the baby.

"I thought you'd be going into labor before Lane," Mom admitted as she joined me on the couch.

"Yeah, me too honestly! She still had three weeks to go. Mom, thank you again for getting Gracelynn fed and off to school this morning. And for cleaning, you know you didn't have to do that."

Mom gave me another hug. "You're welcome, and I'm more than happy to help," she said, tucking a strand of hair behind my ear like she did when I was a child. "Are you hungry?"
I shrugged. "I suppose I should eat." I still didn't feel hungry, I assumed because of all the adrenaline.

Mom helped me stand. "Where is that husband of yours?"

"He's already out in the barn," I told her with a sleepy yawn.

"Well I will just have to take something out to the men then," she said as she led the way to the kitchen where pancakes, bacon, scrambled eggs, and toast waited.

"Oh wow! Thank you Mom, you really didn't need to do all of this." I cradled my stomach as I sat at the table while my mom put a little bit of everything on my plate. "Smells good," I told her as she joined me with a plate of her own.

"Would you like some water or juice?" she asked, standing up.

"Juice sounds nice," I said through a bite of scrambled eggs. I sighed with pleasure, I did love Mom's breakfasts. "This is delicious!" I told her as she placed the juice beside my plate.

We ate together, talking about Lane and the baby. "6 lbs 15 oz," I told her.

"Perfectly healthy, I will pay them a visit on my way home," Mom said with a smile.

"Lane would love that," I told her as I finished my breakfast. I leaned back in my chair, satisfied.

"Soon, it will be your turn! Oh, I can't wait to hold my grand-baby!" Mom said as she began making plates for the men.

"You know what? I think I will just have them come in to eat, is that alright?" Mom asked. It was a lot of food, and it would be silly to carry it all the way outside.

"That would be fine," I told her.

Mom went outside and soon, the table was crowded with hungry men. I went to the living room to get away from the smell.

"I will be cleaning up that kitchen as soon as they all get back outside. I don't know how you handle that stink!" Mom said in a soft whisper, even though we were alone. I couldn't help but laugh.

"Well Bobby is good about keeping his work clothes in the mud room, and washing up before coming into the house," I told her.

"Well they can certainly go out through the mud room to get back to the barn," Mom said, plugging her nose.

I covered my mouth to stifle another laugh. "It does take some getting used to," I admitted. I leaned back against the sofa, making lazy circles against my stomach. *Two more weeks.* I thought with a secret smile.

"I wonder if I will be going into labor early," I said out loud, a little hope in my voice.

Mom snickered and rubbed my shoulder. "Don't count on it sweetheart. That normally only happens after you've already had your first. But, you never know. She will come when she's ready," Mom said, patting my stomach lightly, earning a few kicks.

We both laughed as my stomach fluttered with the movement before settling back down. She didn't move much at all anymore, and I knew that was because I was nesting. It was getting so close to time. "I just hope it's an easy birth," I admitted.

"I'll be right there with you sweetheart," Mom said, pulling me into a hug. She smelled like lavender, vanilla, and a little like maple syrup.

Later, we brought Gracelynn up to the hospital so that she could say hi to Lane and meet the new baby. She sweetly stroked the soft skin of the baby's cheek. "She's so tiny!" she whispered. Then she looked at me. "Will my sister be this tiny?" she asked.

"She might or she could be a little bigger," I said with a shrug. I knew though, that she would be bigger. Dr. Ray confirmed that during my last appointment. She'd be at least 7 or 8 lbs.

"My sister came before yours did," Malachi taunted, like it was a race.

Gracelynn shot him a look.

"It's not a contest, Mal," Lane said sleepily from the hospital bed.

"Sorry, Mom," Malachi mumbled before standing next to Gracelynn. "Sorry, Gracey," he said with a small pat on her back.

"It's okay," Gracelynn said, and they held hands as they gazed at the sleeping baby girl.

"She's so tiny, Mom? Was I this tiny?" he asked curiously.

Lane smiled, she looked amazing even after just giving birth. "You weren't this tiny, but you were pretty little," she admitted, running her fingers through her son's hair affectionately.

"When can we take her home?" Malachi asked

"Should be good to go tomorrow or the day after," the doctor said as he walked in and checked over little Ella. "She is healthy as can be, you are doing great! Did she eat?" Lane's cheeks turned a pretty shade of pink as she nodded. "Looks like as long as you are able to eat, and get around okay we will be able to release you," he said with a smile before leaving us again.

"Mom? Do I have to stay in this hospital the whole time?" Malachi asked. I almost laughed at the horror in his small voice.

"Oh honey no, I'm sure Justin will want to go home," her husband raised his brow.

"I'm not leaving your side," he replied from the side of the room.

We all laughed. "Why doesn't Malachi stay with us?" I said before I thought more of it.

"Oh can I, Mom?" Malachi asked excitedly.

"Katie, are you sure?" Lane asked, her eyebrows raised to her hairline.

"Of course I'm sure!" I waved her off and glanced at Bobby, who nodded in agreement.

"If it's okay with you guys then it's okay with me," Lane said.

I gave a nod, and that settled it. We left the hospital a little while later so that Lane could rest. Gracelynn and Malachi chattered all the way out the door, through the waiting room and outside. Bobby helped me into the truck, and then we were off. We stopped by the taco place for dinner, to which the kids in the back gave a 'Whoot Whoot!' I happily ate my taco, I wouldn't have felt much like cooking after such a long and busy day.

After eating we made our way back home, where Malachi and Gracelynn watched a movie, and then went upstairs to play on Malachi's portable video game. I smiled as I listened to their laughter.

Justin came by with a bag packed for Malachi's stay before heading back to the hospital to be with Lane and the baby. The evening was filled with so much energy that by the time it was bedtime, I was sure I was asleep before my head even hit the pillow.

Twenty-Nine

I happily held Ella while Lane gathered a diaper, wipes, and a tube of diaper cream from the enormous pink and gray diaper bag on the floor beside her. "Alright Baby-Love," Lane crooned when Ella gave a grunt as she took her from me.

I rubbed my giant stomach and sighed. "With any luck, I will be holding my baby girl very soon!"

"When are you due again?" Lane asked, eyeing my stomach. I couldn't imagine getting any bigger, I felt like a whale!

"I was due four days ago," I mumbled dryly. Dr. Ray had assured me everything was fine, and the baby was doing great. She just wasn't ready to come out yet. *Well, I am ready for her to be out!* I thought.

"She'll be here soon," Lane said as she snapped up the adorable pajamas she'd put on her daughter. It was a soft pink fleece that said "Mommy's little angel" on the front.

"I am so tired of being pregnant." I pouted, and then gazed longingly at the baby cradled in Lane's arms. "I'm so ready to meet her!" I whined.

"And you will," Lane told me softly, she placed a hand on my leg and looked at me sympathetically.

"She will come when she's ready and not a minute sooner," I said with a groan, mimicking the words I'd heard at least a hundred times.

Lane barked out a laugh. "Oh Katie! I think this is the most you've complained your whole pregnancy," she said with a shake of her head.

"Nope, summer sucked!" I corrected her.

"Ha! That it did my friend. That it did," Lane confided, standing when Ella suddenly let out a wail.

"Shh. Alright Ella, alright baby." She hummed, walking and softly bouncing the baby in her arms. "She really likes to move," Lane explained.

"Mmm" I hummed, absentmindedly stroking my stomach. I had to apply lotion four times a day, my skin was so stretched and dry. Sometimes the stretch marks would even bleed, it hurt, and itched something fierce!

"I'll give you some lotion for that," Lane said, glancing at my stretch marks. I tugged my shirt back down over my stomach and grunted.

"Will it help?"

"Mmhmm, it helps," she said, as she lifted her shirt.

"Ugh! I'm so jealous!" I groaned. Her pale skin was barely marked, and she was thin to boot! She only had just the slightest bit of baby belly.

"I just said I'd give you some lotion!" Lane said with a small laugh.

"Here, you hold Ella. I'm going to make you some tea." Lane was handing me the baby before I had a chance to reply.

I knew I was being kind of grouchy, but I was tired! Tired of feeling enormous, tired of being tired! I wanted to cry. I looked down at the sleeping baby in my arms, and began rocking her softly so that she wouldn't wake. "You're so beautiful," I whispered, smiling as her lips puckered.

Lane came back into the room carrying a steaming cup of tea.

"Chamomile tea for you, cranky pants," she teased, sitting the cup beside me on the end table.

"Thank you." I laughed. It was almost impossible to continue being cranky holding the baby in my arms. "I don't mean to be irritable," I said, glancing up from the sleeping Ella.

"I know," Lane replied, smiling down at her daughter. "Gosh I just want to cuddle her all the time. She's such a good baby, she rarely cries. Mal cried all the time," she said with a laugh, recalling the past.

"She does seem very content." I glanced down at her again. I began reminiscing of Gracelynn being so little and in my arms. Back then I had been so terrified, but then, I'd really only been a kid myself. Having just lost my best friend, it had been so hard to take care of her.

I blinked back tears and fought to bring myself back to the present. Yes it had been hard, but it had been so worth it. Gracelynn makes my life complete, she's my piece of Beth.

"Hey, you okay?" Lane asked, bringing me back out of my thoughts.

I nodded, though I felt like crying. "I'm fine, just a little emotional is all." Lane offered to take Ella and I nodded. Once my arms were free, I grabbed the tea, now cool enough to drink, and took a sip. It felt good, warm and soothing. "Thank you," I told her as I set the cup back down.

"You're welcome, everything will be okay, Katie," she said suddenly, and I felt my lip tremble.

"I'm so ready to have this baby."A tear slid down my cheek. Lane sat beside me and rubbed my back.

"Hey, it's alright," she soothed.

Bobby chose that moment to walk into the room, immediately rushing to my side. "Honey what's wrong?" he was suddenly kneeling down so that he was eye level.

Lane scooted out of the way, a huge grin on her face. "She's tired of being pregnant," she said as I wiped my wet cheeks.

Bobby smiled sympathetically. "I know, baby. She will be here soon," he said, capturing my hands in his and then kissing my forehead softly. I inhaled his familiar scent and sighed, feeling myself begin to calm down. He'd always had this effect on me, with a soft peck on my lips he stood. "You gonna be okay?"

"Yeah," I replied with a nod.

"Alright, you holler if you need anything," he said, glancing at me and then Lane.

"She'll be alright," she assured him.

Bobby went back outside, and Lane looked at me again as she placed Ella in her carseat while she slept. "Hungry?" She asked.

I shrugged. "I guess I could eat," Lane helped me up off of the sofa.

"Let's go find something for lunch," she said, and once I was on my feet she let out a breath, I assumed because I weighed a ton.

"Sorry," I mumbled self-consciously .

"No need to be sorry. Come on, let's get you something to eat." She led the way to the kitchen, I waddled behind her as quickly as I could.

"Every time I stand I feel like I'm going to burst!" I groaned and walked toward the bathroom, hearing Lane chuckle behind me.

When I went back to the kitchen, Lane was already whipping something together. I didn't question her, I ate just about anything these days, and whatever it was she was doing over there did smell awesome!

"I'm making vegetable omelets, I hope that's okay, you have a ton of veggies!" she called over her shoulder as she worked.

"Smells fantastic! And yes, we do," I replied as I sank down onto the stool. I rested my head on my arms and watched Lane move around the kitchen. She seemed in her element, and it was kind of fun to watch her concentrate on her task.

Lane crossed over to me carrying a plate, fork, and a cup of juice. She placed it in front of me, and my eyes widened. The omelet was huge, full of veggies and topped with shredded cheese! Soon, she finished and before sitting down, she made sure to clean up after herself.

"Thank you," I said before bringing the fork to my mouth. "Omigod!" I moaned as I chewed my first bite.

"Good?" Lane asked as she took a bite of hers. "So good," she said before I replied.

"So good!" I agreed with a laugh, quickly shoveling in another bite, earning a giggle from Lane.

"Well you're welcome, thank you. I love to cook."

"You're really great at it, you're hired!"

Lane and I laughed together, and made small talk while we ate our delicious omelets. Ella was soon awake and crying for a feeding so I joined Lane back in the living room. She covered herself while she fed Ella and I was content as I held my stomach, once again wishing I were already holding my daughter.

I had begun to feel as if time were deliberately moving at a snail's pace, mocking me somehow. *Well I can't be pregnant forever!* I thought to myself. I was terrified, yes, but so ready!

"Malachi asked me if I was going to give him a brother," Lane said, breaking the silence.

I let out a laugh and shook my head. "Oh my! What did you say?" I asked curiously.

"I told him it might happen, but not for a while. He told me he likes having a sister though, honestly I was worried he'd feel jealous or left out or something."

My eyes widened, *why hadn't I thought to talk to Lane about my concerns about Gracey when the baby arrived?* "I have been so worried about the same thing! I am so afraid of her feeling left out, or less ours, you know?"

Lane shifted Ella in her arms since the baby had fallen asleep, fixed her shirt, and looked at me. "I can imagine it is different for you, Gracey has always been yours though, Katie. You guys have taken such good care of her, raising her as your own, and she knows about her mom. I have always admired your strength and your courage, raising a baby isn't easy. I can't imagine raising a child who lost their mother." Lane's voice was a mere whisper.

A tear made its way down my cheek slowly and I whisked it away with my hand. "Thank you Lane, that really means a lot." Lane stood and gave me a hug.

"You are doing an amazing job, and both of your daughters will feel equally loved. You guys are such wonderful parents. You've got this." She said, giving my back a little pat before sitting back down.

"I guess I better get ready to go, the kids will be out of school in about an hour. Me and Little Miss have been here all day!" She laughed.

"I don't mind," I told her honestly. "I enjoy your company, and I love seeing this little one," I said as I stroked Ella's cheek lightly. Such soft, delicate pink skin.

After seeing Lane and Ella off, I decided to clean up the house a little bit before propping my legs up for a while, noticing that my ankles were beginning to swell. I still had a while before Gracelynn would be getting off the bus. I closed my eyes, allowing myself a quiet moment to rest and relax.

I must have dozed off, I woke with a start when the door popped open. Gracelynn came in and then quietly shut the door behind her. "Did I wake you up?" she asked, peering at me apologetically.

"It's okay sweetie, I hadn't planned on falling asleep," I admitted, sitting myself up. Gracelynn crossed the room and plopped down beside me, resting her small hand upon my stomach. "Still no sister yet," she said with a sigh.

I couldn't stifle the laugh that bubbled out of my throat. "Nope, not yet. She's taking her time." Gracelynn seemed almost as eager for the baby to arrive as I was. *Almost.*

"Well I wish she would hurry up cause I wanna meet her!" she said with a frown.

"Me too Gracey, me too." I agreed.

"What's taking so long anyway?" Gracelynn asked as she gestured toward my stomach. "I don't think you're gonna get bigger," her eyes widened and she gasped dramatically "What if you got bigger?"

I snorted. "Oh Gracey, I sure hope not! I can barely get around as it is!"

"Well, you're still pretty," Gracelynn said with a quick peck on my cheek, she truly warmed my heart.

"Awe thank you so much! How was your day?"

"It was okay, I don't have homework," she shrugged before standing. "I am going to go put my bag up. Is it okay if I have a snack?"

I nodded. "Yes you may." She thanked me before rushing upstairs, the noise sounding like a herd of elephants as she ran. I shook my head as she barreled back down the stairs and into the kitchen.

"Well don't hurt yourself," I called out.

"I won't, but I'm starving!" Gracelynn said as she came back into the room with a banana already half eaten.

"My you are hungry," I agreed, watching her finish the banana within just a few bites. Her appetite had been increasing a lot lately which told me that she was about to hit another growth spurt. Soon enough, she'd be needing new jeans again.

"Yeah, we had to run laps today in gym," Gracelynn said, collapsing exhaustively in the chair beside me.

"I don't miss those days," I admitted, recalling my days in elementary school. It seemed like ages ago really.

"Yep, I don't really like to run that much. Also, gym class is right after lunch and that sucks!" Gracelynn said.

I nodded as I listened intently while she chatted about her day. It wasn't long though before she headed back up to her room, claiming that she had to send Lilly a message because she hadn't heard from her in a while.

I decided I'd better get up. I stood and stretched, my body still feeling rather languid from my impromptu nap. I moseyed toward the kitchen where I searched for ideas on what to fix for dinner. I was still pretty full from the rather large lunch I'd had with Lane but I knew Bobby and Gracelynn would be eager to eat after their day.

I frowned and leaned against the wall for support as a sharp pain shot through my back making me gasp. "Ouch!" I called out. I rubbed at my back, maybe I'd slept wrong. I stood straight again and took another step. "Ooooh." I groaned as another burst of pain shot through the same tender area.

"Mom? Are you okay?" Gracelynn was looking at me from the doorway.

"I think so," I said softly, attempting to move again.

Another sharp pain, this time through my side and stomach, seeming to stretch all the way to my pelvis region. I gasped and panted, placing a hand on my stomach. *Something is wrong!* My mind screamed.

I felt Gracelynn's hand on my back and my eyes searched hers, my lip quivered. "Honey, you need to go get your dad."

"Oh my God! Mom!" Gracelynn screeched as hot liquid unexpectedly splashed onto the floor. I let out a small cry of surprise.

"Sweetheart, I'm okay I promise, but I need you to go on and get Dad. I think the baby is coming," I said, trying to keep my voice calm.

I leaned heavily against the wall praying to God that the baby would be alright.

"Hurry… hurry," I mumbled, cradling my heavy abdomen as another rush of water tumbled down my legs and onto the floor. My stomach tightened uncomfortably and I fought to stand on weak knees.

Suddenly I was being held. "Bobby, Bobby!" I groaned as pain rocked me anew.

"Gracey honey, please go get the bag off of the dresser okay?" Bobby called out.

"Honey, we are going to walk to the car, can you make it?" Bobby asked tenderly.

"I think so," I mumbled. It felt like an eternity to get outside and into the car, everything hurt, I was so tired. Bobby helped adjust the seat so that I was more comfortable, and then we were tearing down the road toward town.

I did my best to block everything out and focus on breathing through the pain.

Thirty

I barely recalled the trip as I was whisked into the hospital in a wheelchair, the cool air hitting my sweat slicked skin. Gracelynn was crying, and I wanted so badly to comfort her. "It's okay sweetheart, I'm alright," I soothed, choking back tears as pain tore at my abdomen.

Bobby filled out paperwork quickly when we made it to the maternity ward. Dr. Ray spotted us, and her face lit up with a huge smile. "Ready?" she asked, following us to the delivery room.

My heart was in my throat, I felt this crazy mixture of terrified excitement. My whole body seemed to ache all over but I managed a nod and a smile that probably looked more like a grimace.

I was hoisted onto the uncomfortable bed, Dr. Ray washed her hands and then slid on her gloves as I was put in a hospital gown and my legs shoved into stirrups. *Well this is attractive!* I thought sarcastically as Dr. Ray began checking my cervix. I tried with all my might to sit still through the pain and discomfort.

Soon Dr. Ray pulled off her gloves nodding with a smile as she washed her hands. "Everything looks really good Katie! You are dilated to about four centimeters, what I'd like to have you do is walk around a little bit before we give you your epidural."

"Walk?" I croaked in disbelief. I couldn't imagine even sitting up, let alone walking!

"Walking really helps, and you can rest during contractions," Dr. Ray said, her voice soft, and encouraging.

I nodded, summoning up the strength to sit up with Bobby's help while the nurse assisted in helping get me down. Once on my feet I swayed under the pressure of my swollen stomach. "Is it supposed to feel like she's going to fall out?" I asked, my eyes widening with fear.

Dr. Ray let out a sympathetic laugh. "She won't fall out," she assured me, patting my arm. "I want you to walk for about ten minutes, then you can come back to rest and I will check you again, okay?"

I nodded, not really having the energy to respond. I just wanted to get this over with! I looked at Bobby who walked hurriedly to my side to hold my hand. Together, we walked into the long hallway. Gracelynn and my mom were standing not far from the delivery room.

"Mom!" I cried as she rushed over to give me a hug.

"Sweetheart! Are you doing okay?" she asked, rubbing my back in small circles. It felt good and I struggled not to lean against her.

"It hurts," I admitted as I pulled away and put an arm around Gracelynn who was rubbing her red eyes.

"It's okay Gracey, everythings going to be okay," I told her, giving her my best smile.

"What if you die like my mom did?" Gracelynn asked as she burst into tears. My heart ached for her, my chin quivering with the effort to control my own tears threatening to spill over.

"Oh honey!" My throat constricted painfully, I found it hard to breathe. *Don't take me away from her too!* I pleaded silently.

Bobby grabbed Gracelynn in a fierce hug. "Everything is going to be okay, Princess," he murmured, rocking her side to side as he used to when she'd been much smaller.

"How do you know?" Gracelynn asked, her voice muffled against Bobby's shoulder. I could tell from his pained expression that he didn't know how to answer that question, I didn't either.

My mom offered to take her and Bobby nodded, his eyes full of unshed tears. Gracelynn held onto my mom tightly. Dr.Ray promised Gracey to give her updates, and it seemed to help soothe her some. Mom gave the doctor a smile of gratitude, and hand in hand they left the room. Bobby's parents walked in then, and I didn't think I could handle any more crying so I offered a smile in hopes to reassure them that I was okay. They each gave me a hug, Bobby was wrapped in hugs from his parents as they congratulated the both of us and let us know they'd be right there.

Together, Bobby and I walked down the hallway. I came to a stop when a contraction hit, leaning against Bobby for support. Once it was over, we slowly walked back toward the room. I didn't want to stray too far, but it hadn't been ten minutes of walking just yet.

Finally, with the help of my husband and my nurse, I was on the bed leaning back against the pillows. I was exhausted, and thirsty. The nurse fled to get some ice chips as Bobby held my hand, watching me intently for signs of another contraction.

Dr. Ray bustled in, washed her hands, and slipped her gloves on. "How did that walk treat you?" she asked as she got ready to check me yet again.

"I think it was alright," I said rather dishonestly. I swallowed hard, trying not to think of the possibility of something going wrong. I studied Bobby as Dr.Ray examined me.

"Alright Katie, breathe through this okay?" she encouraged me. Bobby stroked my hand, giving me a sweet smile, that special smile that was only for me.

"Okay, time to get that epidural." Dr.Ray smiled.

My eyes widened and Bobby kissed my hand with a cheerful gleam in his eye. Everything happened quickly, I was rolled to my side when the anesthesiologist came in. He asked me to bring my knees up in a fetal position the best I could and instructed me to let him know as soon as a contraction hit. I whined uncomfortably when the contraction came on, and told him it was time. He moved for the huge needle.

"Oh God!" I groaned trying not to look at it. *You can't be serious!*

"Alright Katie, you're going to feel a bit of pressure here. Let me know if you have any ringing in your ears, any pain or numbness, okay?

I nodded, unable to respond through the contraction. "Honey, honey look at me okay?" Bobby urged. I brought my attention to his face before closing my eyes and crying at the pressure of the needle.

The nurse and anesthesiologist helped me roll back onto my back and Bobby readjusted my pillows. Everything began going numb from the waist down.

"Doing alright?" Dr. Ray asked as she came back into the room. I nodded, feeling much better. "Good deal, you have a visitor," she said.

Lane rushed into the room. "Oh Katie! Are you okay?" I laughed and cried as she pulled me into a hug.

"I'm so happy you're here," I told her with a laugh. "I'm okay now, I can't feel my legs." I said honestly.

Lane moved aside as a monitor was attached around my stomach. "This is to monitor your contractions and the baby's heart rate. See?" Dr.Ray pointed to the screen. I nodded excitedly. *This is really happening!*

"Your mom is chomping at the bit," Lane said, dabbing at her eyes with a Kleenex. I imagined I looked quite the mess, but I honestly didn't care anymore.

I peered at Dr. Ray. "We can only have three in here okay? It's just a little difficult to work with too many bodies in the room," she explained.

Lane piped up. "I'm leaving so that she can come in, I'll stay with Gracelynn okay?" she said in a rush.

"Are you sure?" I asked, feeling badly that she couldn't stay.

"Katie, if my mother had given a crap she would have been in that delivery room both times instead of you. I'd love to be here for you like you were for me, but you need your mom," she told me matter-of-factly.

I nodded and gave Lane another hug before she waved and disappeared. My mom breezed through the door.

"How are we doing?" she asked Bobby as if I weren't able to talk for myself.

I rolled my eyes. "Mom, I'm okay." She was holding my opposite hand in no time, murmuring encouraging words and beaming with excitement.

"How's Gracelynn?" I asked.

"She's alright, poor thing cried herself to sleep," she confided.

My shoulders sagged. "Thank you so much for looking after her, for being here, Mom. I love you!" Mom gave me a hug.

"Alright Katie, I'm going to check you again. Ready?" Dr.Ray interjected. With my nod, she got on her stool, her head pretty much disappearing. "Alright, it is time to start pushing, I see the head!" Dr.Ray said loudly to the room. Bobby squeezed my left hand, my mom squeezed my right. Both nodding.

"You're going to feel some pressure okay? I want you to push, count to ten and hold it Katie," she instructed. The instructions sounded so confusing, but my body seemed to instinctively know what to do.

They counted to ten, and I leaned back with a loud sigh, catching my breath.

"So close Katie, let's try again!" Dr. Ray encouraged.

"I can't!" I panted.

"Honey, you can do this. We're right here, you've got this, let's get this baby girl out!" Mom urged me on.

I glanced at Bobby's tear streaked face giving him a weak smile before I nodded.

"I'm right here, baby," he said, just for my ears, planting a small kiss on my sweaty forehead.

"Alright, push, push!" Dr. Ray cheered me on.

There was a huge burst of pressure. "Oh God! Ooooh!" I cried out as I bared down with all my might. My face was hot, I was exhausted.

"Great job, Katie!" Dr. Ray shouted with glee. Then, a heartwarming wail filled the room and my heart.

"Oh she's here! She's here!" Mom shouted through tears.

"She's so beautiful! You did it, baby!" Bobby was crying, big tears of joy as he smoothed back the hair from my face.

"Oh, Everly!" I cried as she was cleaned up and placed on my chest. *I did it!*

"What a beautiful name! Dr.Ray said, congratulating us before she resumed her work between my thighs.

I stared down at the beauty of my new daughter. "Oh she's gorgeous! She's so perfect!" I blubbered, bringing my lips to the sweet, smooth skin of her forehead. Bobby leaned his forehead against mine as we gazed down at our new baby.

My chest was so full of love I felt like I might just burst from it. Everly was taken from me to get her weight and I felt naked without her warmth. I didn't want to let her out of my sight. Dr. Ray placed Everly in Bobby's arms and I felt myself fall in love with him all over again. *We did this, we created this beautiful baby.* I felt tears slide down my cheeks, but this time it was from an enormous amount of love, happiness, and pride as I watched my husband cradle our daughter.

I heard my mom snapping photos and groaned when she snapped a picture of me laying on the hospital bed.

"Oh, Mom!" I laughed pushing my hand out in front of me.

"You are so beautiful!" Mom gushed, planting a kiss on my forehead. She tucked her phone into her back pocket. "I'm going to go let everyone know she's here!" She rushed out of the room.

Bobby came back to my side and placed the searching Everly on my chest so that I could nurse her. It took a while for her to latch on, but she finally did. I closed my eyes, feeling fatigued. Having a baby was hard work! My body felt defeated, as if I'd been in a fight. Each one of my muscles hurt. I winced as I moved my legs trying to find a comfortable position. The epidural had worn off, my legs tingled and ached unpleasantly.

Noticing my discomfort, Bobby leaned in toward me. "What can I do, love?" he asked, concern in his eyes and voice. I felt myself shrug, I really didn't know what, if anything, would help, except maybe to rest. Everly had stopped suckling so I repositioned her to snuggle in the crook of my arm.

"Babe? Could you raise the bed a bit so I can sit up a little?" I asked.

Bobby raised the bed slowly, waiting for me to let him know when I felt more comfortable. I nodded when I was up enough to look around the room easier. Bobby resituated my pillow, and put a pillow under the tired arm that held Everly. *Oh that's better!* I thought with a small sigh. My eyes fluttered closed, feeling heavy.

There was a tap at the door and I opened my eyes smiling when my mom, dad, Gracelynn, and Lane stepped into the room. Gracelynn came to the bed first, with the sweetest smile on her face as her eyes darted to me and then to Everly. She reached a hand out to touch her sister's hand, and I felt my throat constrict. She was going to be such a wonderful big sister.

"Mom, you did it! You're okay?" Gracelynn asked, huge green eyes looking me over.

"I'm okay," I said with a nod. "Come here," I told her, and she leaned against my chest. Her strawberry shampoo engulfed my senses. I closed my eyes. *This is what home is. Bobby, Gracelynn, Everly. This is everything.*

"Why are you crying?" Gracelynn asked.

"I'm just so happy," I assured her.

"When can we go home?" Gracelynn asked with a yawn.

"Honey, you will probably have to go home with Grandma and Grandpa for a couple of days before I can come home."

Gracelynn pouted. "I don't want to." Her lips twitched as she pondered other options. "I guess I will have to though," she shrugged.

"Everything will be okay sweetheart, and we will come back tomorrow okay?" my mom told her.

My mom and dad both held the baby while Gracelynn sat with me, holding my hand. I stroked her back softly, smiling as her curls bounced against my arm. Then, Lane got to hold the baby. I thanked them all for coming before they left to allow me to rest, and then Bobby's parents came in to see the baby, and to congratulate us both.

By the time everyone left I was more tired than I could stand. I could hardly keep my eyes open. Bobby stroked my hand. "Get some sleep, sweetheart. I'll keep an eye on the baby," he said with a soft peck on my lips. I sank down into the pillows after Bobby lowered the bed back down. I heard him move around and smiled when I saw him lovingly looking after our baby girl. I closed my eyes, finally finding sleep.

Thirty-One

Oh it feels good to be home! I thought with a sigh as I slowly sank down on the sofa with Everly cradled safely against my chest. After being in the hospital for three days, home was a welcome sight. Grace-lynn would be home from school in four hours. For now it was me, Everly, Bobby, and my mom.

Mom and Bobby worked on getting things put away while I rested. My back was tender from the days spent in a hospital bed. As tired and sore as I was though, I also felt this overwhelming sense of happiness and a sort of energy from being back home. I took in my surroundings. Mom had obviously cleaned up before I got here, there were welcome home balloons attached to a bouquet of vibrant flowers gracing the table.

After they were finished bringing things in from the car, Mom offered to hold the baby so that I could nap and shower if I wanted. "I'd love to get the smell of hospital off of me," I admitted with a short laugh.

"Well you go on and do what you need to do. Holler if you need anything!" Mom said as she scooped the sleeping Everly out of my arms. Everly grunted her disapproval, but quickly snuggled into the crook of my mom's arms. I smiled thoughtfully, remembering when we'd held Gracelynn this very way.

I cleared my throat and stood. Bobby quickly offering his help, I grabbed his hand. "You good?" he asked, nodding toward the bathroom. I was getting around better and did my best to assure him that I'd be okay.

I walked slowly, taking my time as Dr. Ray had instructed. Once I made it to our bedroom I inhaled and exhaled deeply. *My clothes, my bathroom!* I made my way to the dresser and picked out a thin pair of cotton pajamas and one of my maternity shirts that would be comfortable. I then made my way to the bathroom where I grabbed my favorite soft and thick towel from the shelf. I turned on the water to the shower, stepped out of my clothing and into the awaiting stream. The water was warm, and felt wonderful against my skin. I rotated my shoulders and neck, releasing tension, and simply stood under the water for a while before washing.

I lathered and washed my hair first, beginning to feel relaxed. Then I washed my body with my pink rose water scrub, I leaned down, *OUCH!* My whole body ached as I bent to scrub at my feet. I slowly stood taking a few deliberate breaths.

Allowing myself to indulge, I enjoyed the heat of the shower a little longer before shutting off the water and wrapping myself in the towel. I felt and smelled significantly better, I thought, as I dressed and left the bedroom feeling fresh and languid.

I made my way to the kitchen where my mom was rocking the baby while making lunch. I offered to help but mom shook her head. "I've got it sweetheart, you just relax." I sighed and shrugged, sitting myself down on the stool. I was tired of being treated like an invalid, but I knew they were all just trying to help. I vowed silently to keep my sour mood to myself as I sat there and smelled something delicious from the stove.

"Potato soup?" I asked, hope rang clear in my voice.

Mom whipped around to look at me and smiled. "How did you know?" she asked.

"I love your potato soup!" I said as I did a little happy jig in my seat.

Mom laughed, earning a grunt from Everly as she stirred awake and started suckling at her fingers. "Well, I suppose you'll have to take over now," Mom said as she walked the baby over to me and placed her in my arms. I fed her, watching her curious dark eyes study my face. I knew at this stage she couldn't really see me so I cooed to her, letting her hear my voice and know that she was safe and so very loved. As I peered down at her sweet face I wondered if she'd look more like me, or have more resemblances of Bobby.

"She looks like you," Mom said, as if reading my mind.

I smiled wistfully, "I wouldn't mind if she had Bobby's eyes," I told her. I wasn't in any rush for her to grow up though, I had learned from experience that they grow up fast. I wanted to treasure each moment, every milestone. To watch her grow into herself, as I've witnessed Gracelynn doing. I looked forward to watching my girls grow together.

A steaming bowl of delicious soup was placed in front of me, and I adjusted the now-sleeping Everly against my shoulder to lightly pat her back. Once my soup was cool enough, I began eating. Mom sat beside me with her own bowl, and Bobby joined us—fresh after a shower and shave. He kissed me soundly on the lips, and then stroked Everly's cheek before making himself a heaping bowl of the savory soup and plopping down beside me.

"Want me to take her?" he offered, so that I could eat.

Though I appreciated the thoughtfulness, I shook my head. "Thank you. I've got her." We ate together and made small talk. After lunch, I allowed Bobby to take Everly, smiling as I watched him tenderly cradle her in his capable arms. Then, I stood to help Mom with the dishes, even though she tried to protest against it.

"I'm fine Mom, really. It honestly feels good to be doing something," I assured her. She elbowed me playfully but nodded in defeat.

After Mom left and Bobby had fallen asleep with the baby on the recliner, I lay myself down on the sofa. A nap sounded amazing, and as they say "when the baby sleeps, so should mommy." I smiled, taking another glance at my husband and our new baby girl before drifting off to sleep.

My head shot up as the door shut and I peered up at the delightful, brilliant green eyes of Gracelynn. She placed her bag down gently and walked over to me. I scooted myself back so that she had room to give me a hug.

"Am I going to hurt you?" she whispered.

I shook my head. "No sweetheart, you won't hurt me. Come here, oh I've missed you!" I said, a soft cry in her strawberry scented curls.

"I missed you too," Gracelynn said with a sniff.

I pulled back to get a look at her. I'd only been gone three days but she looked older to me…I knew that I was probably just being silly. Bobby's eyes opened and he grinned widely at Gracelynn and I. "Hey sweetheart," he said to Gracelynn, and she moved to give him a hug, careful not to wake her sleeping sister.

She glanced down at the baby. "She's so little," she said with a soft smile.

"You were once about this little too," Bobby said, before I could. Gracelynn carefully stroked Everly's pink cheek.

"Can I hold her?" she asked skeptically.

Bobby looked at me in question and I sat up, nodding. "Come sit over here by me sweetheart, and honey, you can bring Everly here to Gracey," I instructed. Gracelynn settled in carefully beside me, smiling widely as Bobby walked toward her with her baby sister.

"Okay, now hold your arms like this." I showed her. "Yes, that's right. Now make sure to support her head, okay?" I said as the baby was placed in Gracelynn's arms.

"Oh, wow!" Gracelynn squeaked, her eyes huge as she looked down at Everly. "Hi there," she said, her throat thick with emotion. I blinked back my own tears, and then grabbed my cell phone, standing up to take a picture. *Or ten!* I thought with a private smile. I snapped wildly, eager to capture the sweet moment.

I studied the photos after Everly was placed in my arms and Gracelynn began working on her homework upstairs. *I am going to have to invest in a good camera,* I thought as I studied each picture. I'd taken quite a few, capturing so many expressions from Gracelynn and even a few with Everly seeming to be studying her sister.

Later that evening, after Everly was fed, bathed, and changed, I placed her in her bassinet. Bobby went to bed early because he had to get back to his duties. Since she was sleeping in our room, I didn't have to bother with the baby monitor. He'd wake up if Everly woke, and I'd likely hear her fuss anyway. I peered down at my sore chest. *Yep, I have built in radar!* I thought.

Padding off to the kitchen, I heated some water for tea and sent Lane a message.

Well there you are! Lane's reply was quick and I couldn't help but smile.

I hope I didn't wake anyone. I just got Everly to sleep and wanted you to know that I was thinking of you. Thank you again for being there for me at the hospital. And visiting after.

I put the phone down while I took a sip of my hot tea. I hummed in content. Tea had this wonderful way of soothing and relaxing my body and mind.

Girl! Don't even fret, I'm always here for you. You didn't wake me, I'm up feeding Ella yet again. Hey, you feel like a used up cow yet?

I covered my mouth with my hand to silence the bubble of laughter and shook my head.

OMG lol! Not yet, I guess I have that to look forward to!

Well sorry to break it to ya, but yea… pretty much. Girl I don't know how much longer I'm going to go before I start giving her a bottle. I read over her message and pondered it. I know that a lot of women say that it is best to breastfeed for as long as possible, but I also felt like it should definitely be the mother's choice.

Well that is certainly up to you, I'm sure every woman feels differently about it. I said finally.

Yeah, you are probably right there. At least I have someone to bitch about it to though! Lane replied

It is nice having someone to talk to that understands what you're going through. Thank you for being my friend, for helping me through this. I confided. Lane had been a major help, it was so easy to talk with her.

You're welcome! You are my best friend Katie, I appreciate your help and I am happy to help you too.

I pushed tears out of my eyes. Lane and I messaged back and forth for quite some time before she later told me that she'd finally gotten little Ella to sleep and that she was going to try to catch some Z's. I admitted to her that I should also do the same. The tea had worked wonders to relax me and I was rather tired. We said goodnight, and I turned off the lights after rinsing my cup.

Once in the bedroom I closed the door quietly. I changed into a t-shirt and made my way to check on Everly. She was sleeping peacefully. I studied her for several moments.

Her eyes moved behind closed lids as if she were dreaming and I couldn't help but wonder what she may be dreaming about.

I bent and kissed her brow, earning a frown and a pucker of lips for disturbing her slumber. After another glance at Everly I made my way to my side of the bed and curled up next to Bobby. *Oh it does feel good to be in my own bed again!* I thought as I snuggled in beside my husband.

I yawned sleepily. Everly had woken up several times during the night, and a couple of times Bobby had woken to take care of her so that I could get some rest. We took turns, and when the alarm went off I felt like I'd just gotten to sleep.

Everly slept through Gracelynn getting ready for school, even when she kissed her plump cheek before leaving. Bobby was out working in the barn so the house was quiet. I stretched out on the sofa, deciding that I needed more rest after a long night with little sleep.

Rest didn't last long, for Everly was awake and ready for another feeding after only thirty minutes. *It had felt good to take that cat nap,* I thought, as I fed and burped her. Then, I leaned back to relax with her cuddled in my arms. I smiled as she yawned and smacked her little lips.

A knock sounded at the door and I called "come in" from the sofa. I wasn't in any kind of position to stand. I was surprised when Lane rushed in with the baby in her arms and a huge smile on her face. "I hope I didn't wake you or the baby. I just had to see you!" Lane said as she made her way over to me. "May I?" she asked, glancing down at Everly.

She handed me Ella, still in her carrier, and she gently picked up Everly. I smiled at Ella as she scrunched up her brow unsatisfied at being in my arms instead of her mother's, but since she could hear Lane, she seemed okay.

"Oooh my goodness! Katie, she is going to look so much like you!" Lane said in a babyish voice. Then she giggled, glancing at me. "Sorry I didn't mean to talk to you like a baby."

I snorted a laugh, shaking my head. "It's okay." Lane smiled and looked down at Everly again.

"Ella is getting big!" I said as I repositioned her, not used to her weight.

"Yeah, well, she eats like, all the time!" Lane said dramatically. "You can lay her down on the floor if you'd like, she loves it!" Lane said as she glanced down at her daughter with a smile. Lane was glowing! She looked so happy, and thin!

I glanced down at myself. "I'm sorry, I would have changed if I knew you were coming."

Lane arched a perfect brow. "Pssh, don't even! You just had a baby," she said before smiling down at Everly. "Your momma is so silly, yes she is!" She cooed and I couldn't help but laugh.

Once Everly was asleep and Ella wailed for Lane, I took Everly while Lane cuddled Ella close, murmuring soothing words. She calmed almost as soon as she was placed in Lane's arms. "She is such a momma's girl," Lane said. She meant to sound exasperated I was sure, but she held such love in her voice that I knew she was happy and very proud.

Our little ones were asleep in no time, and I told Lane that she was more than welcome to lay Ella down beside Everly. It was so sweet seeing the two of them together that we both took out our phones and began snapping photos. "We are hopeless," Lane said with a giggle and small shake of her head.

"You want some coffee?" I asked.

"Oh my god, yes please!" Lane said as she followed me into the kitchen. She sat down and sighed. "I don't think Ella slept more than two hours last night," she confided.

I nodded sympathetically. "I'm not sure how much sleep I got, but it definitely didn't feel like enough." I stirred my cream and sugar into my steaming cup of coffee and sipped, and my back gave an involuntary shudder as Lane took a long drink of her black coffee. "How can you drink it black?" I asked

Lane shrugged. "I've honestly been drinking it like this since I was around sixteen." I remembered a time long ago when Lane had been so different. She'd been edgy, popular, and hung out with the "cool kids." She had to learn how to take care of herself at a young age. Back then, I had been quick to judge.

I sat down beside Lane and we talked over coffee for some time. We each had two small cups. When the pot was empty I offered to make her more but she shook her head. "Girl, if I have any more coffee I am going to be so jittery and probably not get any sleep at all!" She laughed.

I snorted. "It's decaf!"

"Wow… really? I couldn't tell," she said with a shrug. "Tasted good to me, maybe I should try drinking decaf for a while."

"I read that drinking caffeine while you breastfeed is a bad idea."

"Yeah well, everyone has an opinion," Lane said dryly as we moved to the living room to keep an eye on our sleeping babies.

Lane and I enjoyed one another's company. She stayed for lunch with Bobby and I, and later decided she'd better get home to try to nap before school let out. I thanked her again for coming as we said our goodbyes, then I settled down on the sofa. My ears began to ring in the silence. Everly was in and out of naps, she'd wake for a while and simply stare quietly and then her eyes would flutter shut.

I still had quite a while before Gracelynn would be home, and it was such a beautiful day that I yearned to be outside. I stood and stretched my tired muscles. *A little fresh air might do me some good*, I thought as I looked out the window. Making up my mind, I got Everly dressed in a warmer outfit since it was only in the mid 60's, and then I changed my own clothes. I put on a loose pair of jeans and a sweater, and then tied my hair back. *There!* I thought as I studied my reflection. I looked better than I had in days!

I held Everly, grabbed up my purse and keys and after letting Bobby know I was going for a drive, we headed down the road under a clear blue sky.

Thirty-Two

"Sweetheart, are you almost ready?" I asked Gracelynn. She'd been looking forward to our day together for a while. While I was too, I was also leaving Everly's side for the longest period of time since her birth. Everly, who was almost two months old!

"Just gotta grab my letter!" she hollered before charging back upstairs. We were headed to the cemetery to visit Beth. It was a tradition of ours to do this, we'd go out for lunch together and then sit and read a letter, or just talk to Beth. We'd begun the tradition when Gracelynn was around five years old, that was when she had confided that she'd liked to see where her mom was buried. We would go on Beth's birthday, as well as every year around this time, when the leaves were changing colors and it was cool, but not yet cold.

As I waited for Gracelynn I scooped up the smiling Everly with her big hazel eyes. Instead of my brown, or Bobby's beautiful gray-blue, Everly's eyes were a little of both. So wide and expressive, rimmed with thick, long lashes. She also had the sweetest smile, and the softest, palest blonde hair. She did look a lot like me, but she had many of Bobby's features too. His stubborn chin, his smile, she even had his toes in the way that they tended to curl under at the tip. Everly squealed at me, bringing me out of my thoughts.

"My sweet girl," I cuddled her. I felt a bit nervous to leave her, but I knew with Mom and Dad she would be in great hands. Once Mom got in the living room, she reached for Everly eagerly.

"Come to Grandma!" she cooed. Her salt and pepper hair was scooped in a bun, as Everly loved to grab it in her strong little fists. She had quite the grip, too.

Gracelynn rushed downstairs and after saying bye to her grandma, grandpa, and her little sister, she ran to the door. "Well hang on sweetie, don't forget your coat! I will be right there," I told her with a laugh. I grabbed the envelope from the end table and slipped it in my purse. I'd written Beth a letter as well, it had been quite some time since I'd written one. I knew it probably would seem silly to some, but it was my way of telling her I still missed her. That she was so loved and treasured.

It was my way of not saying goodbye, but keeping her with me always. I thanked my parents for watching Everly and then stepped outside into the brisk fall air. I smiled, Gracelynn was playing hop-scotch with Bobby.

I giggled as Bobby tripped and then pretended to injure himself, making Gracelynn double over with laughter, a tinkle of bells that went straight to my soul. "You aren't really hurt are you?" Gracelynn asked as she peered down at him quizzically. He grabbed her swiftly, bringing her down to the ground and tickling her.

"Oooh nooo! I fell for it!" she cried with glee. I watched the pair of them, feeling my heart swell with love and pride.

Noticing me, Bobby cleared his throat and stood, crossing over to me while brushing dry grass off of his coat and jeans. He bent and gave me a kiss. "You ladies have a great time," he said to Grace-lynn and I as she came to stand beside us.

"We will!" Gracelynn told him.

I nodded and then gave him another kiss before Gracelynn and I walked to the car and buckled up. I turned on the heater, it was a chilly day and I was glad that Gracelynn had chosen to wear a sweater and her coat. "Ready?" I asked, my eyebrows rising as I looked at her in the rearview mirror.

Gracelynn's head bobbed quickly. "So ready, and it will be nice to just be with you!" She said with a smile. I returned her smile, but wondered if she were feeling left out.

"I hope you haven't been feeling left out sweetheart," I told her, wanting her to know it was something that I worried about.

"I don't feel left out, well not exactly. I know you are busy with Everly and everything and I've got school and all. I just sometimes miss when it was just us." She paused and worried her bottom lip with her teeth, something she did when she felt like she said the wrong thing. "Not that I don't want a sister! I just…Ooh I feel like I'm not saying this right." Gracelynn peered at me with sad green eyes and I offered her a smile.

"Oh honey, I know what you mean! I miss spending time with you too!" I reassured her.

Gracelynn smiled again, her eyes lighting up with their usual brilliance. She truly was such a sweet and special soul.

"Okay, so what are you hungry for?" I asked her as I stopped at the red light on the highway.

"Hmmm. How about the Club House?" Gracelynn asked. I felt my lips curve in a smile.

"Did you know that your dad took me there on our first date?" I asked.

Gracelynn's eyes widened. "Really?"

"Yep, we were seventeen!" I said with a wistful smile.

"Wow, you were young," she said, eyes wide and expressive.

"Yes, we were."

"I don't mean you are old or anything," Gracelynn said suddenly. I couldn't help but chuckle at her affronted expression.

"It's okay, I know what you meant. You are very thoughtful for respecting my feelings though. Thank you," I told her, wanting to acknowledge her thoughtfulness.

"Well, Malachi is so rude sometimes! I always tell him he should be thinking about what he says instead of just saying whatever pops in his brain!" I watched Gracelynn's eyes roll as she gazed out the window.

"Did you and Mal get into an argument?" I wondered

Gracelynn shook her head. "Well not exactly, he's just mean sometimes to other people. I think he likes me a little more than a friend sometimes." My eyes widened at her admission.

"I'm not ready for a boyfriend or anything, this girl Sadie, she already has a boyfriend and she's my age!" Gracelynn made a disgusted sound and I bit back a laugh. *Well good. Why were kids getting interested in dating at such a young age anyway?* I thought to myself.

"Well I have to say I'm happy you know what you aren't ready for."

The topic was forgotten as we pulled up to The Club House. When Gracelynn and I made our way in the door, I was hit by a wave of nostalgia. It looked almost exactly the same! The benches and round tables. The salad bar in the middle of the restaurant was a new addition. There were also picnic-style linen clothes covering the round tables. The radio still blared songs from the 80s and 90s. I felt my head bob to a Backstreet Boys song as we waited for a hostess.

"Hi, seating for two?" A peppy young girl greeted us. She couldn't have been more than seventeen, she had long straight dark hair and huge made-up eyes.

"Wow you're pretty!" Gracelynn complimented her.

The girl's cheeks took on a faint pink hue as she smiled. "Aww thank you! You are very pretty too! How old are you?" she asked.

"I'm nine, I'll be ten soon though!" Gracelynn said with a smile. *Soon meaning next spring.* I thought with a smirk.

"That's so cool!" The girl said as she led us to our seats.

Gracelynn and I sat at the round table and the waitress took our drink orders. I told Gracelynn she could get whatever she liked. She chose hot cocoa, and said she might get soda after that if it was okay. I ordered myself a soda. Ever since I'd had Everly, I had this crazy indigestion and the Sprite bubbles soothed the irritation.

Dr. Ray had assured me that it was normal to experience that and told me that I could take a simple antacid. Since I didn't really like Rolaids with their chalky texture, I chose to drink the carbonated soda instead.

After our drinks were brought to us, we were ready to order. I usually ordered for Gracelynn and was pleasantly surprised when she took charge and ordered for herself.

"Can I have the cheeseburger please, with no onions, and instead of fries can I have onion rings?" she asked. The waitress nodded, taking down her order and then peered at me.

"Oh, I think I will have one trip through the salad bar, and how about I go ahead and try a bowl of butternut squash soup."

The waitress nodded. "The soup is amazing! I hope we do this again next fall," she said as she took the menus from us.

"Well I can't wait to try it," I told her.

She walked off and then returned quickly with my salad plate. "I'll be right back," I told Gracelynn, waving my little plate.

"Kay," Gracelynn said simply as she sipped her steaming hot cocoa.

I made my way to the salad bar, it looked really good, fresh, and all the vegetables in a colorful display. I fixed my salad and grabbed a few slices of avocado. Once I was satisfied, I headed back over to our table.

"Oooh avocado!" Gracelynn beamed as I told her that I'd gotten some for her.

She put it on her napkin and ate the slices with a little salt and pepper. It wasn't long before our food was ready, and we ate our lunch happily. The soup was indeed good, creamy and rich, with buttery notes. I offered Gracelynn an opportunity to try it. She gave me a skeptical look before dipping her spoon in and bringing it to her lips. She blew softly and then took a bite.

"Wow, that's good," she said with surprise. Then, she finished her cheeseburger and worked on her onion rings slowly.

After we were done eating our lunch, I left a tip with the waitress, paid the bill, and then we were off. As we got to the car I told Gracelynn she could sit up front with me. She scurried in and buckled up. "Oh my gosh I am so full! Thank you for lunch, Mom."

"You are very welcome, I think I am a little stuffed myself."

"It was good though," she said as we began our trip to the cemetery.

A few times I found myself glancing back at the empty car seat out of habit and sighed. I already missed Everly, but I knew that Gracelynn and I both needed this time. Besides, we had to do this— no matter the tears and pain it may bring.

As we made our way to the secluded cemetery, Gracelynn drew quiet as she usually did before we arrived. She smiled, but her eyes held emotion as she unbuckled and got out. She waited by the car, holding her letter in her hand.

"Wow! Look at the trees!" she said as she looked around.

I smiled, taking in the vibrant shades of red, green, and yellow of the tree leaves. There were piles of leaves by the trees, and when the wind picked up now and then, the trees would shed a few more leaves. I zipped up my coat the rest of the way, and then Gracelynn held my hand in hers as we made our way through the headstone maze until we came upon Beth's name. It was near a row of towering oak trees, their leaves a beautiful, deep red-brown color.

Gracelynn sat cross-legged on the ground in front of the headstone. She placed a hand on the surface and closed her eyes. I kept close, but not too close, giving her the space and time she needed. I could see her mouth moving, but couldn't hear the whispered words she spoke. She usually didn't speak loudly enough for me to hear, and I'd assured her many times that it was okay. I didn't need to hear what she wanted to say, unless she wished for me to hear it.

I watched emotions play on her face, how her cupid bow lips would tremble as she spoke, how her eyes deepened to a jade green as they filled with tears. Even then, as she was close to crying, I didn't move. I knew by now that she would seek me for comfort when she was ready.

I swallowed past the hard lump that formed in my throat and looked up at the sky. Swirls of soft pink and purple could be seen to the east in the mostly blue expanse, small puffs of clouds here and there. The sun's rays broke through these few clouds, gracing us with warmth.

A small cry brought me out of my thoughts and I watched as Gracelynn dug up the small box of letters and drop the one she'd written inside. She stood then, wiped her face with her coat sleeve, and sat in my lap with her head against my shoulder.

"You okay?" I asked against her hair

"Yeah, I don't think this will ever stop hurting though," she said with a sniff. My chin quivered with effort not to cry.

"I understand sweetheart. We find ways to heal, and we keep her right here," I said, pointing to my chest.

"Momma Katie?" she asked. She hadn't called me that for awhile, having settled on just calling me Mom.

"Yeah?"

"I know that this is hard for me, but sometimes I feel like it maybe hurts you more." Gracelynn took a breath and then looked at me with her tear-stained face. "She was your best friend, like your sister. I think that you are very strong," she said in thought.

A tear slid down my face, unable to restrain them any longer. I smiled sadly as Gracelynn wiped at my tears with her small hand, then she embraced me in a huge hug. "I love you sweetheart," I mumbled in her hair.

"I love you too. I'm going to go walk around a little by the trees while you have your turn, okay?" she asked.

"Thank you. I'll be done in just a bit, okay?" Gracelynn nodded and then shrugged in thought.

"You don't have to hurry, you need your time too."

I watched her walk away toward the little grove of tall trees just across from me. For a little while I just sat there, looking at the headstone, and like Gracelynn had, I placed my hand against the cold surface and closed my eyes.

I felt the breeze kick my hair up and around my shoulders, and I heard Gracelynn giggle, so I glanced behind me to see her spinning as the wind blew her hair around. I smiled and brought my eyes back in front of me. With a swallow, I took the envelope out of my coat pocket. I'd taken it out of my purse when we'd driven up so that I wouldn't have to carry my purse along.

It felt heavy in my hand as I tore it open carefully, not really knowing why I bothered to seal it to begin with. When I took it out of the envelope, I opened it slowly. I usually ended up crying every time, but it was also a kind of therapy. A few breaths helped me steady my voice as I began to read aloud what I had written with my heart.

Dear Beth,

It has been a while since I've written, but I feel like you know that you're always in my thoughts. Sometimes I swear I can still feel you with me, that might be because of Gracelynn...God Beth! I wish you would have been able to meet your daughter. She is such an amazing little girl, she is growing so quickly and every day she looks more and more like you. The resemblance is remarkable really, especially now that she is getting older. She even has those freckles on her nose that you used to complain about.

She also has your quick wit, your love for wild and bold colors, she is so incredibly sweet-natured and sensitive. You were that way too even though you wouldn't admit it... You always put up a strong front.

I cleared my throat, emotions making it difficult to read aloud. My vision became blurry with unshed tears. I struggled to take hold of the emotions. I glanced behind me again, Gracelynn was still playing with the fallen leaves and after a few deliberate breaths, I continued.

You always had to be strong though. I read your diary, and I got your letter. Gracelynn has your letter as well, and though she hasn't shared it with me, I know she treasures that letter with all of her heart, as I treasure mine. Beth, I had been so moved by your letter to me. Even more, by reading your diary. Wow, that diary! It took me on one hell of a journey. It had been hard to read, but also in a way, I felt like I was getting to know a part of you that I hadn't known before. I was surprised that it was so full of secrets, but I wasn't angry with you for not talking about it. I hurt for you...I hate that you'd had that kind of life. You deserved so much better than the life you were brought into.

I am ever thankful we were able to take you in and provide friendship, support, and safety, thankful to be your best friend. As much as it hurt to read about so many of the things you'd gone through, I admire your courage and your strength so much, and I know that your daughter carries that strength and courage in her too.

She will always have a safe home with us, always have a life of love and laughter. Now she gets to share this space with her new baby sister.

Yeah, I'm a mom now! Sometimes I can hardly believe it, even though I gave birth to her almost two months ago already! Her name is Everly Elizabeth, she's beautiful, and I wish so much that you were here to meet her, too.

Gracelynn is such a good big sister, and I am so happy that our daughters get to grow up together. It is something I know you would have wanted too, if you were still with us.

It took so long to heal from that overwhelming absence of you. There were so many times that I would almost expect you to walk through the door. To call or text me, and it was years before it finally seemed to dawn on me that you really were gone. That you couldn't walk through my door, that I couldn't hear your voice.

Sometimes it feels like ages have passed since I last heard your voice, held your hand, gave you a hug...and others it feels like just yesterday. Time is kind of funny like that. But no matter how much time passes, I hold you in my memories, I hold you in my spirit, we hold you in our hearts.

Until we meet again my sister,

Katie

I folded the letter back up, placed it in the envelope, and then tucked it in the box with all of the others. With an audible sniff I sank my fingers into the earth and covered the box with the dirt and grass. Placing my hand on the headstone once more, I allowed myself the time to cry.

On shaky legs, I rose and turned to walk toward Gracelynn. Stopping just a moment as I watched her toss a handful of colorful leaves into the air, and then spin in a circle as they cascaded gracefully around her. She lifted her arms above her head in the air, her hair swinging out as she twirled, her eyes focused on the sky above her, a secret smile on the corner of her mouth. She looked so peaceful and free. I stood and watched her for a while, her happiness was contagious, and I found myself smiling.

When she noticed me standing there watching, she scooped up a huge armful and walked over to me. "Try it, it's a lot of fun!" she giggled.

"Let's do it!" I said. She tossed the leaves into the air and I swirled and twirled with Gracelynn as the leaves fell all around us. We both collapsed onto the ground as the earth spun. My breath came in heaves until my heart began to slow and I let out a laugh.

"That was so fun! Thank you."

"You're welcome, Mom," she replied.

I turned and propped myself up on one elbow to look at her. Her eyelashes cast dark shadows on her flushed cheeks as she lay there with her eyes closed, the sweetest smile on her face. She opened her eyes, her green gaze finding mine. "Let's go home."

Together we stood, and Gracelynn held my hand in hers as we walked to the car and headed home. Gracelynn's soft hum filled the air as I drove that familiar road. I joined her in her little tune. My heart felt full, my soul at peace, happy.

I don't know what the future holds for us, what lessons we may learn along the way, what mistakes we will make, but what I do know is that each new day brings new possibilities. I think that's what makes it so sweet, what makes it so perfect.

Epilogue

Dear Mommy, I don't no what to say so I will say hi. Katie brings me here and she writes you alot. I wanted to try. I want this to be for you and me, so I didn't show anyone it. So I'm six today. I'm not a great speller yet, but I do my best. Katie talks about you to me alot. I feel sad on my birthdays cause I didn't got to meet you before. I don't want Katie to be sad, so I try to be happy. I have a pixure of you by my bed. I look at it alot. I have your hare,, and eyes, and smile too. Well I like school sometimes and movies and to be out playing with friends. I like music too, I wonder what you sound like. So today for my birthday I had school but it was okay. They sang and we had cupcakes too. they were good. My favorit is chocolit. Well I better go now I got a party... I will write again.
  Love Gracelynn

Acknowledgments

First and foremost, Mom: I want to thank you for always being here for me. For encouraging me when I was down on myself, for cheering me on all of the way. You've always supported my dreams, and have always told me that I can do anything that I set my heart on. Thank you for being you, I love you.

To my husband, thank you for being my best friend, for your love, your support, your commitment to our family, your excitement for our journey together, and your encouragement for my dreams. I don't think there are enough words to express my love and gratitude for you.

To my three incredible and brilliant children. You've made my life so beautiful, from the moment each of you were placed in my arms, I knew my heart would be forever full. Thank you for your sweet smiles, your precious hugs, for each and every "I love you, Mom." Thank you for your laughter, for your humor and your quick wit. Thank you for challenging me, and for believing in me. I love you all so much. Remember that you can do anything you set your mind and heart on, and I'm always here for you every step of the way, with a happy heart, and a proud smile.

To my Mom and Dad in law: Thank you for being here for us, for walking this journey with us. For the countless times you've helped pull us out of some tough situations. And Mom, for the many hours spent visiting, laughing, encouraging me to keep writing, and for being my writing buddy! Love you guys.

To my family. I love you, thank you for your support, and your friendship. For all of the memories, and all of the learning moments along the way.

To my amazing friends, each of you are incredibly wonderful. I want you to know I appreciate your support, and your faith in me.

A very special thank you to Robin! Meeting you and getting to know you has been a gift. You opened a door for me that I never imagined for myself, and I have so much gratitude for you. Girlfriend, you are such an amazing woman! Thank you for your support, and the hours of editing dates. I love you and am forever thankful and grateful for our friendship.

Hearts Unleashed Publishing House

Abigail Gazda, you are a true inspiration. Thank you so much for being such a wonderful, kind hearted soul. Thank you for your faith in me. For your words of wisdom, encouragement, and motivation. Thank you for taking a chance on this small town gal! I consider myself blessed to have you as my friend and publisher!

Jill Weeks, you are incredible! I love your excitement and your energy, thank you for all of your support on this journey.

Valerie Irvine-Karinen, my amazing editor! Once again, thank you for doing such lovely work, thank you for your dedication, and for your friendship.

Susan Harring, I appreciate and thank you for your beautiful work, and dedication to making my book look so gorgeous!

Last but never least, I want to thank my readers! Thank you for supporting my journey, you encourage me to keep writing, and I hope that I encourage you to keep reading! Remember that you can achieve all of your dreams, believe in yourself and your worth.

With Deepest Appreciation,
Samantha Vitale

In Loving Memory of Golya Sterling